CULT OF THE
WARMASON

More novels featuring Xenos from Black Library

GENESTEALER CULTS
by Peter Fehervari

DEATHWATCH
by Steve Parker

DEATH OF INTEGRITY
by Guy Haley

SIN OF DAMNATION
by Gav Thorpe

MISSION: PURGE
An audio drama by Gav Thorpe

DEATHWATCH: IGNITION
by various authors

DEATHWATCH: XENOS HUNTERS
by various authors

STORM OF DAMOCLES
by Justin D Hill

THE TAU EMPIRE
by various authors

BLADES OF DAMOCLES
by Phil Kelly

CULT OF THE
WARMASON

C L WERNER

BLACK LIBRARY

For Lindsey, who has sharp eyes and cunning wit.

A BLACK LIBRARY PUBLICATION

First published in 2017.
This edition published in Great Britain in 2017 by
Black Library,
Games Workshop Ltd.,
Willow Road,
Nottingham, NG7 2WS, UK.

10 9 8 7 6 5 4 3 2 1

Produced by Games Workshop in Nottingham.
Cover illustration by Raymond Swanland.

Cult of the Warmason © Copyright Games Workshop Limited 2017. Cult of the Warmason, GW, Games Workshop, Black Library, The Horus Heresy, The Horus Heresy Eye logo, Space Marine, 40K, Warhammer, Warhammer 40,000, the 'Aquila' Double-headed Eagle logo, and all associated logos, illustrations, images, names, creatures, races, vehicles, locations, weapons, characters, and the distinctive likenesses thereof, are either ® or TM, and/or © Games Workshop Limited, variably registered around the world.
All Rights Reserved.

A CIP record for this book is available from the British Library.

ISBN 13: 978 1 78496 614 0

No part of this publication may be reproduced, stored in a retrieval system, or transmitted in any form or by any means, electronic, mechanical, photocopying, recording or otherwise, without the prior permission of the publishers.

This is a work of fiction. All the characters and events portrayed in this book are fictional, and any resemblance to real people or incidents is purely coincidental.

See Black Library on the internet at

blacklibrary.com

Find out more about Games Workshop
and the world of Warhammer 40,000 at

games-workshop.com

Printed and bound by CPI Group (UK) Ltd, Croydon, CR0 4YY

It is the 41st millennium. For more than a hundred centuries the Emperor has sat immobile on the Golden Throne of Earth. He is the Master of Mankind by the will of the gods, and master of a million worlds by the might of his inexhaustible armies. He is a rotting carcass writhing invisibly with power from the Dark Age of Technology. He is the Carrion Lord of the Imperium for whom a thousand souls are sacrificed every day, so that he may never truly die.

Yet even in his deathless state, the Emperor continues his eternal vigilance. Mighty battlefleets cross the daemon-infested miasma of the warp, the only route between distant stars, their way lit by the Astronomican, the psychic manifestation of the Emperor's will. Vast armies give battle in His name on uncounted worlds. Greatest amongst his soldiers are the Adeptus Astartes, the Space Marines, bioengineered super-warriors. Their comrades in arms are legion: the Astra Militarum and countless planetary defence forces, the ever-vigilant Inquisition and the tech-priests of the Adeptus Mechanicus to name only a few. But for all their multitudes, they are barely enough to hold off the ever-present threat from aliens, heretics, mutants — and worse.

To be a man in such times is to be one amongst untold billions. It is to live in the cruellest and most bloody regime imaginable. These are the tales of those times. Forget the power of technology and science, for so much has been forgotten, never to be re-learned. Forget the promise of progress and understanding, for in the grim dark future there is only war. There is no peace amongst the stars, only an eternity of carnage and slaughter, and the laughter of thirsting gods.

CHAPTER I

Kashibai felt the hum of heavy machinery pulse through the ceiling of rock above her. Was it a trick of the promethium lamps or were the walls of the tunnel visibly shivering? She found herself listening for the patter of pebbles and dust, the grinding groan that would presage a crack in the roof. Some small part of her heart sickened at the thought of Tharsis, capital city of Lubentina, smashing down on her head in all its sacred vastness.

Not for the first time, Kashibai whispered an imprecation against the atavistic dread she continued to hold for places such as the Cloisterfells. Even a segmentum away from the rolling plains of her home world, the old anxiety about being underground refused to die away completely. But if the fear lingered, it was only an echo of itself. No longer was it Kashibai's master. The steely discipline of faith and duty had subjugated all fear. Anything, good or ill, that might compromise her usefulness to the Order of the Sombre Vow had been stripped away from her soul, leaving only the resolve to serve the God-Emperor of Mankind.

'The Emperor is with me,' Kashibai said. She pulled her gaze away from the roof overhead, looking across the winding tunnel down which they'd been advancing. She could see the black and crimson armour of her companions illuminated by the flickering lights bolted to the rock walls. A dozen Battle Sisters stealing through the ancient tunnels beneath Tharsis, impelled upon a mission of both mercy and violence.

Forsaken and shunned by Tharsis' establishment, the Cloisterfells were far from deserted. Disgrace and reverses in fortune and integrity had forced many to eke out a troglodyte existence far from the sculpted spires and ornate sanctuaries of the city. Some of these wretches watched the Sisters from the doorways of hovels cobbled together from the garbage dumped into the underworld. Some of them gazed upon the armoured warriors with obvious fear; others considered the Adepta Sororitas with reverence and piety. Most, however, were so lost in the squalor of their circumstances that they simply stared with fatalistic dejection, indifferent to this intrusion into their shadowy world.

Appearances, however, belied the reality. Not all those who dwelt in the Cloisterfells were so resigned. Far from the attention of Lubentina's leaders, buried away from the Emperor's light and the Imperial Creed, strange ideas and curious ambitions festered. Sometimes the rot would erupt in a spate of crime and sedition that wafted up from the depths to defile the city above.

'Be vigilant,' Kashibai warned her squad through her

helm's vox-bead. 'We're near the objective.' There was no need to elaborate. The staccato wail of a heavy stubber firing further down the tunnels was explanation enough. Kashibai pressed a finger to the brand upon her cheek, the sacred flower that symbolised the Adepta Sororitas. She whispered a short prayer and touched the purity seal bound to the trigger guard of her flamer. She accepted the caustic machine-spirit of her weapon and the danger of being so reckless as to fail to appease it before entering combat.

To the chatter of the heavy stubber there was now added the muffled roar of an explosive and the sharp crack of an autogun. Shouts, screams and animalistic shrieks drifted down the tunnel. The honour of leading the attack had been bestowed upon Kashibai and her squad.

Kashibai turned to her Sisters. 'Our duty is before us,' she said. 'God-Emperor guide and guard our deeds.' At her command, her squad quickened their pace, rushing ahead.

The noise of combat intensified as Kashibai's warriors raced down the winding passage. They ignored the side tunnels that opened into the corridor, leaving them to the attentions of the second squad of Battle Sisters following behind them. The ramshackle shelters and their scruffy inhabitants were likewise bypassed. Kashibai would allow nothing to compromise the momentum of the advance. Such were the orders she'd been given.

Hurrying down the tunnel, the charge of Kashibai's Sisters was drowned out by the swelling din of gunfire and violence that rolled down the passage. With startling abruptness the corridor opened into a wide gallery, a subterranean vault dozens of metres across and nearly half again as deep. At some point in its existence the chamber had been connected to the infrastructure of Tharsis. Great pipes and conduits slithered down from the ceiling and crawled along sections of the floor. Puddles of industrial effluvia seeped from one corroded pipe, the distinctive reek suggesting to Kashibai that the muck was a by-product of the incense manufactured to anoint the Warmason's Cathedral and Lubentina's numerous lesser shrines and chapels.

'How can anyone live in such a stink?' Sister Reshma wondered. The sharpshooter of Kashibai's squad, Reshma was close beside her leader as they entered the vault.

'This isn't living,' Kashibai said. 'Without the Emperor there is only existence, not life.'

In defiance of the stench, the shanties and scrap-huts of the under-dwellers littered the vault, squatting beneath the huge pipes and pressed between nests of conduit and cable. It was amidst the disorder of this slumland that a fierce combat now raged. The beams of lasguns flashed across the cavernous chamber, stabbing through flimsy walls and scouring corroded pipes. The bark of slug-throwers and autoguns smashed through the doors of hovels and ripped knots of cable from the walls. Somewhere the grisly blaze of a meltagun shot outwards to transform a shack into a snarling inferno.

'We've found the missing patrol,' Kashibai reported, as she gazed across the violent harvest strewn about the vault.

Mangled bodies wearing the green and gold of Lubentina's local militia were sprawled amid the confusion of shanties or slumped beside the massive pipes. Far fewer in number were the bodies of their enemy, grubby men arrayed in a riotous assortment of coveralls and cloaks, the only unity of their appearance effected by the dominance of purple and red in their vestments. Whether they signified gang colours or the heraldry of some seditious political sect, Kashibai didn't know, but she was grateful the malcontents so boldly announced themselves. It would enable her Sisters to identify the enemy from any slum-dwellers who'd been caught in the middle of the fighting. They'd come here to find the missing militia platoon, not massacre hapless bystanders.

'Confirmation of contact,' Kashibai repeated. 'Heretics distinguished by purple and red costume.'

'Are there survivors, Sister?' The question crackled across the vox. Kashibai could detect the tension in Sister Superior Trishala's voice. They'd descended into the Cloisterfells charged with rescuing the soldiers. If that duty was impossible, then the only penance to redress that failure would be to exterminate the heretics responsible.

'None visible, but the heretics appear to be concentrating their fire on a cluster of shacks under some drainage pipes. God-Emperor willing, there are soldiers who haven't succumbed,' Kashibai said.

'Relieve the pressure against any survivors,' Trishala ordered. 'Do all that is needful to draw the enemy away from that junction. Visit the Emperor's justice upon them.'

Kashibai activated her flamer and swung the weapon around. She could see a clutch of figures stalking around the curve of a two-metre wide pipe, trying to flank a cluster of shanties where the intense discharge of las-beams bespoke a concentration of local militia soldiers. Before the slinking figures could rush the position, the Order of the Sombre Vow announced their presence upon the battlefield.

'Emperor guide our wrath,' Kashibai swore, motioning her squad forwards.

At Kashibai's signal, the Battle Sisters fired upon the enemy. The roar of boltguns boomed through the vault as high-explosive shells slammed into their targets. Scarcely human shrieks rose from the stricken foe as flesh and bone were torn asunder by the devastating fusillade. The attempt to flank the militia strongpoint disintegrated, its impetus shattered by the sudden and brutal impact of the Sisters' firepower. Creeping shapes collapsed as the bolters ripped through them, autoguns and pistols falling from dying hands. Prowling foes in coveralls crudely stained purple and red crumpled in the dark beneath the industrial pipes, their arms clawing at the air as vitality fled from their mangled frames.

Survivors of the Sisters' initial volley swung about, seeking to extricate themselves from the gap between the huge pipes. The cover that had hidden them from the attentions of the local militia now acted as an obstacle to their escape, funnelling them into a killing ground the Adepta Sororitas were quick to exploit. Ten, twenty, even thirty of the enemy were shot down as Kashibai's warriors poured their fire into the reeling foe. It was butchery, but of a sort that didn't trouble the Sisters of Battle. Those who took up arms against the forces of the Imperium, who profaned the dominion of the God-Emperor by thought and deed, were entitled to neither mercy nor pity. Their lot was extermination without compunction or compromise.

Eradication of the flanking force relieved the immediate menace to the local militia holdouts, but it turned the violent attentions of the enemy upon Kashibai's squad. The local militia patrol had numbered a hundred soldiers when it went missing over ten hours before, losing vox contact with the surface after a brief report of contacting hostile elements. Only a considerable force would challenge such an incursion into the Cloisterfells, much less spring an ambush so ferocious as to find those soldiers cut off and surrounded. The creeping assault party had been but a small part of the enemy's strength. Now the Sisters felt the full fury of the foe.

Out from the cluster of huts, a riot of gunfire blazed away at the Sisters. Autoguns, lasrifles, stubbers and shotguns all barked away from among the shanties. A lance of searing light scorched a hideous gouge across the slums, shearing through shacks and conduits like a daemon's fiery claw. Sister Bishaka dropped to the ground as the cleaving laser came at her, slashing through the wall of the shanty she'd been using for cover.

'Cover her,' Kashibai told her squad, redirecting their fire to the enemies targeting Bishaka. While she crawled back towards her comrades, rounds from a slug-thrower glanced off her power armour. A burst from Sister Reshma's bolter shredded the side of a shack and reduced the shooter to a gory mess.

'I should have settled that faithless cur once I recovered my bearings,' Bishaka complained as she reached the squad's position.

'In His beneficence, the Emperor has provided enough heretics for us to share,' Reshma declared.

An autocannon now added its vicious fire to the assault, its shots obliterating entire shacks, sending burning debris bouncing off the ceiling overhead. Entire swathes of the slums were being flattened by the furious assault. Between the autocannon and the scything beam of the big laser, the enemy seemed intent on depriving the Sisters of any measure of concealment.

Except from one quarter. Kashibai was swift to notice that there was a several-metre wide strip that was being ignored by the brutal retaliation. At once her suspicions were aroused. Her Battle Sisters had already experienced something of their opponents' penchant for ambush and misdirection. Here, she felt certain, was another sampling of the foe's skulking methods.

'Watch my left,' Kashibai told Sister Reshma. Among the warriors of her squad, there was none who married accuracy and speed so well as Reshma. If her suspicions played out, speed would be more important than precision. 'The rest of you continue to return their fire. Keep their attention fixed on you.'

Orders given, Kashibai swung her flamer towards the undamaged strip of shacks. 'The Emperor protects,' she intoned as she thought of the under-dwellers who might still be hiding in the shanties. The choice between compassion and duty was never a comfortable one, but the demands of duty would brook no hesitation. The shanties were being spared by the enemy deliberately to cover their own purposes. She was certain they were using the strip as a corridor to bring fighters directly against the Sisters.

With a searing roar, fire erupted from the nozzle of Kashibai's gun. Liquid flame jetted out across the shanties, immolating those closest to the Battle Sisters and setting those further back ablaze. Screams of horror and anguish rose from the conflagration. Reeling shapes stumbled out from the smoke and flame, bodies wrapped in orange tongues of fire. Reshma's bolter cracked away, picking off those who tried to flee the havoc wrought by Kashibai's flamer. A few lasguns and autopistols growled from behind the crackling mass of fire, striving to silence Kashibai before she could inflict further damage.

'Well struck, Sister,' Bishaka called out.

'Too well,' Reshma declared. 'They're going to rush your position.'

Tightening her grip upon the flamer, Kashibai sent another scorching blast into the slums, prosecuting her campaign against the enemy assault force. More screams rang out, and figures dressed in purple and red scrambled away from the burning ruins, smoke rising from their scorched clothes and seared skin. Reshma maintained her grim vigil, dropping enemy after enemy with crippling shots, pitching many back into the very flames they'd sought to escape, leaving others wounded and writhing in the shadows.

Their assault broken, the enemy now loosed an even more abandoned barrage against the Sisters. Autocannon and laser joined with the smaller weapons in assailing the position adopted by Kashibai's squad. Slivers of rock gouged from roof and floor glanced off the black power armour that protected the Sisters. A stony splinter struck Reshma's helm before spinning away into the gloom.

The local militia survivors tried their best to support Kashibai's squad, intensifying the volleys of las-fire they were directing at the enemy positions. It was a gallant if fruitless effort. Kashibai knew it would need more than a few embattled soldiers to break their foe. Fortunately such a force was near at hand. While Kashibai's squad had been holding the enemy's attention, a second squad of Sisters had been taking the field. Keeping to the perimeter of the vault, they'd kept to cover while circling around the combat, biding their time until they were in position to strike.

'Sister Kashibai, we are starting our advance,' Virika announced across the vox. 'It would be a disgrace if we allowed you to keep all the heretics for yourselves.'

'You are welcome to claim your portion,' Kashibai replied, wiping blood from her brow. 'Emperor grant you good hunting.'

The boom of frag grenades revealed that Virika's squad was moving into the slum. Clouds of debris rose from demolished shacks while steam and sludge gushed from damaged pipes. Howls of surprise rang out across the cavernous chamber, almost subhuman in their sound. The thunderous snarl of Sister Nagina's heavy bolter silenced the cries nearest Virika's squad, raking across the concealed enemy and the shacks hiding them.

The barrage that had only moments before seemed nigh overwhelming now began to falter. The autocannon had been silenced, either eliminated by Virika's Sisters or else withdrawn by the enemy. The fury of the smaller weapons lessened as gunmen fell to grenades or retreated away from the threat they presented. The big laser made a few spiteful stabs at Kashibai's squad, nearly managing to strike Sister Mridula with one of its shots. Kashibai tried to gauge how far back the vicious laser might be sited, but a far closer menace soon presented itself.

Directly before Kashibai was the strip of slums her flamer had turned into a burning inferno. All about the edges of the conflagration were the smouldering bodies of those caught by the fire or dropped by Reshma's speedy shots. Even being grazed by a bolter's shell was enough to cripple an ordinary man, much less leave him with the ability to fight. Kashibai had discounted the wounded left by Reshma as posing no further threat. Now she discovered a reason to rue her assumption.

Lunging out from the smoke was a huge man, his skin blackened by the flames, his clothes reduced to steaming strips of rag. Blood gushed from a ghastly wound in his side, a fist-sized hole punched through his abdomen by Reshma's bolter. Instead of lying down to die, however, the urge to kill drove the brute back to his feet and sent him charging straight towards the woman who'd shot him. Before Reshma could react, the man was attacking her, swinging a crackling power pick at the Sister. The energised mining tool slammed into her, tossing her armoured body into the air like a child's doll.

Kashibai swung around, ready to burn the pick-armed thug with her flamer. The sight of Reshma sprawled on the floor restrained her. It was just possible her comrade's power armour had blunted the force of the blow. If she still lived, a blast from the flamer might finish her.

The hulking brute turned away from Reshma. He glared at Kashibai from the charred crust of what face he had left. She shuddered at the impossible viciousness of that gaze, the depthless hate that shone in his blemished eyes. She drew back, intending to scorch him from an angle that wouldn't see Reshma in harm's way. Again she underestimated the grisly vitality of her foe. By rights the thug should be dead on his feet, barely able to move with that wound in his side. Instead the man rushed at her even more quickly than he'd charged at Reshma.

The other Sisters in Kashibai's squad were trying to suppress the sporadic shots coming at them from behind the pipes and hovels. It was left to Kashibai to deal with her hulking attacker. The injuries he'd suffered made him seem scarcely human. His body was disfigured by the knots of muscle that rippled beneath his charred skin, a physique of such grotesquery that she doubted even a lifetime in the ore-mines of Lubentina's polar reaches could inflict upon human flesh. The man's head seemed at once both compressed and elongated, as though his skull had been squeezed from the sides until its very shape became distorted. The broad hands that clenched the power pick were bound about in thick windings, crude mittens that couldn't quite hide the alarming fact that he had only three thick, stumpy fingers on each extremity.

Mutant! The unclean word rang through Kashibai's mind. The bestial nature and prodigious endurance of her enemy were explained. A mix of righteousness and disgust filled her as she met the brute's attack. She felt the sizzling impact of the pick course down her arm as she parried the man's assault with the barrel of her flamer. She winced as the barrel collapsed under the blow, nearly bent in half by the fury of the energised tool. She would offer a eulogy for the weapon's machine-spirit when she returned to the convent. Allowing she survived to do so.

Kashibai's right arm felt numb from the impact of the power pick, but her left was unimpaired. Deftly she plucked the combat knife from her belt and drove the blade up into her foe's wound. She felt the blood of her antagonist – hideously cold and viscous – spurt across her face as she plunged the knife upwards, trying to dig her way to any organ vital enough to put the brute down.

The monstrous foeman screeched an atavistic cry of pain. The power pick fell from his hands as agony pulsed through his immense frame. But he failed to fall, refused to die despite the Sister's stabbing blade. One three-fingered hand came whipping around, smashing across Kashibai's face. The blow knocked teeth from her jaw and sent her tumbling to the ground. The thug glowered down at her. He reached into the wound in his side, plucking the knife from where she'd left it embedded in his flesh.

Before the brute could spring at Kashibai, the armoured figure of a Battle Sister interposed, setting herself between the subhuman hulk and the fallen woman. The rescuer wore a mantle of black silk over her ornately adorned power armour, purity seals and campaign honours fixed to her gorget, the badge of the Adepta Sororitas marked in gold upon her pauldrons. No helm concealed her dusky countenance nor hid the vengeful aspect that now possessed those features. Her eyes were like pits of iron as they matched the enemy's glower.

'Your breath has defiled this world long enough, filth,' the warrior spat. The bolt pistol she held in her left hand barked once, bursting apart the brute's shoulder and spilling him to the floor.

From where she lay on the ground, Kashibai cried out a warning to her commander. 'Sister Superior! He's still moving!'

True to Kashibai's warning, life yet clung to the brute. He was crawling towards the power pick, reaching for it with his disfigured hand.

Sister Superior Trishala was in action even before Kashibai's shout. Smoke still issued from the barrel of her bolt pistol when she moved against her stricken foe. In her right hand she held a gleaming sword, its guard fashioned in the shape of the aquila, its pommel aglow with the frightful energies ready to be unleashed by the blade. Even as the thug's fingers closed about the grip of the pick, Trishala's power sword was chopping down. The man's malformed skull was reduced to pulp beneath the coruscating aura of blue light that rippled down the power sword's blade.

Kashibai had regained her feet when Trishala turned away from the slain brute. The Sister Superior frowned when she noted the state of Kashibai's flamer. 'Virika's squad is pressing them back on the left,' Trishala said. She handed Kashibai her bolt pistol. 'I need your squad to close the gap. Catch them between two fields of fire. By the Golden Throne, we'll purge these mutants from Tharsis.'

'Wasn't our objective to find and relieve the militia patrol?' Kashibai asked.

Trishala's gaze remained a thing of ice and iron. 'I've been unable to make contact with them over the vox. The platoon's vox-caster must be unusable or the underground is interfering with transmissions. If we can't coordinate with the survivors, then the safest way to extricate them is by exterminating these heretics.' She noted that Kashibai was looking past her to the sprawled body of Reshma. Sister Pranjal had broken from cover to drag her injured comrade to cover. 'Make an appreciation of her wounds,' she said, 'but understand that duty comes first. She must be left behind and you can spare no one to linger with her. We will need every gun.'

Kashibai felt Trishala's command cut into her. She knew Trishala was right, but that only made it worse. She handed the bolt pistol back to the Sister Superior. 'I'll take Reshma's bolter,' she said.

'We'll need every gun,' Kashibai said, echoing Trishala's words.

Trishala noted the disapproval in Kashibai's voice as the squad leader hurried away to muster her warriors and discover Reshma's condition. The reaction was to be expected. The hardest thing for any warrior was to leave a comrade on the battlefield, yet there were times when it was necessary. Kashibai might dislike the order, but she was disciplined enough to execute it without protest. It was that dependability that made her so valuable to Trishala.

It was only a matter of moments before Kashibai's squad was following Trishala through the devastated slumland. The Battle Sisters fanned out, sweeping ahead in an arc that would swing around to close up with Virika's warriors, the point held by the militia survivors acting as the fulcrum of their advance. Moving through the destruction, their bolters blasted away at the sporadic gunfire still being directed against them by the enemy. The diminished capacities of their foe troubled Trishala more than any resurgence could have. There were any number of undocumented tunnels and passages running through the Cloisterfells, excavations wrought by work crews and expansions dug out by the wretches who called the underworld home. The fear in Trishala's mind was that the bulk of the enemy had withdrawn, stolen back into the shadows of some secret network of forgotten corridors, leaving behind a rearguard to ensure the Sisters couldn't follow their line of retreat.

'Make haste!' Trishala gave voice to the urgency that pounded through her veins. 'By the Golden Throne, we can't let them escape!'

The cry was barely given when the slashing light of the laser came stabbing out from among the shanties. The cutting beam ripped across the shacks, sending several of them crashing down. The Sisters could see a gang of men moving about beyond the rubble, each of them draped in cloaks of purple and red. Kashibai's warriors opened up on them, picking off three and sending the rest scurrying for cover. Then the laser was stabbing out at them once more.

'Where are they firing from?' Kashibai called out, trying to focus her squad against the weapon that had bedevilled them since their entry into the vault.

'There! In the pipe!' Trishala shouted, triggering a burst from her bolt pistol at a huge section of pipe standing among the hovels. Crouched in the open face of the disused metal cylinder was a clutch of enemy fighters. They were clustered around the bulky frame of a large excavation laser that some fanatic had transformed into a vicious weapon by profaning its range inhibitor and perverting its safety thresholds.

The range was too great for Trishala's pistol, but as the rounds clattered against the shacks around the laser's crew, she succeeded in diverting their attention away from Kashibai and the other Sisters. The purple-garbed gunners pivoted the makeshift weapon on its crude framework and unleashed its malignant energies towards the Sister Superior.

Countless hours of training and years of experience to hone both reflexes and instincts saved Trishala from the cutting beam. She ducked down just as the laser came cleaving through the hovels. Shacks collapsed around her, spilling debris on top of her. She heard Kashibai shout in alarm, then her subordinate's voice was lost in a renewed fury of gunfire. Bolters snarled as they answered the coughs of autoguns. Savage shrieks and snarls sounded from the enemy fighters as they broke cover and rushed at Kashibai's warriors.

Trishala shoved against the rubble piled across her back, the enhanced strength afforded by her power armour allowing her to easily shrug aside the weight. As she extracted herself from the debris, she caught sight of something that flashed across one of the narrow paths between the shanties. It was just an impression, a blur of purple and crimson, but there was a quality about the way it moved that sent a chill rolling through her. Echoes from long ago strove to fill her mind with fear. Trishala beat the fear back with the white-hot heat of hate.

'Sister Kashibai, continue your attack on the pipe,' Trishala commanded. 'There's something moving on our flank. I'm going to see what it is. That will free your squad to achieve the objective.'

'May the Warmason watch over you and the Emperor guide your steps,' Kashibai voxed back.

Trishala drew her power sword from its scabbard and ran down the passage between the shacks. Her every sense was keyed to picking up the trail of the thing she'd so briefly glimpsed. She listened for the sound of its rushing feet, looked for the shiver of the flimsy shanties as it forced its way between the ramshackle shelters, tried to follow the cool oily stink it left in its wake. The mangled bodies of local militia troopers and underworld dregs flickered through her awareness; even the pale, gruesome corpses of enemy fighters couldn't distract her from pursuit of her quarry.

From ahead there sounded the distinctive chatter

of Sister Nagina's heavy bolter. The shooting abruptly stopped, cut off by Nagina's anguished scream and a grinding shriek that didn't issue from anything human. Turning towards the violent sounds, Trishala drove her armoured body through the crude walls of the shacks, smashing through the hovels. Her violent passage through the slums soon brought her into an open space a few metres in width... and face to face with a horror that had haunted her dreams for a lifetime.

Sister Nagina's body lay in a pool of blood, as did the corpse of another of Virika's warriors. Their power armour was ruptured, broken open by the slashing claws of the thing that now loomed over their bodies. Its colouration diverged from the creatures Trishala had seen as a girl, its bony carapace a deep purple in hue while the exposed sinew and muscle between its shell-like segments were a bright red. Yet it was unmistakably of the same breed that had brought death to the hive cities of Primorus, a bestial humanoid with angular dorsal plates running down its hunched back, an abbreviated stump of tail protruding from its spine and vicious talons growing from its hoof-like feet. Two sets of arms grew from the abomination's shoulders, one pair ending in dextrous fingers while the other terminated in scythe-like claws. The fiend's head was a squashed bulb covered in a leathery hide and sporting a set of broad jaws lined with needle-like fangs. Its eyes were pale yellow, the pupils little pinpricks of black that shone with a malignance belonging to neither beast nor man.

Sight of the multi-armed horror stunned Trishala. For a terrible instant she found herself unable to move. In that instant, the monster sprang at her, uttering the same shrieking ululation it had voiced when slaughtering Nagina. Instinct rather than thought brought Trishala's sword sweeping out, striking at the pouncing monstrosity. The energised blade slashed across the abomination. The shriek that sounded from its fanged jaws was now one of pain. It drew back, every muscle growing taut as its body tensed for another spring. Then the creature's eyes grew distant, somehow disconnected from its surroundings.

To Trishala it seemed nothing less than the God-Emperor's intervention when the monster spun around and retreated down a pathway between the hovels. Behind it, spattered with a glistening green ichor, the creature left one of its clawed hands, shorn away at the wrist by her sword.

The Sister Superior recovered quickly. She controlled the urge to chase after the stricken monster. It wasn't the danger of trailing the wounded creature that held her back. Trishala had recognised the thing. She knew what it was and what its presence here meant.

Subduing her disgust, Trishala retrieved the severed claw from the floor. For weeks she'd been warning Palatine Yadav that the trouble building in the Cloisterfells was more than increased ganger activity or some upwelling of sedition among the dispossessed of Tharsis. Now, perhaps, he would listen to her.

The clamour of many bodies racing through the slums drew Trishala's attention back to the narrow paths between the shacks. Charging towards her were a mass of men dressed in grubby coveralls and brandishing a motley variety of weapons. She saw one of the men, his face dominated by an inhumanly elongated mouth and bulbous forehead, point at her with a shaking fist and cry out a single word.

'Infidel!'

A shot from Trishala's pistol exploded the man's malformed skull, but his shout had served its purpose. Provoked to a crazed fury, the rest of the mob surged towards her. Trishala sent shot after shot into the charging mass, dropping another half a dozen of them in the space of a few heartbeats, but even that wasn't enough to stem the tide. Las-beams scored her armour, marring the surface but unable to pierce the heavy ceramite. Slugs from more primitive firearms ricocheted off, dancing away into the slums. The ineffectiveness of their shots only swelled their frenzy. Soon, Trishala's sword was slashing out, hewing through writhing bodies as the mob converged on her.

'Cleanse the mutant! Scourge the heretic!' Kashibai's shout sliced through the tumult as she led her Battle Sisters to stem the surge of enemies.

From the shacks behind Trishala, Kashibai and her squad sent a withering hail of shells into the enemy. The mob disintegrated under that fusillade, torn to bloody ribbons by the concentrated fire. A few survivors turned and fled back into the slums, but the majority of them died trying to reach Trishala, climbing over their own dead in their obsession to kill the Sister Superior.

The power sword crunched down through the sternum of the last enemy, a bald-headed youth who would never see his twentieth cycle. His features weren't as abnormal as many of the others, somehow making the fanaticism gleaming in his eyes even more terrible to see. As he slumped at Trishala's feet, he pawed at her belt with a trembling hand, trying to free the claw she'd cut from the monster.

'Defiler,' the youth snarled as life abandoned him.

With a shudder he fell to the floor amid the wreckage of purple-clad bodies.

Trishala stared down at the youth, then laid her hand on the alien claw she'd taken. Turning towards Kashibai, she gave her subordinate new orders. 'I need a liaison with the local militia. They have to pull out as soon as the way is clear. Impress that point on them. I want them out of here as fast as they can manage.'

'You are conceding the field to the enemy?' Kashibai wondered. 'We've captured the pipe and their laser battery. We have them on the run.' Timidity was something she'd never expected to hear Trishala express. She should have known retreat wasn't her intention.

'They can't be allowed to run. We're done fighting where and how the enemy expects us to fight,' Trishala declared. She pointed at the bodies of Virika's warriors. 'As soon as our people are out, we secure the approaches to this vault and put it to the torch.'

Kashibai nodded, but again Trishala could see the discomfort the brutal command provoked. She shook her head. 'Don't fear for the inhabitants. The cleansing fire will be the greatest mercy we can bestow on them.' An edge of pain crept into her voice and there was a faraway look in her eyes when she spoke. 'If you trust me in nothing else, Sister Kashibai, trust me when I say this.

'There are perils far worse than death that wait to lay claim to mankind.'

Cold black eyes watched as the Sisters turned the vault into a roaring inferno. The crackle of flames, the flicker of fire, the sickly smell of roasting flesh, these drifted back to the ventilation duct like phantoms from a dimly recalled dream. The only thing that was real, the only thing that was substantial to those staring eyes was the commanding figure of Sister Superior Trishala.

The great eyes stared past the armour and flesh of Trishala, peering through them at the woman's soul. Carefully, ever so carefully did Bakasur set his psychic feelers probing her essence. Hers was a strong spirit, bolstered by an innately resolute willpower and honed by decades of the droning devotions of the Imperial Creed. It was certain that with some slight effort, some exertion of his gifts, the magus would be able to punch through such mental defences as she could boast, but to do so would serve small purpose. The abrupt cognitive demise of Trishala would agitate the Order of the Sombre Vow even more than she was already doing. No, the prudent course was to tread carefully until the time was right.

Bakasur slipped through the corridors of Trishala's mind. He didn't press his powers, didn't strengthen his intrusion so that he could read memories and intercept thoughts. He maintained a light touch, avoiding the stray chance that she'd be aware of his spying. He contented himself with impressions, hints and extrapolations that together formed a worrying trend.

For some time Trishala had been a menace in Tharsis, pressing for increased measures to subdue the unrest in the tunnels and among the city's dispossessed. The escalation of local militia incursions had been a product of her campaigning. Now she'd been so bold as to bring her Battle Sisters down here from their priory. This much was known to him already, but probing her mind he found surprising revelations as to why she'd been such a persistent nuisance.

Skimming the currents of Trishala's mind, Bakasur saw clues to a motivation buried deep within her. She'd gone through this before. How much did she know and how much did she merely suspect? More, what did she intend to do about it?

A soft hiss shuddered through Bakasur's mind. The magus was drawn out of his contact with Trishala's psyche, reacting to a far more immediate and familiar intelligence. A sympathetic wince of pain whipped across his pale features, thin lips peeling away from needle-like fangs. The magus sent a soothing vibration through the mind of the pained creature. Normally he wouldn't dare to profane one of the Inheritors with his touch, but its suffering was a thing he couldn't abide. It was out of concern for the Inheritor that he'd compelled it to forsake combat with Trishala after her sword struck it. After what he'd glimpsed in the woman's memories, he wondered if it might have been better not to interfere, to give the Inheritor a chance to remove that threat.

'You are safe, revered one,' he told the three-armed Inheritor crouched beside him behind the duct's grilled grate. 'She won't hurt you again.'

Bakasur reinforced his words with a mental image of comfort and security. The Inheritors were far beyond the dull workings of human comprehension; it was difficult for them to lower themselves to human concepts. Bakasur's physiology combined the attributes of both the Inheritors and humans, a hybrid of both mentality and biology. It was this blending that gave him his powers and his authority. Alone of the many enlightened that lurked in the shadows beneath Tharsis, it was the magus who communed with the Great Father. It was he who carried the commands of the source to its manifold generations of progeny.

The Inheritor looked up at Bakasur, some measure of calm now subduing its agitation. It wasn't fear, or even hate, that moved the alien's mind to such animosity towards Trishala. No, it was the understanding of what had been done to it, the diminishment wrought upon it when she cut away its claw. That was an injury not upon the Inheritor alone, but against the Great Father's grand design, a weakening of the skein that had been so cautiously created.

Unlike the hybrids, unlike those in whom brute mammalian emotions still held sway, the Inheritor had no sense of selfishness to goad it into something as inconsequential as vengeance. When the Sisters interposed themselves into his ambush of the local militia, Bakasur had commanded a withdrawal, committing only a small rearguard to sacrifice themselves. But when one of the sacred Inheritors was maimed by Trishala, a fanatical rage had seized upon the cultists. Dozens had swarmed back into the vault to strike down the woman who dared set her hand against one of the holy ascendants. The result had been a massacre. Determination and ferocity were poor replacements for craft and strategy.

Bakasur focused again upon Trishala. Yes, he felt that same urge to kill this desecrater, the same feeling of outrage thundered through his flesh. But he wouldn't indulge such primitive drives. He could see ahead, fix his vision upon that pattern being crafted by the Great Father.

The outrage of the moment was easily forgotten when balanced against the promises of the Great Father. Bakasur would die, all in the Cult of the Cataclysm would die, but in death all would be reborn. Reborn into a perfect unity with the cosmos itself.

Of what consequence the travails of the flesh when set against the wonders of eternity?

CHAPTER II

The soft melody of nigh-primordial orisons rippled through the mammoth halls of Tharsis' Sovereign Spire. Raised ages ago by the first Cardinal-Governor of Lubentina, the tower had served many roles in its time. Now the planet was led by Cardinal-Governor Sephtok Murdan, a ruler who took pride in his piety and devotion to the Imperial Creed. The incongruous blend of hubris and humility that constituted the core of Murdan's personality had served to transform the Sovereign Spire once again. The tower was now a showpiece, an opulent display of one man's devotion to the God-Emperor. Lavish tapestries depicting scenes from the Great Crusade had been exactingly restored after generations of neglect, hanging once more in their ancient splendour. Grand sculptures had been commissioned to accent the many antechambers and sanctuaries until no room within the tower was without the inspiring countenance of a saint, primarch or revered scion of the Ecclesiarchy staring down from the walls. Flocks of winged servitors had been dispersed into the halls, an omnipresent choir of cherubs that filled the corridors with the litanies of sacred psalms and holy chants, rich incense spilling from the censers crafted into their chests.

The Cardinal-Governor himself was far less impressive than the magnificence of his residence. He was a spare man, his body trending towards emaciation. His flesh had a yellowed tinge to it, lending his skin a quality not unlike old parchment. The overriding impression conveyed by his long, drawn features was one of weariness. The thick robes of his office seemed to overwhelm him, fairly smothering him beneath their ostentatious bulk. His gait was a creeping shuffle that made any official procession twice as lengthy as that of his predecessor.

It was in Murdan's eyes that a petitioner would get a glimpse of why this man controlled Lubentina, for there alone could one glimpse the unremitting resolve that filled the current Cardinal-Governor. It was only in the eyes that the tired, sickly appearance was disrupted and the zealous strength of the soul within shone through.

Those eyes were closed while Murdan sank back into the depths of his alabaster throne and listened to the bickering of his councillors. The attitude of restful oblivion was deceptive, for he paid the keenest attention to every word spoken in his presence. Like some reptile basking in the sun, Murdan let the discourse flow into him, building up until that moment when, without preamble or warning, he would snap from his repose and seize upon some factor raised by an unfortunate councillor.

From where she was seated among the councillors, Sister

Superior Trishala closely scrutinised the Cardinal-Governor, trying to gauge how Murdan was reacting to the details he was hearing. Despite her vigilance, he remained an enigma, keeping his thoughts close and his impressions hidden behind his withered visage. After a time, Trishala diverted her attention to the man currently addressing the council.

'...are growing worse,' the clipped tones of Colonel Hafiz rang out. Commander of Lubentina's Planetary Defence Force, Hafiz was the opposite of Murdan in almost every way and far easier for Trishala to read. Strongly built, with broad shoulders and a thick, bull-like neck, he punctuated each point he raised with an animated shake of his fist. Fierce, almost primal, in his mannerisms, Hafiz was all physicality and action. There was passion and conviction in his eyes, but these qualities lacked depth. They were more a veneer laid atop the unquestioning discipline drilled into the soldier. Initiative and independence weren't encouraged among Lubentina's militia.

'But is it a genuine increase or a reaction to the growing presence of your troops in the Cloisterfells?' The question was voiced by the black-robed Palatine Yadav. Among the highest-ranking priests on Lubentina, he was the keeper of the Warmason's Cathedral, a great and prestigious position to hold. Yet these responsibilities weren't enough for Yadav. He aspired to greater things and since taking on his duties several decades ago, he'd done everything in his power to improve the flow of pilgrims journeying to the shrine world. Anything that might present a disruption of the throngs of faithful visiting the cathedral was, to Yadav, the most abominable of sins.

'There have been disturbances in the Cloisterfells for

some time, palatine,' Hafiz reminded Yadav. 'Those disturbances have been spreading into the hab-units of the laity. Thefts, disappearances, murders – even an increase in mental breakdown in certain sections.' The colonel clapped his hand down upon the onyx surface of the council table. 'The use of the local militia to patrol the tunnels is a reaction to this unrest, not a provocation.'

Yadav shook his head, irritation pulling at his features. 'I have perused the same reports you have, colonel. After considerable evaluation of the evidence I see nothing to support your claims. A handful of isolated incidents don't constitute a pattern. What *does* is the marked expansion of criminality since your troops began their campaign in the tunnels. The number of occurrences hasn't been the only increase, but also the scope and violence of these outbreaks.' He looked down at the data-slate resting on the table beside his arm, manipulating the runes displayed upon its crystal face until the device recalled the report he was seeking. 'Here is an example for you. Forty days ago Argos Mineral Hoarding VII suffered an intrusion during their maintenance cycle. One Ares-pattern mining laser and twelve power cells were stolen in the incident. This theft was executed in such a fashion as to avoid the attention of the hoarding's personnel until well after the robbery was accomplished.' Yadav again consulted the data-slate. 'Let us move forwards to three days ago, well after your patrols began. The same hoarding was again violated, but this time the perpetrators seized six mining lasers, a hundred power cells, seven cases of delving charges and a gross of power picks, maul-hammers and plasma-drills. We also have to address the fact that they murdered sixty-three workers when they staged this outrage.' Yadav peered closely at Hafiz. 'Your patrols aren't quelling the unrest in the tunnels, but have made things worse.'

From across the council table, the corpulent Minister Kargil interjected his own opinion on the subject of escalation. 'What has made things worse, palatine, is the trespass by the Order of the Sombre Vow into the Cloisterfells.' He waved a pudgy, bejewelled hand towards Trishala. 'They should be content with the prestige of serving as protectors of the cathedral. Instead we find them charging around underground getting into gunfights with gangers and damaging the infrastructure of Tharsis.'

Trishala leaned forwards, ready to offer rebuke to Kargil. It was annoyance enough that the council saw fit to waste time with debate and discussion when action was called for. That she'd been summoned here when she should be organising her Battle Sisters for a more thorough incursion into the Cloisterfells only worsened her temper. Verbal abuse from a profiteer like Kargil was the final indignity.

'It is a simple thing to speak of obligation and duty for someone to whom those are just words,' Trishala said. 'What duty do you know beyond growing your wealth? Do you feel any obligation to the pilgrims who come to Lubentina but lack the resources to leave? No, you leave them to sink into the Cloisterfells where they and their descendants lose the Emperor's light and become a breeding ground for heresy and worse.'

Kargil rapped his rings together in a petulant gesture. 'The dregs of the Cloisterfells have only to climb to the surface to do homage to the God-Emperor. They are too lazy to rise to such effort. You accuse me of being faithless, yet you make excuses for them? For that matter, if the tunnels are such a hotbed of heresy and rebellion as you say, why is it only now that the Order of the Sombre Vow has taken an interest in them? Is it perhaps that your boldness is reserved for festivals and pageants?'

Colonel Hafiz made a slashing motion of his hand. 'I'll hear none of that,' the officer snarled. 'If not for the Sisters the entire patrol would have been wiped out.'

'You know that for a fact, do you?' Kargil asked, unable to keep a sneer from his visage. 'You know that your troopers wouldn't have been able to acquit themselves perfectly well on their own? I know your men suffered terrible losses, but how many of those losses were inflicted by these seditious elements and how many were lost when the Sisters became over-zealous and started setting everything on fire?'

Hafiz glanced at Trishala, a look of apology in his eyes. When he swung around to face Kargil, there was no trace of softness in his gaze. 'You have the wrong of it,' he said, each word carefully enunciated, exactingly stripped of the emotion boiling inside him. 'The situation was critical. Without Sister Superior Trishala's intervention, none of us would have got out of that vault.'

'None of *us*?' Kargil repeated, a malignant glow rushing into his face. 'Is it the usual protocol for the commander of a planet's defence forces to personally lead a simple patrol? By the Throne! And you wonder why this scum came against you in such force?'

'You see how your decisions have exacerbated the situation?' Yadav asked the colonel. 'Going down into the tunnels yourself could only make things worse. Your presence could serve only as a rallying cry for these seditious elements. Do you appreciate the coup they could effect by killing you? In the deluded minds of such men they would consider such an accomplishment as legitimisation of their grievances, something to embolden their wayward scheming still further.'

'It needn't be sedition,' Kargil said. 'We've not had serious trouble with rebels here for generations. The grumblers and complainers we do suffer aren't the sort to take up arms and go shooting up platoons of soldiers. I say the culprits are gangers. They learned Colonel Hafiz was coming into their territory and decided that the ransom they could demand for him was big enough to–'

'The enemy isn't gangers or rebels,' Trishala declared. 'There is a xenos infestation underneath this city.'

From the metal casket she'd brought with her she removed an object wrapped in rough fabric. 'I have the proof,' she added as she slammed it down on the table. The fabric fell open, exposing the purplish claw she'd cut from the monster in the vault.

Trishala's display was met with a stunned silence. Murdan seemed to sink deeper into his voluminous robes, retreating before this shocking claim. Kargil's face grew steadily redder, his fat body swelling with indignation. A tremor shook Yadav, one of his hands closing about the aquila medallion he wore around his neck, as if to ward away some evil omen. Hafiz stared down at the claw, studying it with intense scrutiny. The other councillors looked at one another in both alarm and confusion.

It was Kargil who finally broke the awkward silence. 'Xenos,' he scoffed. 'Are you asking us to believe that after millennia of human habitation an alien threat has only now chosen to make itself known?'

'There is no denying that talon is an offence,' one of the other ministers said, quickly averting her eyes when she chanced to look at the limb.

'Mutation,' Yadav said. 'It is a lamentable reality that the bodies of those who have withdrawn from the Emperor's light can harbour the most grievous abnormalities. Corruption twists both flesh and soul. Where the mutant is found, the rot of heresy isn't far away. It is a terrible slight upon all of us that a shrine world could exhibit this kind of manifestation. It is a warning that we haven't been vigilant. That we haven't been zealous enough in our duties to the God-Emperor.'

Trishala turned to the palatine. 'This claw came from an alien, not a mutant.' She let her gaze stray to Kargil. 'And I didn't claim this xenos was indigenous to Lubentina.'

Kargil cut her off with a huff of laughter. 'I was unaware that you had been trained as a magos biologis as well as a Battle Sister. You must have been to make such an assertion.'

'Sister Superior, isn't it possible you're overreacting?' another councillor suggested, trying to mollify the mounting tempers around the table.

'I fought it,' Trishala stated. 'It was my sword that cut that arm from its body.'

Kargil pounced on Trishala's words. 'There you have it then. In the heat of combat, in the turmoil of fighting for your life, your recollection has become distorted. You've turned a particularly noxious mutant into something entirely different. Something that maybe a Sister Superior can feel no shame for allowing to get away.'

He licked his lips nervously when he saw the fury his last barb provoked in Trishala.

Yadav interrupted Kargil's harangue. 'It is certain that the malefactors killed in this incident are a divergence from acceptable human stock,' he said. 'One has only to look at the rampant malformities readily evident in the carcasses recovered from the vault.' His tone became conciliatory as he turned towards Trishala. 'Yet there is nothing there so divergent that it needs some obscene xenos biology to explain it. However debased, these were men.' He looked past Trishala to Colonel Hafiz. 'Wouldn't you agree?'

Hafiz nodded his head. As indebted as he felt to the Sisters for their rescue of his command, he couldn't lend his support to something he didn't believe. 'Mutation,' he said.

'I know what attacked me,' Trishala repeated. 'It was nothing human.'

Kargil rolled his eyes. 'On the moon of Tarsus Nine I saw a creature that was almost two metres tall, covered in fur and with a frill of horns growing out of its shoulders. That atrocity was a mutation of an asteroid sapper whose radiation suit failed and left him exposed to the unfettered rays of Tarsus for a twelve-hour work cycle.'

'It is a truism that those in whom the light of the God-Emperor is feeble are susceptible to the most pernicious genetic divergence,' Cardinal-Governor Murdan declared. 'We must consider the squalor and disorder of the Cloisterfells, an environment where the weak of spirit may find their faith tested. All too many fail that test and in doing so they invite into themselves not merely the heretical ideas that pollute the mind and soul, but likewise the contaminants that befoul blood and biology. The righteous will seek absolution through termination once they appreciate their degenerate condition.'

Murdan wrung his bony hands together, a deep regret in his eyes. 'The faithless, however, fear the judgement of the God-Emperor. They cling to even such a miserable existence and, in the lowest pits of their wretchedness, they breed amongst themselves and perpetuate generations of polluted spawn.'

'It needs no xenos to explain the monstrous qualities of these malcontents,' Yadav agreed. 'Mutation, spiritual and genealogical degeneracy are far more reasonable explanations.' There was almost a tone of appeal in the priest's voice as he spoke to Trishala.

Kargil was more brusque in his manner. 'I can understand why the Sister Superior insists this incident be magnified beyond its proportions. This excursion, this "exercise" as she terms it, has cost the city considerable resources. The damage done to the vault has inflicted a disruption to incense production, reducing output to thirty per cent. Efforts to redress the disparity have forced conscription squads into the tunnels to recruit extra labour for the factories.' He turned towards Murdan. 'Forgive me for pointing this out, Excellency, but it would create a poor impression on the pilgrims visiting Lubentina if they were unable to express their devotion through the purchase of properly sanctified incense sticks to burn in the Warmason's Cathedral.'

'There must never be any disruption inflicted upon the faithful,' Murdan agreed. 'The pilgrimage to Lubentina is one that should strengthen the faith, not cause it to be questioned.'

'Then that is why you won't listen to me?' Trishala asked. 'Because you don't want to disrupt the pilgrimage or disturb the pilgrims?'

'Understand the gravity of your accusation,' Yadav pleaded. 'If there is a xenos presence on Lubentina then we would be compelled to dispatch an astropathic call for assistance. The Imperium would send Space Marines and Imperial Guard to impose a quarantine while the situation was being evaluated. Maybe even the Inquisition to investigate. There would be no pilgrims allowed to pay homage at Vadok Singh's cathedral, to restore their faith by seeing the Warmason's relics. Word would spread that there was a blight on Lubentina. The faithful would go elsewhere. Even when things returned to normality it would take a long time to repair the damage.'

'It might take years, even decades, for the pilgrimages to resume,' Kargil elaborated. 'Think of what harm that would inflict upon our economy. All the devotionals left unsold, the incense unburned. Empty hostels...'

'Such concerns are transitory,' Murdan said. 'But it is the loss of prestige Lubentina would suffer. A place of holiness, a shrine world devoted to the God-Emperor's Warmason, the noble Vadok Singh! How should the blemish of such a taint be effaced? It isn't simply our own honour, our own position that is jeopardised but the legacy of Vadok Singh himself! How many might have their faith shaken, their minds left vulnerable to all manner of heresies, should we be found unworthy custodians of the duty entrusted to us?'

Trishala looked towards Colonel Hafiz. 'You were there,' she told him. 'It was your men who were killed by these things. Will you sit here and say that they were nothing but mutants and rebels?'

Hafiz looked up from the table, forcing himself to meet her accusing glare. 'I saw nothing that couldn't be explained in such terms.'

'Then we are agreed,' Yadav said. 'This incident was nothing more than a mutant uprising.' He propped himself up in his chair, looking across at the other councillors. 'An additional tithe shall be levied to fund more missionary work among the unfortunates in the Cloisterfells, that the Imperial Creed may draw them away from the confusion and madness that threatens to overwhelm them.'

'That is the long view, palatine,' Kargil said. 'I prefer more immediate and practical solutions. We can evaluate each sector, each individual section if need be, based upon how indispensable they are to the city as a whole. Those that offer nothing vital can be sealed off and isolated.'

'You would entomb the innocent along with the guilty,' Hafiz warned the minister.

'Necessary casualties to curtail this unrest,' Kargil huffed. 'If it eases your conscience, think of them as martyrs. Sacrifices to the prestige and prosperity of Lubentina.'

Trishala slammed her palms down on the table. 'You can't eradicate a xenos infestation by simply sealing it away and trying to ignore it. Their taint must be purged, cleansed utterly before it destroys everything.'

'I have heard your claims, Sister Superior,' Murdan's voice bristled with annoyance. 'Your course would inflict injury upon the legacy of Vadok Singh and inflict upon this world a blemish that might forever tarnish it. There is *no* xenos presence here. There will be *no* distress call sent. What we have is a rabble of brazen mutants and malcontents that will be dealt with by *our* forces.' He pointed at Kargil. 'Initiate the conscription of another four thousand soldiers to augment the local militia. I leave the details of financing such an endeavour to you.' The Cardinal-Governor turned his attention upon Yadav.

'Amend the sermons of your priests to include a call to arms. Muster the frateris militia – draw your recruits from off-world pilgrims if need be. We will seal such areas of the underground as are feasible, but the rest of the tunnels will need to be cordoned off and purified.'

Murdan leaned back in his throne and contemplated the anger he saw in Trishala's face. 'Confine your Sisters to their duties at the Warmason's Cathedral,' he ordered her. 'There will be no more exercises in the tunnels. I will hear no more stories about aliens crawling through the bowels of Tharsis.'

The Cardinal-Governor's fingers drummed against the arms of his throne, an agitated tattoo that echoed through the hall. 'We will handle this,' he repeated. 'There will be *no* distress call.'

'Your obstinacy before the Cardinal-Governor was unacceptable.' Palatine Yadav's voice was subdued as he walked along the great archway that spilled down from the upper reaches of the Sovereign Spire and into the statue-lined expanse of the Starfold Plaza. Throngs of pilgrims in robes of grey and white could be seen prostrating themselves before the towering sculptures, sometimes setting sticks of smoking incense into the sand-filled pits that spread before the base of each eidolon. The congregations were largest around the colossus that depicted Vadok Singh himself, but none of the statues was without at least a few score petitioners seeking a blessing from the legendary hero or revered saint they depicted.

Trishala stalked in silence beside the palatine. The discourse in the council chamber, the reprimand issued by Murdan, these were things that had cut deep. A pompous profiteer like Kargil would say that her pride had been wounded, but the injury wasn't so shallow as anything she recognised as 'self'. The intransigence of the Cardinal-Governor had challenged her sense of duty. For the first time since taking the sombre vow, she felt doubt. Not doubt in her own abilities or her own worthiness, but in the very nature of the calling she'd taken onto herself, the obligations she'd accepted as a Sister Superior.

'My own home world was despoiled by xenos,' Trishala said. 'Smoke and fire spilling through the streets, the screaming and the shooting. The shrieks of aliens as they scuttled through the devastation. The whole of my family was lost. By the time the Inquisition came there was little left to save.' She fixed a stern gaze on Yadav. 'Whatever I have to do to keep that from happening here, whoever I offend or insult, by the Golden Throne I will. It won't be by my inaction that such a thing happens again.'

Though Yadav knew Trishala's background, had read her history, never before had he heard her speak of it. No pain, no regret crept into her voice, only a steely harshness. Whatever sorrow she'd felt, whatever hurt she'd known, it had been buried so long that it had been transmuted into something entirely different. What the priest heard in her tone was hate, strengthened and sharpened by the purity of righteousness. Yadav had seen many times the awful power of such hate. It could fuel the most astounding valour, drive someone beyond endurance and reason, push them to feats that trespassed upon the realm of miracles. At the same time he'd seen the demands hate put upon both soul and body, a relentless taskmaster that left nothing of comfort and tranquillity to succour the mind.

'By defying decorum and protocol you will only hinder

your course,' Yadav warned. 'There are ways to get things done, but we must all of us abide by the strictures of status and position.'

'No one wants to hear an unpleasant truth,' Trishala said. 'They have to be forced to face it. Dragged out and made to confront it if need be. There isn't time for courtesies and diplomacy. This world is threatened by xenos and you need to accept that reality.'

'The only one certain of that is you,' Yadav pointed out. 'Colonel Hafiz was there and he saw nothing to make him believe what attacked his men were more than rebels and mutants. Yet you are convinced that it is you who is right and everyone else wrong.' The priest shook his head. 'Isn't it more reasonable to consider that maybe your belief is wrong? Some similarity between this mutant's abnormalities and the xenos that attacked your home world has brought all those old memories rushing back. Distorting your perception.'

'There are some things that retain their clarity no matter how much time has passed,' Trishala said. 'Don't you think I have meditated on this? Don't you think I've prayed that I'm wrong? But I'm not. That claw is from a xenos. And it would be reckless to assume that where there is one alien there aren't others.'

Yadav tried a different tack. 'Would you have the Inquisition here, the Ordo Xenos set loose on Tharsis? You of all people know what would happen then.'

Trishala's eyes were cold as steel when she looked at Yadav. 'Don't mistake me, palatine. I understand that what the Inquisition did to my home world was necessary. All taint of the xenos had to be purged. In such a situation, mercy could only be the most unforgivable weakness. To risk the alien taint rising again... or spreading to other worlds and other people.'

'You took your vows as a way of fighting back?' Yadav asked.

'No,' Trishala said. 'I became an Adepta Sororitas because I sought a way in which I could strengthen the Imperium, a way to be of service to the God-Emperor. Even to play the smallest part in His design, to defend all that He has built.'

'Yet you are still haunted by your memories,' Yadav persisted. 'For all the valour and strength and discipline that the Order of the Sombre Vow has given you, somewhere in your heart you still hold on to this ember of hate.'

'To despise the xenos is virtue, not sin,' Trishala recited from one of Yadav's own sermons.

Yadav frowned at the reproof. 'Without context, wisdom decays into foolishness. Hate can be servant, but it must never be allowed to become master. There must always be the understanding that what ennobles us is far more than hate. There is devotion and there is faith and there is obedience.'

The stress the priest put upon the last word wasn't lost on Trishala. 'I can't sit back and do nothing,' she told him.

'You aren't doing nothing. The Order of the Sombre Vow has been entrusted with protecting the relics of Vadok Singh and the Warmason's Cathedral,' Yadav said. 'The council is taking steps to deal with this unrest – whatever its nature. The expense will probably upset Minister Kargil and the merchant guilds, but they will rise to their responsibilities. An expanded local militia supported by several thousand frateris militia will settle things.

'Your experiences when you were a child have clouded

your judgement. The trouble down in the tunnels made you think back to what happened on your home world.' Yadav tapped a finger against the side of his tonsured head. 'In some corner of your mind you expected to find xenos down there and when you encountered a severely deformed mutant, that part of your mind latched onto it, transformed it in your imagination into the same sort of monster that killed your family.'

'I know what I saw, what I cut with my sword,' Trishala stated. 'I've been ordered to keep my Sisters stationed in the cathedral. You need have no fear that I will disobey those commands. But nothing you tell me will change what I know to be true.' She waved her hand at the plaza below, at the tiers of towers and minarets that rose beyond the statues to stab upwards into the sky.

'My prayer is that you will see I'm right,' Trishala said. 'That you will forget your fears about lost revenue and lost prestige. That you will send the call for aid before it's too late.'

Far beneath the windswept spires of Tharsis, away from the cold light of a distant sun and the chill kiss of a polar wind, the air was hot and dank, mephitic in its cloying humidity. A dull, persistent pulse of orange light glowed from just beneath a skin of mineral encrustation built up over millennia.

Beyond the orange glow was a place of shadows, a writhing darkness that sent flickering protrusions out across the pulsating walls. There was an intensity about that blackness, an antiquity that reached beyond the roots of this planet, stretching away into lightless voids cosmic and primordial.

Bakasur bowed his head as he hastened towards that darkness. He stifled the fearful adoration that surged through such of his being as remained weak and anthropoid. He composed his thoughts, turning his mind to patterns that transcended mammalian flesh. He brought his intellect into that state of harmony that was receptive to the darkness, that could synchronise itself with the visions of the Great Father.

The magus could hear the scuttle of the Inheritors as they stirred in the dark. He felt regret that he wasn't like them, that his own form wasn't cast in such wondrous shape. He could never be accepted by them as he was, only tolerated as a necessity, a means towards a divine end. But with that end, he would earn ascension. He would be cleansed and cast anew, drawn into purpose eternal and wondrous.

Out of the shadows, Bakasur felt the Great Father brush against his own consciousness. The magus exulted in the contact, aware that he was blessed to commune with the master in such a profound manner. He opened his mind to the psychic touch, cast aside the barriers and defences that warded him from the notice of the astropaths and psykers that attended Lubentina's Cardinal-Governor. Here, in the very lair of the Beast, there was no need of such precautions. The might of the Great Father was indefatigable and unyielding, more than equal to hiding both of them from scryers and telepaths.

The Great Father's intelligence poured into Bakasur, flooding through his mind like a raging tempest. The magus shrivelled in the ecstatic agony, his identity drowning in the psychic splendour of his master. Like a stalking hound, the Great Father's mind probed into every corner of Bakasur's being, exploring every facet of his individuality. Each experience, each memory and thought was turned over, examined, digested and then discarded. Higher and higher the floodwaters rose; Bakasur could feel his essence smothering, fading away beneath the enormity that had supplanted it. Terror, beautiful and radiant, suffused his being. He would be consumed, drained and devoured, absorbed into the majesty of his master.

Bakasur collapsed, gasping for breath, feeling his organs shuddering in agony as nervous sensation was restored to them. His skull throbbed with pain, a tortuous pounding that seemed it could only end by bursting from his cranium. Most terrible of all, however, was the sense of emptiness, the dreadful diminishment that always followed communion with the Great Father. After housing even a fragment of his master's mind, his own mind felt small and empty. A grisly loneliness clawed at the magus. Only the knowledge that the sensation would pass made it bearable and gave the magus the strength to rise from the rocky floor.

'Your unworthy servant awaits your bidding, master,' Bakasur told the darkness and the thing that brooded beyond the shadows. Dreadful anticipation gripped him when he felt the Great Father's mind again reaching out to his own.

This time Bakasur wasn't smothered beneath the flow of his master's presence. There was no loss of identity, no threat of being consumed. Having extracted what it needed from him, now new knowledge was pouring into him, revelations that crackled like fire through his brain. The wisdom of the Great Father streamed through Bakasur's synapses, a torrent of plot and counter-plot. The situation on Lubentina had changed at Trishala's instigation, but where Bakasur had seen a threat the Great Father saw promise.

Trishala had tried to warn the rulers of Tharsis about the Inheritors and the Cult of the Cataclysm. Bakasur's spies revealed that such warning had been dismissed. There would be no distress call, no appeal to the Imperium for aid. The Lubentines intended to quell their 'rebel problems' on their own.

Bakasur reeled at the ambitious seeds the Great Father planted in his mind. They would use this, they would harness the fear and dread of Lubentina to achieve far more than their initial design. The slow, gradual spread of the Great Father's blessing was at an end. No more would they need to be satisfied with clutches of pilgrims waylaid before their return to the spaceport. The opportunity for a far bolder strategy now stood before them.

All it needed was the right application of pressure to make things happen.

The time had come for the Cult of the Cataclysm to emerge from the shadows.

CHAPTER III

From the upper reaches of the Tomb-Cutters' Guild, Colonel Hafiz spotted a motley swarm of purple and crimson come scrambling out from the waste-runs that dipped away from the vast tomb-yards. The officer shuddered as he noted the horrible malformations that distorted the bodies of the maniacs. Though he refused to accept Sister Superior Trishala's claims that their enemy was the product of some xenos contagion, there was no denying that they were some perversion of human stock. They crawled and squirmed through the waste channel with frenzied abandon, heedless of the acidic muck that was the runoff from the tomb-cutters' chemical etchers. It was a sickening sight watching them trudge through the toxic filth, steam rising from their bodies as the acids burned their skin.

The searing flare of a plasma gun blasting away at the Guild Hall was a fearsome reminder to Hafiz that, however brutish and deformed the cultists were, they'd managed to arm themselves in a most formidable fashion. Much of the weaponry he'd seen them using looked to be cobbled together from mining tools and industrial implements, profanely debased towards purposes far from those ordained by the Machine God. Other weapons looked to have been stolen from the Arbites and from the stocks of Lubentina's militia, plunder stripped from the bodies of slaughtered patrols and overwhelmed positions.

Attempting to quarantine the Cloisterfells had proven disastrous. Hafiz hadn't anticipated an enemy as organised and numerous as that which waited in the underworld. This insurrection must have been years in the planning, for the enemy had excavated a number of new tunnels and passages, routes by which they could circle around barricades and strongpoints to fall upon the soldiers and militia from supposedly secure areas. Trying to fight them underground was a losing prospect, so with Cardinal-Governor Murdan's approval, Hafiz had withdrawn to the surface, intending to confine their adversaries to the slumland below.

As he looked out across the funerary complex, Hafiz was confronted with the reality that even this much was proving beyond the capabilities of his soldiers. The responsibility, he knew, ultimately rested with him. He'd made the most disastrous error any commander could. He'd underestimated the enemy.

'Alert Lieutenant Abhav,' Hafiz told his comm officer. 'Have his platoon concentrate fire on the crypt-presses. I want that sun gun eliminated.'

He turned back to the window as his orders were being voxed to Abhav. The crypt-presses, gigantic mechanisms of rockcrete and plasteel, were lined up across the boulevard adjacent to the tomb-yards. Their dark facades were splotched with streaks of white-grey, molten splashes of marble-dust expelled from the huge store-towers that loomed above them. The integrity of one tower had been compromised so completely that the structure now sagged at a gravity-defying angle and had spilled a huge mound of powdered marble onto the engravers' sheds across the street.

Those store-towers had offered the first challenge to Hafiz's plans. When the alarm had reached his headquarters that the enemy were breaking into the tomb-yards, he'd thought to send them scurrying back to their burrows with a display of force. Six Chimera armoured assault transports had been the vanguard of his attack. Two of them now stood burning in the street, blasted from ambush by missiles launched from the towers. The violence of his command's reprisal had riddled the towers with las-fire, but even now they were a source of sporadic shots. He suspected that the enemy had breached the dispersion pipes that hung from the underside of each tower and were crawling up through them to enter the superstructure.

Out of the corner of his eye, Hafiz could see the pudgy figure of Captain Debdan moving towards the window. 'Do you want the men to open up on the towers again?' he asked, noticing the direction of the colonel's gaze.

Hafiz shook his head, gesturing angrily at the tomb-yards where swarms of the enemy could be seen darting behind the pressure-kilns or boldly rushing through the glaze-showers despite the toxic chemicals puddling the floor of each stall. He saw a huge brute loping around a line of prefabricated mausoleums, what looked to be a lascannon tucked underneath his arms.

'If we divert too much fire to the towers then that scum will just walk right in,' Hafiz cursed.

'We could try a counter-assault?' Debdan proposed. 'Use two of the Chimeras and move the men up after them.'

Hafiz grunted a caustic laugh. 'Into that?' He pointed at the steaming pools of acid forming between the pressure-kilns, the clouds of yellow gas venting from hoses and pipes holed by the shooting. 'The tomb-cutters use servitors to operate that machinery and even those have to be recycled after a year. I send my troops out there and six months from now every one of them will be confined to a hospice spitting out bits of his lungs.'

'They must be mad,' Debdan said.

An ugly growl rattled at the back of Hafiz's throat. Angrily he snapped off a shot with the laspistol in his hand. His target was one of the shapes slinking around by the glaze-showers, a tall rebel robed in purple. This enemy had his arms wrapped about a severed section of pipe nearly twice as tall as himself. Tied to the apex of the pipe was a loathsome icon, a fanged and leering visage, inhuman and monstrous. The colonel's shot exploded the clay icon into a thousand fragments. A second shot pierced the icon-bearer's neck and pitched him backwards into one of the toxic puddles.

'Worse than madness,' Hafiz snarled. 'Heresy. They have done more than forsake Murdan's authority. They've abandoned the God-Emperor Himself.'

The flare of the plasma gun bloomed once more from the crypt-presses. This time the shot immolated a swath of the Guild Hall's annexe, vaporising a three-metre stretch of the building's roof. The suppressing fire coming from Abhav's platoon lost its intensity as most of the survivors hurriedly quit the roof.

'Raise Abhav again,' Hafiz ordered his comm officer. 'Tell him to get those men back in position.'

A flurry of motion among the stacks of funerary slabs the tomb-cutters used to seal the faces of their construction drew the colonel's attention, making him forget the plasma gun and Abhav's routed men. It was only a glimpse, a blur, but something about the way the thing moved prickled the hairs at the back of his neck. For a moment he kept his eyes on the stacked slabs, ignoring Debdan's questions and the vox operator's failure to contact Abhav. His focus was entirely on the slabs and the ghastly apparition he'd glimpsed.

Horrified fascination held Hafiz when he saw the creature come sprinting out from behind the slabs, charging towards the burning wreck of a Chimera. Hafiz was amazed by the thing's speed as much as he was revolted by its inhuman anatomy. The claw Trishala had cut from the monster in the vault didn't begin to conjure such a nightmarish...

Hafiz was about to class the thing a mutation, but then he saw a second come loping out from the stacks, both so similar in aspect that they might have been poured from the same mould. Trishala's insistence that the menace threatening Tharsis was alien rang once more in his ears and sent a shiver through his body.

'Withdraw,' Hafiz hissed, now watching the four-armed monsters slipping out from among the stacks. Just one of these things had killed two of Trishala's Battle Sisters, its claws shredding their power armour as though it were parchment. 'Withdraw!' he shouted, turning from the window and seizing the vox-caster from his startled comms officer. In hurried tones he broadcast the order for retreat to his men.

'You can't concede the tomb-yards to these... cultists,' Debdan objected. The captain didn't put too much animation into his protest. He'd been after a promotion for some time and if Hafiz were dismissed for cowardice in action then Debdan might be able to jump a few ranks in short order.

'We can't fight them,' Hafiz snapped. 'Not here. Not with only a few platoons. Not against creatures that can kill Battle Sisters.' He turned away from Debdan, barking out orders to the rest of his staff, hurrying them to quit the brief headquarters they'd established.

They had to pull out. Leave the tomb-yards to these aliens and their cult. Hafiz would bring every piece of artillery in the militia's arsenal to bear against the zone and pound it into rubble. The area was largely uninhabited to begin with. Let the cultists have it, then bombard them from afar. It was too much to hope they'd crush the cult by such tactics, but maybe they could make them think twice about trying to gain a foothold on the surface.

Of one thing Colonel Hafiz was certain. Cardinal-Governor Murdan and his council were going to have to rethink the gravity of the problem and how much they were willing to expend to reach a solution.

From the heights of the Warmason's Cathedral, Trishala was afforded a sweeping view of Tharsis. The cathedral was the tallest building in the city, mightier than even the Sovereign Spire. From the lowest step outside the Great Gate to the protective gargoyles that crouched atop the loftiest of its seventy bell-towers, the cathedral was one hundred and eighty metres. To this height was added that of the great summit upon which it had been built – Mount

Rama. Formed from the spoil dredged up by the mines that had once been the lifeblood of Lubentina, the heap had grown and expanded until it assumed gigantic dimensions and dominated the landscape around Tharsis.

Karim Das, whose mineral exploitation swiftly eclipsed that of the other merchant guilds operating on Lubentina, gave credit for his prosperity to the wisdom and guidance of Vadok Singh. Adhering to the principles of the Warmason's craft Das was able to accumulate a vast fortune and even marry one of his children into a noble house on Terra. To repay the bounty he'd benefited from, he set about creating a shrine to his holy patron. With the help of the Ecclesiarchy he was able to erect the Warmason's Cathedral on Mount Rama and house within it some of the most sacred of Vadok Singh's regalia. For those who belonged to the Cult of the Warmason, there was now a way to venerate their patron without making a pilgrimage to holy Terra itself.

The cathedral was a monolithic structure, its thick outer walls forged from plasteel and reinforced with interior balustrades of ferrocrete to support the weight of the upper floors and outer towers. Immense glassaic windows peppered the exterior, each showing fabulous scenes from the Great Crusade and the Golden Age. Colossal reliefs depicting the instruments used by Vadok Singh and the constructions shaped by the Warmason's designs stretched across the walls. Gilded walkways and ornamented balconies jutted out from the building, hovering between the lofty bell-towers and the slopes of Mount Rama far below.

It was downwards that Trishala cast her gaze. The slopes of Mount Rama were always characterised by the throngs of pilgrims slowly ascending the approaches to the Warmason's Cathedral. The route taken by those off-worlders seeking to pay homage to Vadok Singh was strictly dictated by revered tradition and venerated customs. The Ladder of Obeisance was the most arduous of the paths a pilgrim could choose, a winding stairway that circled nearly the whole of the mountain and counted over ten thousand steps in its ascent. Those who mounted the Ladder were considered the most pious and devoted of the Warmason's cult, though a wealthy pilgrim could claim the same prestige if he hired one of the city's professional penitents to make the climb for him. For those less stout of either body or spiritual conviction there were six other approaches to the cathedral, each one less taxing than the last, the least of them being the Chastened Road, which led directly from the heart of Tharsis up to the cathedral. The short journey upon the Chastened Road allowed little time for reflection or privation and pilgrims on the path, except for those brandishing the flag of their hired penitent, were subjected to the voluble scorn and jeers of the Lubentines whose habitations and vendor stands abutted the street.

Normally the indignity of the Chastened Road kept it largely free of traffic while the distinction of the Ladder meant the stairway was often a creeping mass of humanity. There wasn't a better indicator of how much Lubentina's situation had altered than the change that had beset the approaches to the cathedral. The Ladder was all but devoid of travellers while the easier paths and especially the Chastened Road were packed with those seeking the holy halls of the Emperor's Warmason. Nor were pilgrims the prevailing majority of those seekers; they'd been supplanted by Lubentines, locals alarmed by the turmoil afflicting their city and hastening to the most venerated shrines. Many of the Lubentines sought to ease their minds, reflecting on the wonders of Vadok the Builder and how his works had endured through the millennia. Others sought the blessing of Vadok the Defender, to beg his protection from the trouble afflicting their city. A few came to appeal to the Warmason's martial aspect, to find strength and courage to join the fight.

Trishala turned from her view of the city and stared through the window behind her. She watched a group of petitioners file past an onyx plinth upon which rested the Gauntlet of Vadok Singh and the stasis field generator that had preserved it for millennia. Trishala could almost see the despair rising from them; seeing them make the sign of the aquila with their hands, hearing them recite the High Gothic chants, observing them as they moved off along the angular corridor to hunt down the next shrine to render up their prayers.

The sound of Kashibai's boots on the grated floor of the balcony drew Trishala away from the window. She returned the salute Kashibai rendered her, then directed her comrade to study the pilgrims beyond the crystalflex sheet.

'Look at them, Kashibai,' Trishala said. 'How much greater would their fear be if they knew what truly threatened them?' She turned her head to regard her companion. 'More than just mutants and rebels.'

'They're frightened enough already,' Kashibai told Trishala. Though she wouldn't vocally contest the Sister Superior's claim that there were xenos on Lubentina, Trishala knew she held the same attitude as Palatine Yadav on the matter.

'When the armour of ignorance is pierced, fear is the first wound.' Trishala closed her hand around the aquila she wore. 'I pray the God-Emperor will spare them the truth. At least a little longer.'

'You sound doubtful. Are you saying prayers have no power?' Kashibai asked.

'I am saying the prayers most apt to earn attention are those accompanied by deeds,' Trishala said. 'If Palatine Yadav would only give us liberty to assist in repressing these... rebels.' She shook her head, a bitter smile on her face. 'Our duty is here, of course. To defend the cathedral and guard its relics, especially the precious Shroud of Singh and Warmason's Casket.'

Kashibai nodded. 'I recall someone once told me that there was no honour in a duty that wasn't burdensome.'

Trishala scowled at her companion. 'I said that to a young initiate who didn't want to memorise her orisons.'

'Such wisdom must surely have other applications,' Kashibai persisted. Her expression grew serious. 'I have faith that the God-Emperor has put us where we need to be.'

'If I could share that conviction,' Trishala said, 'it would be a great solace to me. I feel that it is in battle that I can best serve the Emperor.'

Another group of petitioners bowed their way into the corridor, struggling to keep their balance in the strangely tilted hall. Though the floor was level, the angle of the walls created the illusion that the entire passage was rolling over onto its side. It was an architectural peculiarity that the Sisters had long become accustomed to, noticing it only by clumsy reactions of visitors to the cathedral.

'Are there not other ways to earn the grace of the Emperor?'

Kashibai countered. She looked away from Trishala to acknowledge the respectful genuflection of the passing petitioners, a courtesy the Sister Superior didn't extend. 'Surely devotion and fealty have some value. The mine-serf working away in the dark to wrest ore from the ground to build the machinery of the Imperium, or the grox-herder tending his beasts to feed worlds he will never see.'

Trishala watched the petitioners walk to the shrine. She was always alert for some zealot whose adoration of Vadok Singh would drive him to fanatical excess. Even in times of calm there'd been those who'd tried to lay their hands upon the artefacts ensconced in the cathedral. With Tharsis swiftly losing its peaceful veneer, Trishala had posted sentinels to watch over all the major artefacts, augmenting the protection afforded by the cathedral's acolytes. As she looked at the rotund attendant standing behind the plinth and matched him against the steady flow of petitioners, she re-evaluated the Gauntlet's importance. A single Sister in her black power armour would present far more of a deterrent than the current guardian.

'Assign Sister Reshma to this hall,' Trishala told Kashibai. She gave her a reproving look. 'The Imperium is too vast for any individual to be vital or even important. The time of the primarchs and the saints is gone, all that are left are lesser beings. If your grox-herder fails and falls, another will take his place. So too with us all. The fact we have lives is of no significance to the God-Emperor. It is what we do with those lives that endows us with worth. Deeds are our measure, and the greater the sum of our deeds the more the Emperor's light burns inside us.'

'Each of us venerates the God-Emperor in our own way,' Kashibai said.

The expression on Trishala's face made it evident she had no interest in entering a discussion on dogma. Stiffening her back, Kashibai snapped a hurried salute to her superior. 'I will post Reshma to guard the Gauntlet's Retreat.'

Trishala returned Kashibai's salute before leaving the balcony and marching off down the hall, following the rotation of passageways and antechambers that would lead her to the great narthex that opened out from the cathedral. Those she encountered in her circuit, pilgrims and petitioners alike, gave way before her. They pressed close to the ancient whorlwood panels that lined the walls, forgetting the curious vertigo imposed by the curl of those walls in their eagerness to avoid impeding the stern-faced Sister Superior.

Sensing the anxiety rolling off the crowds, Trishala could only be thankful that she'd grown beyond such weakness. Uncertainty bespoke a lack of faith, just as fear indicated a lack of resolve. Those who truly embraced the Imperial Creed didn't have such failings. They were firm and steadfast, unyielding in their convictions. No matter what was demanded of them, they looked to the Imperial Creed to dictate their choices. She appreciated the viewpoint Kashibai held, a belief in the ultimate mercy and justness of the Emperor. It wasn't a wrong belief, but it was a naïve interpretation. The Emperor's design was one that encompassed all the untold trillions of humans in the Imperium. To think that great design could be altered for the benefit of any individual was the worst kind of hubris.

A last crowd of robed pilgrims parted before Trishala and she made the descent down the broad stairway that rippled its way to the obsidian floor of the narthex. Polished to a mirror-like sheen, stepping out onto the black surface was still a thrilling sensation. It was like walking across the cosmic space between worlds, an effect that was made all the more real by the thousands of tiny lights suspended from the hall's lofty ceiling, their glow reflecting in the obsidian floor. At regular intervals, a hidden projector sent the hololith of an ancient warship flying through the illusory starfield, much to the awed admiration of the congregants.

Trishala smiled at that. The artifices of the architects who'd laboured on the Warmason's Cathedral were indeed remarkable, but there were places where their craftsmanship had been wanting. Even in a place as resplendent as the narthex there were discreet blemishes. An incongruously ponderous beam clawing its way down one wall, a crazily angled pillar, the outline of a doorway that projected a few centimetres from the middle of the ceiling. Within the upper levels of the cathedral there were even more instances of such oddities. Windows that stared into blank walls. Stairways that vanished into ceilings. Crude statuary that crouched in shadowy niches, their outlines as disturbing as they were indistinct. All were echoes of the ancient past, facets of a design Karim Das never implemented.

An honour guard of Sisters flanked the gigantic bronze doors that opened from the narthex onto Cathedral Plaza. Standing nearly ten metres high, the doors had been cast to mimic the grain of some ancient Terran wood. Each portal was surrounded by plascrete castings of the Warmason's sacred works, an assemblage of gargantuan fortresses and bridges rendered in exacting detail. Just above the doors, standing upon a projecting base of marble, was an effigy of Vadok the Builder, the principal aspect of the Warmason. The Sisters guarding the entrance were arrayed in white rather than their customary black, holding their bolters against their chests and maintaining an expression as stony as that of the Warmason's statue. Though their pose might be statuesque, the guards were alert to their surroundings, keeping a vigil that was much more than simply symbolic.

Emerging from the solemn confines of the cathedral, Trishala stepped into the bedlam of the plaza. The square was vast, fifty metres across at its widest and surrounded on all sides by the bulky stone buildings that hosted the many businesses that catered to the pilgrims who flocked to Lubentina. Some of the oldest structures were squat, blocky affairs, while others boasted heights of a dozen floors and more. Those closest to the cathedral had great load cranes and the skeletal frames of elaborate scaffolds rising from their roofs while those farther away displayed signs that alternately reminded those who gazed on them of their duties to the God-Emperor or advertised the services of some Lubentine enterprise.

A babble of hawking, haggling and arguing rose from the columns of stalls that edged the plaza, where vendors tried to sell pilgrims everything from flasks of sacred unguents and bundles of incense sticks to Lubentine prayer bells and hololiths of the Warmason himself. Most numerous of all, however, were those selling every manner of victual to the pilgrims as they completed their ascent of Mount Rama, whether they came by Ladder or Road.

Trishala found her gaze lingering on a crew of labourers erecting a scaffold against the side of the cathedral. A truck loaded down with several rockcrete tombs was parked a small distance away, the symbol of the Tomb-cutters' Guild etched into the sides of the cab. Though the rebels had seized the tomb-yards, the Guild had enough funerary receptacles stored across the city to keep busy for a few weeks yet. Except for the lowest levels of the cathedral, the whole of the structure was encased in rings of crypts and tombs. The graves were cemented against the towering cathedral, allowing the wealthy dead the chance to be ensconced near the Warmason's relics. Such was the profusion of these attachments down through the centuries that new ones were now being layered atop older ones. The effect, to Trishala's eyes at least, was like the encrustations of parasites upon the body of some marine leviathan. Indeed, watching the stacked tombs climb upwards it was easy to forget that the cathedral itself wasn't situated vertically but rather projected at an angle over the further slopes of the mountain.

How unlike the conventional towers of the Sovereign Spire. For all the roles the governor's palace had played down through the centuries, it hadn't been the subject of such confusion. Right or wrong, Murdan and the Cardinal-Governors before him had maintained a purity of vision and purpose. Turning away from the cathedral's funerary encrustations, Trishala stared down upon Tharsis and the mighty tower at its heart. Palatine Yadav had summoned her to another council meeting. Her duty now was to disturb Murdan's resolve and make him waver in the course he was set upon.

It was a daunting prospect, but as Trishala looked past the Sovereign Spire and at the thick plumes of smoke rising from the tomb-yards, she had reason to believe it wasn't an impossible one.

* * *

'Impossible!' Minister Kargil's objection boomed through the council hall like a peal of thunder. He shook an accusing fist at Colonel Hafiz. 'You can't seriously propose that we flatten the tomb-yards with artillery? Do you have any conception of how much damage that would inflict on production? We have faithful from across the segmentum who have already paid for interment on Mount Rama. What should we tell them? "I'm sorry Sejanus but you can't die, at least until the crypt-presses have been rebuilt." Loyal, devout subjects of the Imperium have placed their trust in our ability to provide for their...'

Hafiz slammed his hand down on the table, returning the minister's glower. 'Don't prattle on about obligations and trust, minister. It is the money bloating your coffers that worries you. You'd hate to see that steady stream of wealth disrupted.'

'Don't act superior to me, Hafiz,' Kargil snarled back. 'Yes, I am worried about the prosperity of Lubentina, as should be everyone at this table.' He turned away from the colonel to regard the other councillors. 'The services we've provided for the Cult of the Warmason have made this a rich world. Lubentina has built a reputation for itself as a monument to the glory of the God-Emperor. We have become a favoured shrine world, respected by the Ecclesiarchy for our exacting attention to efficiency and detail. All of that will be jeopardised if we submit to panic. Consider what would happen if some influential off-worlder were to come here to bury one of his household only to find us incapable of fabricating a tomb to his specifications. He would be certain to let others in his circle, his peers in society, know of the inconvenience he was subjected to. Lubentina's reputation would be tarnished, and if enough visitors left here with such stories, the blotch upon our record might never be expunged.'

'How much production is being accomplished with the tomb-yards in the hands of these cultists?' one of the other councillors asked. 'The disruption you describe has already happened. It seems to me that the colonel's plan is the quickest method to resolve the situation.'

Kargil shook his head. 'It would take years to rebuild if we condone Hafiz's operation. Years and considerable expense. Right now, such damage as has been caused to the facilities could be repaired in a few weeks, a month at worst.' He spun back around and faced Hafiz. 'What we need is for the colonel to compose himself, rally his troops and go back in there. How a rabble of mutants and heretics can overcome an organised and professional military force is a question we can set aside until after the conflict has been resolved.'

Seated beside Palatine Yadav, Trishala listened to Kargil's speech with a steadily mounting outrage. The minister refused to hear anything that would jeopardise his expected profit margins. Playing the hypocrite, he accused Hafiz of ignoring the long-term effects of his strategy while blissfully ignoring the hazards of his own. Without decisive action, the uprising would grow.

'The enemy is more than mutants and cultists,' Trishala said. 'They are a xenos infestation. You have heard Colonel Hafiz describe what he saw in the tomb-yards.'

Palatine Yadav leaned forwards, his eyes roving across the table, meeting the gaze of each councillor. 'Hearken to Trishala's warning,' he said. 'I must confess that I was in error when I dismissed her concerns before. Since that time I have conducted research of my own and come upon an account in the *Book of Domitian* where he describes the fall of a planet in the Segmentum Obscuras. The invaders were a breed of xenos that used an uprising among the labour-caste to prosecute their conquest.'

Trishala clenched her hands tight while Yadav recited the downfall of that perished world. She felt her heart pounding faster inside her chest, a cold tingle ripple through her skin. She could picture everything the palatine was describing, all of it to the last detail. It was what had happened to her own home world of Primorus.

When Yadav finished his recitation, most of the councillors had a troubled look on their faces. Kargil wasn't one of them. 'An interesting parable, your grace, and I agree that there are similarities to our own circumstances. But Domitian identifies the xenos blight as genestealers. Now I am no authority on xenobiology, I leave that subject to the perverted minds who think it a fit topic for human contemplation.'

'What man knows the intrigues of the xenos?' Yadav cautioned. 'Who can say how many methods the alien may use to usurp the domain of man?'

'All due respect to your position, your grace, but I cannot believe the situation is as dire as you describe,' Kargil said. 'Hafiz wants to turn the tomb-yards into a moonscape and you sound like you want to call the Inquisition down here to burn out anyone who so much as sold one of these cultists a new set of boots.'

From his throne, Cardinal-Governor Murdan's voice lashed out with a question. 'Is that what you're proposing, Yadav?'

The palatine rose from his seat and bowed to Murdan. 'It is, your excellency. It is my conviction that this problem is beyond our capacity to deal with alone. If I may, I should advise that we make an appeal to the Imperial authorities for help restoring order.'

'Your proposal is rejected,' Murdan declared bluntly. The thin governor leaned out from his voluminous robes and gave Yadav a reproving look. 'However this trouble arose, whatever its nature, we will resolve it on our own. Minister Kargil worries over the economic aspects of this situation. My fears are for the souls of all those devout pilgrims whose faith in the Emperor might be shaken if we show weakness. If we call for help, it will be saying that our own trust in the Emperor's mercy is wanting, that we didn't have faith enough to allow our own convictions to see us through our time of crisis. They will wonder at the lack of faith shown by a shrine world and then the cancer of doubt will claw its way into their minds. They will think that if even Lubentina was uncertain of the Emperor's protection, then how much less deserving must their own worlds be.' Murdan closed his eyes and raised his face towards the ceiling. 'No, there will be no weakling's cry for aid.'

'Excellency, it is no weakness to gather the instruments to achieve victory,' Trishala said, standing to address Murdan. Yadav whispered to her, fairly begging her to sit down before she did anything to provoke the governor. She ignored his entreaty and continued, 'There is only one measure of weakness, and that is failure.'

Murdan's eyes bored into Trishala's. 'There are different measures of failure. If you win the battle but lose the war, of what value then is your victory?' He swung around and motioned to Colonel Hafiz. 'When you've assembled your artillery, target the waste-runs and any other connection from the tomb-yards to the Cloister-fells first. After that, I don't expect to hear that so much as a kerbstone is left intact.'

'But your excellency!' All the colour had drained from Kargil's visage as he heard Murdan's orders.

'In every test of faith, there must be sacrifice,' Murdan declared. He looked back to Trishala. 'Sentiment can be afforded no place in the decisions rendered by authority. When the thing must be done, let it be done.'

A disruption at the entryway drew eyes away from Murdan. Soon a servant in the governor's livery was escorting an anxious Captain Debdan to where Colonel Hafiz was seated. There was a brief exchange of whispers, then the colonel addressed the council in a grim tone.

'More cultists have broken onto the surface,' Hafiz said. 'They're reported in the prayer-binders' quarter, the incense factories, and there have been sightings around the reliquary mills. In all, seven different outbreaks, each effected simultaneously with the others.'

The colonel's crisp report brought shocked murmurs from the council. Several of the men who'd supported Kargil's restrained approach now took up Yadav's position and clamoured for a call for aid to be dispatched.

'Lubentina will handle its own affairs,' Murdan snapped, unmoved by the appeals cast upon him. 'There will be no cry for help.'

'All respect, excellency, but the situation has changed,' Yadav said.

Murdan nodded. 'Indeed it has,' he conceded. His next words sent an icy chill through the veins of all within the council room. Even Trishala found herself shocked by the brutal pragmatism of the Cardinal-Governor.

'Now there is much more work for Hafiz's artillery,' Murdan declared.

CHAPTER IV

Agonised screams, shrieks of horror and rage, the snap of lasguns and the bark of autoguns, the sinister whine of power picks and shock mauls, the rumbling crash of collapsing walls, the dull groan of tanks and transports. The streets of Tharsis were filled with a maddened riot of sound, a bedlam that thundered through the air. An auditory confusion that overwhelmed the senses, consuming the very concepts of discipline and obedience, leaving behind only the raw savage urge to fight and to kill.

Behind the cover of a toppled rockcrete obelisk, Bakasur sat in the dust of destruction and focused his mind upon the awesome powers that were the Great Father's legacy to him. Already the smell of smoke and blood and burning promethium had faded to nothingness. The images before his eyes had become shadowy blurs, the immense aberrant warriors charged to act as his protectors were only dark blotches to him now. He turned his focus upon the sounds, deadening them one after another, closing them off and sealing them away as though he were locking doors inside his brain. The noises were the hardest stimulus to reject, for the loudest of them were things not merely heard but came upon him as tremulous vibrations he could feel in his bones. It needed exacting concentration to separate himself from the din of battle. Fortunately the magus was equal to such a strain.

For an instant Bakasur felt a terrible cold and then his consciousness was soaring beyond his body. As he looked down upon himself he was struck by how frail he appeared next to the hulking aberrants. Such a delicate vessel to invest with so many gifts and to entrust with so many things. A terrible fright sped through his mind, a crackle of doubt that he should prove unworthy of all that depended upon him. After all, he wasn't one of the Inheritors. His was a flawed physicality distorted by the taint of lower life. Whatever the powers of his mind, he could never transcend the limitations of his flesh. Not until he rose with the Great Father into the stars for the ascension that would bring him rebirth.

The magus willed himself away from his physical form, chiding himself for the mammalian affectations that caused him to linger over his body. This sense of self was a distraction, a dangerous delusion that would be lifted from him in time. Then he would be one with the Great Father. Then he would be redeemed.

Bakasur's consciousness sped across the battleground. A district of chapels and shrines, their ponderous ornamentation now scarred by gunfire, the greenery of their grounds trampled beneath boot and tyre. He saw a brigade of soldiers in tan uniforms deployed about the pillars of a small temple, a heavy bolter barking away from where it had been concealed under an archway. He watched as a cadre of purple-garbed cultists approached the strongpoint from the left only to be mowed down by the snarling bolter and the flashing lasguns of the planetary militia. Only two of the hybrids reached the cover of a smashed groundcar lying in the street, the rest of their band ending up strewn before the temple in gory disarray. In death, however, the half-human cultists had achieved their purpose. They'd distracted the soldiers from the menace that now fell upon them from the opposite flank. A shrieking rush of Inheritors raced across the temple grounds and charged among the pillars, ripping and tearing with their deadly claws and sharp fangs. To sacrifice their lives for the Inheritors was the noblest purpose that could be asked of any who served the Cult of the Cataclysm.

Away from the pillared temple, Bakasur viewed a platoon of soldiers reinforcing the low walls of an outdoor gallery. Smashing fountains and urns with entrenching tools and rifle butts, the troopers dragged the broken masonry to the perimeter. While the men at the walls piled up the rubble they'd created, some of their comrades took up position among the statues of long-dead priests and missionaries, using their broad plascrete bases for cover. The gallery was sited to afford a commanding view of two intersecting streets and the soldiers promised to make taking those streets a costly prospect.

Bakasur evaluated the defences the soldiers had raised. Against lasrifle or autogun, they might serve well enough. But these were far from the only weapons in the cult's arsenal. It needed but a slight exertion to stimulate the mentalities of the hybrids that could make a mockery of the position. Only a flicker of thought, and the magus sent his plan directly into the brains of the cultists.

For a few moments, the troopers continued to reinforce their position. Lasguns flashed and a sheet of burning promethium shot out as a band of cultists tried to rush the gallery. The attack was quickly beaten back by the soldiers, a litter of dead and dying hybrids sprawled in the road.

Such relief as the platoon felt by repulsing the cultist charge quickly evaporated. The bodies on the street jounced and shuddered as a fleet of immense vehicles came rumbling towards their position. Bakasur could feel the despair that dripped from the troopers. They recognised the machines driving down upon them and appreciated how formidable they were.

Hulking masses of permasteel, the Goliath trucks had been the armoured workhorses of the old mines, built to withstand toxic spills, cave-ins and firedamp. The cult had restored and further strengthened their bodies with layers of metal plating, even going so far as to chain a metre-thick slab of ferrocrete to the front of the leading truck's engine block. Weapons bristled from the cabs and roofs of each truck, sporting everything from heavy stubbers and modified mining lasers to autocannons and cobbled-together plasma guns. The sigils of the cult were painted across each Goliath, proudly boasting their allegiance.

The troopers made an effort to stand their ground. Lasguns flashed, striving to penetrate the cabs and strike the drivers. The platoon's heavy flamer sent another sheet of fire washing over the street, but the blazing promethium made little impression on machines built to withstand the ember-eruptions of Lubentina's slag-drops. The only mark the soldiers' efforts made was to blister the paint of the foremost Goliath and scratch some of the extra plating bolted to the others.

Roaring nearer to the gallery, cultist guns returned the militia's fire. A swath of perimeter wall was blown apart by the pounding inflicted upon it by an autocannon, the troopers behind it shredded by both the high-velocity rounds and the splinters of their own barricade. The beam of a laser seared across one of the bronze missionaries, sending the statue crashing backwards and precipitating a chain reaction that soon found six of the sculptures smashing earthwards. The soldiers sheltering beneath the statues scattered, scrambling to find new cover.

Before the rattled platoon could regain any sort of cohesion, the leading Goliath came barrelling into their position. The perimeter wall shattered as the heavy truck smashed through it, one hapless soldier pulped beneath the machine's enormous wheels. The Goliath rumbled onwards, only stopping when the ferrocrete slab fastened to its hood slammed into one of the statues. As the truck came to a rest, the heavy stubber nestled in its cab maintained a steady fire, forcing the soldiers to keep their heads down.

The iris hatch at the rear of the Goliath swirled open and from the bay set within the truck's body a swarm of cultists spilled out across the devastated gallery. Shotguns boomed as the hybrids surged towards the reeling soldiers while cracking autoguns picked off those men who tried to flee back towards the streets. An enraged aberrant, a huge rock drill clenched in his brawny arms, charged into a group of shaken troopers huddled behind a heap of debris. The churning grinders that tipped the aberrant's crude weapon were swiftly caked in the flesh and sinew of his mangled victims.

The fiery explosion that abruptly engulfed the leading Goliath and flipped the immense truck onto its back snapped Bakasur's focus away from the carnage of the gallery. The magus set his concentration upon the task of finding the enemy who'd inflicted such a blow upon the cult. He found them, another platoon of troopers barricaded in the rockcrete halls of an abbey. Already the men were frantically loading another missile to send against the Goliaths. Bakasur expanded his awareness away from the soldiers, exploring the buildings around them. To the left they were supported by only a few squads, and the building to their right held an entire detachment.

The nature of that detachment gave Bakasur pause. He resisted the inclination to exploit the opportunity to its fullest, however. For the moment it was enough that the platoon with the missile launcher was eliminated. That would require only an unprotected flank to achieve. More direct action could wait.

Again, the magus set his psychic powers to stimulating the minds of his cult, those he'd chosen to serve as extensions of his own will. The hybrids assaulting the gallery divided their forces, some remaining to hold the captured position and to keep the attention of the men in the abbey. The others, shielded by the buildings beyond the gallery, rushed down the street parallel to the abbey. They'd emerge well to the right of the troopers. No alarm would be given by the soldiers in the building that guarded the abbey's flank, nor would the hybrids encounter any resistance until they were upon the platoon

Bakasur had marked for destruction. The magus's telepathic exertions had seen to that.

Bakasur let his consciousness seep back into his body. The risk of drifting too far from his mortal shell was a dire one. Now that the cult was poised to secure the chokepoint that jeopardised their advance, he saw no reason to entertain such danger further. Until he'd outlived his utility to the Great Father, his life wasn't his own to expend. There was still much to be done. Much to prepare before the end.

Before Lubentina outlived its utility to the Great Father in spreading his glory across the stars.

From the balcony set high upon the cathedral's central tower, Trishala stared out across the sweeping sprawl of Tharsis. Entire districts had become smoking ruins, ransacked and despoiled by the rebels. The Tomb-Cutters' Guild had been reduced to a pile of rubble, the factories and works around it turned into acres of desolation. The hab-blocks of the chapel-serfs were empty, blackened ruins. Fighting persisted in the area of the under-temples and the seminaries, the flash of explosions and the crack of gunfire rising from the streets. Brigades of local militia rushed to form cordons around those regions firmly in the grip of the cultists while batteries of artillery lumbered into positions on the outskirts of the city, where they could direct their fire against those areas considered lost to the enemy. Wherever soldiers and rebels were absent, ragged files of civilians staggered through the streets, hurrying towards whatever promised them escape or shelter. Some fled into the wastelands beyond the city, some tried to make their way to the spaceport. Others tried to reach the Sovereign Spire and the governor's district, seeking refuge within the fortress.

The stream of petitioners ascending Mount Rama had swollen into a flood. From all across Tharsis, the frightened masses were rushing to the Warmason's Cathedral. As she observed the tide of desperate humanity packed along the Chastened Road, Sister Superior Trishala felt a bitter sense of déjà vu. She felt that she'd been here before, seen all of this long ago on Primorus.

Then she'd been naught but a girl, a child caught up in an incomprehensible turmoil from which there was neither refuge or respite. When the xenos cult on her homeworld had exploded from the shadows into open revolt, the populace had reacted with the same useless panic and terror. She remembered the hot, smothering atmosphere in the security shelters the inhabitants of her hab-block had fled into, the thousands of trembling people packed into a space intended for only a few hundred. She could still hear the air-cyclers chugging away, their machine-spirits railing against the ordeal of purging the exhalations of so many refugees. Later there had been the other sound... the scrape of xenos claws against the doors.

A groaning shudder passed through the metal balcony Trishala stood upon. She could hear the massive door that led back into the cathedral slowly rumbling open. Plasteel nearly a metre thick, it was an absurdity that such a ponderous construction should open onto something as innocuous as the little balcony. But, like so many of the secret corners and incongruous features of the cathedral, the huge door was a legacy from the past. A reminder of the curious design that Karim Das had chosen with which to pay homage to Vadok Singh.

'I thought I should find you on the Curate's Leap,' Kashibai told Trishala as she walked out onto the balcony.

The balcony had taken its name after a despondent curate had jumped to his death, unable to endure the shame of accidentally destroying an ancient tome dating to the time of the Great Crusade. It was claimed the imprint of his fingers could still be found on the railing where he braced himself before his jump. More substantial was the pattern of cracks and holes that marred the tombs directly below the balcony.

Trishala continued to gaze down at the throngs of Lubentines. 'Have I become so predictable, Sister?'

Kashibai joined her at the rail, her armoured hands closing about the spiral lattice of the mesh. 'I've served under you long enough to know you dislike any disruption of routine. You can only take so much before you need to get away.'

'Solitude bestows tranquillity,' Trishala quoted from the *Angelikite Verses*. 'It becomes needful sometimes to step aside and refocus the mind.'

'You are hardly alone here,' Kashibai said, nodding to the masses in the plaza below.

'One can be alone in the midst of multitudes,' Trishala corrected her. 'I'm not certain even Palatine Yadav has accepted that this is more than a mutant uprising. If he did we should be out there, eradicating these creatures, not hanging back with the refugees.'

'Not all are blessed with the strength to fight,' Kashibai said. 'It is the honour of those with such strength that we can protect those without it.'

'It is a burden, not an honour,' Trishala corrected her. 'If we could be certain the cathedral was secure I could send detachments from our convent to reinforce the militia. I am certain that Palatine Yadav would support such actions now.' She waved her hand at the distant glow of Tharsis, at the conflagration blazing in the seminaries and the Redeemer's District where Hafiz's artillery continued to bombard the rampaging cultists. 'Because of that, I cannot risk sending even a few squads out.'

'More and more people are fleeing the city,' Kashibai agreed. 'Many of them are coming here for sanctuary, seeking the protection of Vadok Singh and the God-Emperor.'

'They seek the protection of our bolters,' Trishala said, her voice dripping with cynicism.

'They don't know how to fight,' Kashibai said. 'How many of those people down there do you think have even held a gun, much less fired one? Their service to the Imperium has been one of labour, not war. Even then there have been many who answered Palatine Yadav's calls to assemble the frateris militia, taking up weapons they've never used to defend their city.'

Trishala gestured to the crowds along the Chastened Road. 'Would that the God-Emperor gave them all such courage, then the Cardinal-Governor's idealistic vision of Lubentina fighting its own battles would be more than a dream.'

'Part of our duty is to protect those unable to protect themselves,' Kashibai said.

Trishala bristled at Kashibai's words. 'Our most sacred duty is that to which we have vowed to be true. Protecting the relics of Vadok Singh,' she said. 'Double the guard on the Palladion and remind the Sisters that no member of the laity is to draw closer to it than the transept. Then I want you to reinforce the honour guard in the narthex. Order has to be maintained. A mob of this size and in this state is beyond the ability of acolytes and militia to control. It needs our attention. If we don't exert control over these people from the moment they cross the threshold we're inviting disaster into our midst.'

'These people are desperate,' Kashibai cautioned. 'It won't be easy to restrain them.'

Trishala only partly heard Kashibai speak. She was listening instead to the scrape of xenos claws against the doors of the security shelter. The aliens never did tear through those doors. Someone on the inside had opened them for the creatures.

'These people are dangerous,' Trishala said. 'Even if you don't believe that, conduct yourself as if you do.'

Palatine Yadav looked across the information on his data-slate, horrified by how swiftly the rebellion had escalated. The local militia had been driven from the Redeemer's District and was now trying to extricate itself from the vicinity of the scholarium. The tomb-yards had been completely obliterated by artillery and the barrage being concentrated against the missal-works would soon see them condemned to the same fate. The incense factories were firmly in the grip of the cultists, shielded from bombardment by the hab-blocks of the perfumers who laboured there. So too were the seminaries and under-temples of the Preachers' Quarter, infested by rebels who'd boiled up from long-forgotten connections to the old mines of Karim Das. Loyal forces still held a firm grip on the governor's district and the complex of bureaucratic buildings that had grown around the Sovereign Spire. The spaceport had yet to come under attack and the approaches to Mount Rama were still open to the Imperials. Still, it was impossible to mistake the rapid spread of the rebels. A fifth of the city was either destroyed or firmly in the grip of the cultists and another fifth was actively being fought over. Sabotage had reached epidemic proportions with power plants destroyed, water sources poisoned, and bridges bombed. It was a grim assessment that he gave Cardinal-Governor Murdan as they walked together.

'By trying to protect everything, we would lose everything,' Murdan said as they walked through the incense-filled corridors of his private apartments. Murdan paused in his steps to contemplate a hololith projecting on the wall across from him, a portrait of his predecessor Rohak. Each time the two men made a circuit of the passageway, the governor stopped to study the image of that long dead hero who had prevailed during the heretical riots of 3637. It was as though by looking into that face he could find the secret of the strength and wisdom that had enabled Rohak to triumph over the heretics.

Yadav didn't think Murdan would find any answers there, even if there were any to be found. He was too unyielding in the beliefs he'd adopted to reconsider his decisions. In the Cardinal-Governor's view, it was better to break than bend. Any compromise, any vacillation was a mark of doubt – something he equated with spiritual failing.

'We can't simply abandon Tharsis to these heretics,' Yadav said, repeating the argument that had dominated their discussion.

Murdan continued to stare at the portrait. He wagged a skeletal finger at Rohak. 'To win the war you must concede the battle. Rohak knew this. He evaluated his resources and made a practical assessment of what he could hold and what he couldn't. If he'd tried to save everything, the enemy would have taken it all.'

'You're talking about withdrawing from almost the whole of the city,' Yadav protested. The agitation in his voice brought Murdan's ivory-coated bodyguards a few steps closer to the men, one of them even going so far as to unbutton the flap of his laspistol's holster. Their loyalty to Murdan was such that they wouldn't hesitate to shoot if they thought the governor was being threatened.

Murdan turned away from the portrait. There was regret in his eyes as he looked at Yadav. 'Colonel Hafiz has lost a quarter of his troops and the militia you assembled to support him has been decimated. The reality is that we don't have the manpower to contain these cultists. They're popping up like weeds. Exterminate them from one street and they show up in even greater force in the adjacent district. If we concentrate on holding the spaceport, the Sovereign Spire and the Warmason's Cathedral, then we can preserve the core of Lubentina. We will have something to build from when the uprising is put down.'

'That means abandoning millions to the enemy,' Yadav objected.

'That is a sacrifice we must make,' Murdan sighed. He raised his lean hand to interrupt Yadav's rebuttal. 'Do you know that after the militia's setbacks in the Cloisterfells Minister Kargil asked me to pour poison gas into the tunnels? I was as aghast at the suggestion as you are now. My thoughts were on the innocents who would perish. If I had focused on the innocents who would have been saved by such a brutal act, this crisis would be over now. No, palatine, I cannot be swayed by appeals to my compassion. My heart has already betrayed my obligations once. I won't allow it to do so again.'

'Then you must give the order for an astropathic distress call to be given,' Yadav insisted.

Anger flared up in Murdan's eyes. 'No, we won't. Lubentina has survived because of its faith in the Emperor and the protection of His Warmason. We will not cast aside our faith because of fear.'

'It is not faithlessness to use every tool the God-Emperor has given us,' Yadav said.

'The subject isn't open to debate,' Murdan declared, cutting off the palatine's argument.

Yadav bowed to the Cardinal-Governor. 'I will pray that you find enlightenment,' he said as he withdrew from Murdan's presence.

The moment the gilded doors at the end of the corridor closed behind Yadav, Murdan waved the commander of his bodyguard to his side. 'Keep a watch on him, Jayant,' he said. 'I am concerned that the palatine may do something reckless.'

Jayant nodded his understanding. 'If he should try to go to the astropath and send the distress call on his own?'

Murdan's gaze was as cold as ceramite when he answered the guard's question. 'If he sets so much as one foot upon the Jade Stair you will kill him.'

Very little of the obsidian floor was visible as Trishala descended towards the narthex. Clusters of petitioners were everywhere, milling about the chamber in dazed bands, their faces blank, their gaze confused. After fleeing their homes, after the turmoil of the Chastened Road and the other approaches to the cathedral, they seemed at a loss now that they'd reached the sanctuary they'd been seeking. Acolytes moved among them, trying to ease the worst of their fears and instil some manner of discipline. Members of the frateris militia did their best to direct the crowds by channelling them away from antechambers and other dead ends. Deacons and even higher members of the Ecclesiarchy led small groups in prayer or delivered quick sermons to comfort the refugees who stopped them at every step.

Uncomfortable memories rose up; the image of her parents wearing just such vacant expressions when they'd finally reached the security shelter. These weren't petitioners or pilgrims now, they were just like the cowering masses in that shelter on Primorus. Displaced refugees retreating to whatever safety they could find. The difference here was that they had more than rockcrete and plasteel to guard them. They had the Order of the Sombre Vow.

They had Trishala.

She ignored the hope she saw on the faces of the refugees as they parted before her on the stairway. She gave no notice to the words of gratitude and adoration the crowds spoke to her. Trishala had no patience for emotionality. Let Kashibai think defending these people was some noble honour; the truth was they were a burden. They would complicate any defence of the cathedral a thousandfold. Even more if they kept clumping together in confused mobs and impeding the already sluggish and disordered flow of people coming in from the plaza.

Trishala marched across the narthex, making towards the gigantic doorway. There were a dozen Battle Sisters at the entrance. The pretence of an honour guard had been cast aside and all of them were arrayed in their black combat armour, boltguns at their sides. She could see Kashibai standing at one doorway, motioning to the crowds outside with gestures not unlike those of some road-prefect directing traffic. The Sisters had assumed the mundane chore after the frateris militia had proven incapable of restraining the masses. It seemed even Kashibai was out of her element. Her efforts were proving inefficient, with entire groups slipping around her.

Starting forwards to reprimand Kashibai for not taking a firmer hand in imposing order upon the refugees, Trishala froze in her steps. Something she'd caught out of the corner of her eye, a flash of skin that struck her with a feeling of wrongness. She spun around, thrusting her way through a crowd too slow to part for her. Ahead she saw the figure that had caught her attention, a little man in a heavy brown coat. He appeared unaware of her interest, making no effort to hurry away. His calm veneer, however, was too deliberate. While the people around him were at least making an effort to move out of Trishala's way, the man in the brown coat gave her no notice at all.

Reaching out, Trishala caught hold of the man's collar. Tugging on the garment she turned him around to face her. His features were heavy, even a bit dull in their expression. Nothing about that face bespoke a mutant taint, but as Trishala pulled on the coat the sleeve was drawn back. Once again she saw the flash of purplish skin that had caught her eye. It had a rubbery, poreless texture, more like the skin of a mollusc than anything human.

The exposed cultist didn't waste time on protestations of innocence. Still with that dull look on his face, he drew a thick knife from under his coat and drove it towards Trishala's belly.

The Sister Superior retained her hold on the hybrid's

other arm. The knife raked harmlessly against her armour while she twisted the prisoned limb around with her. There was a sickening pop as she forced it from its socket. The cultist crumpled forwards. A blow of her armoured fist against the back of his neck spilled him onto the floor, his malformed body twitching as his life ebbed away.

An awed silence had oppressed the refugees while Trishala swiftly dispatched the infiltrator, but now the narthex resounded with a raucous din of screams and cries. Such was the confusion of the moment, Trishala failed to discern that not all of those cries were of fear. Some of them were of fury.

Up on the stairway, a heavy-set labourer threw off his dust-slicker and ripped a fat-muzzled stub-pistol from his belt. A vicious grin split his face as he fired at Trishala, displaying teeth too sharp and numerous to belong to anything purely human. Across the hall other cultists were casting off their disguises to charge at her with a motley array of weaponry. Beneath the curiously angled pillar, a cultist in the robes of a pilgrim began blazing away with an autogun, indifferent to the refugees his shots ploughed through.

The bullets from the cultist on the stair spattered harmlessly from Trishala's power armour. The shooter quickly realised his mistake, turning to flee up the stairs, climbing over the shivering bodies of frightened pilgrims. Before he could reach safety, she had her own pistol in her hand. Snapping off a burst, Trishala sent a shell exploding through the cultist's back. The impact threw him over the side of the stairway and headlong to the obsidian floor below.

Trishala felt something slam against her side. Turning,

she found herself holding the bleeding wreckage of a refugee who'd been struck by the autogun. Pushing the dying man aside she returned her attacker's fire. While the cultist's shots glanced off her armour, two shells from her pistol smashed into the false pilgrim and flung his body across the floor.

Other guns were barking out now. Kashibai and the Battle Sisters at the doors were firing at the cultists, cutting them down with controlled bursts. The flash of enemy guns illuminated the cultists in the dim light of the narthex, announcing their positions with every shot they fired. It was the masses of panicked refugees who forced the Sisters to restraint, thousands of terrified civilians scattering in every direction, screaming and shouting, seeking anywhere to hide from the violence that had abruptly exploded all around them. Despite their caution, it was impossible for every shot that left the bolters to strike an infiltrator as it sped across the narthex.

The exposed cultists were only one menace, however. Trishala raced across the hall to the doors. The panic inside the cathedral couldn't be allowed to spread to those outside. Any instant they might stampede, trampling over each other in their maddened flight. The ones inside the narthex were starting to turn back to the doors, to escape the gun battle by retreating to the plaza.

'Back!' Trishala shouted, firing her bolt pistol into the ceiling. Her other hand drew the power sword from its scabbard, a crackling aura of light rippling about the blade as she swept it through the air. 'Back!' she roared. 'You are subjects of the Imperium! Beneficiaries of the God-Emperor Himself! Comport yourselves as such, not like frightened animals!'

The combination of her withering scorn and the imposing threat of her weapons had an immediate effect on the crowds. Trishala hadn't calmed them. She'd shamed them.

'You will control these people,' Trishala hissed to Kashibai across a secured vox-channel. 'I don't care how pathetic, how pitiful they look. I don't care how hurt or scared or tired they are. You will control them. From the first moment they step inside, we have to maintain order.'

Kashibai lowered her eyes, chastened by Trishala's reprimand. 'It will be done, Sister Superior.'

'Be vigilant,' Trishala warned, raising her voice, letting her words drift back to the crowds. 'Look over everyone you let in. There may be more infiltrators among them.'

The admonition had the desired effect. She could hear the frightened murmurs passing among the refugees. They'd be policing themselves even more carefully than the Sisters at the door, looking for any hint that the man beside them might be something less than human. Such paranoia might not catch any of the cultists, but it might give them an incentive to change their plans about slipping into the cathedral.

Trishala lowered her voice again as she conferred with Kashibai over the vox. 'Remain here. I'll instruct the Ecclesiarchy to have some acolytes dispose of these bodies. Then I must arrange patrols to conduct a thorough search for any others that have got into the cathedral.' She sheathed her sword and nodded at the nearest of the dead cultists.

'We can't assume these were the first enemy to slip inside,' Trishala said. 'But it is your duty to make certain they're the last.'

* * *

Jayant kept at a discreet distance as he followed Palatine Yadav through the halls of the Sovereign Spire. After several hours, he'd just begun to think that Murdan was wrong about his suspicion of the priest. Yadav had spent some time down in the lower levels of the tower, conferring with the monks and confessors who were attending the large numbers of injured being brought into the government compound. Then the palatine had sequestered himself in one of the many chapels that were situated about the spire's central hub. Jayant had spied on Yadav but it seemed to him the priest was meditating rather than plotting.

Now Jayant realised he'd been mistaken to think Yadav's visit to the chapel was so innocent. The palatine had gone there to screw up his courage, resign himself to the course of action he'd decided upon. When he left the chapel Yadav took a circuitous, seemingly rambling route through the tower. Always the course took him higher, always it led him nearer to the Jade Stair and the Crystal Turret wherein the astropath Rakesh was sequestered.

The astropath was regarded as a revolting presence by the Cardinal-Governor's staff and servants. The psychic mutant was useful, even essential to Vadok, but that didn't make him less loathsome to pure humans. Very few servants lingered in the vicinity of the Crystal Turret or even the hallway leading to the Jade Stair. When Jayant followed Yadav into the corridor, there was only a single servant about, a young woman in the surcoat of a sanitation-vassal using a synth-fibre duster to brush dirt from the wainscoting that adorned the walls.

Jayant eased past the servant after giving her a look of such venomous intensity that she quickly turned away.

She was smart enough to keep quiet, but too stupid to go away. He debated whether he should kill her now or wait until after he'd dealt with Yadav. Either way he wasn't going to leave a witness around. The people of Lubentina would endure many things from their Cardinal-Governor, but even they were liable to get upset over the death of the palatine. Jayant didn't intend to act unless it was certain he had to. There was just a chance that Yadav might still turn back.

That chance vanished when the palatine suddenly quickened his pace. Jayant cursed under his breath. He didn't like to kill a priest. Sliding the vibro-knife secreted in his sleeve down into his hand, the guard started forwards to overcome Yadav before he could climb the stair.

Jayant started forwards, but he took only a few steps before all the strength drained out of him. There was a burning sensation spreading from his back and out through his chest. Awkwardly he reached a hand up behind his shoulders and tugged a slender needle of glass out of his skin. His eyes couldn't quite focus on the thing as he held it to his face, but it seemed to him there was some odd smell to it.

The guard slumped onto his side. Jayant could see Yadav far off down the hall as the palatine started up the Jade Stair, but he was powerless to stop the priest. It was all he could do to draw breath into his lungs. Part of his brain was screaming at him that he was dying, but the rest of his awareness was too numb to care. He didn't even react when the servant woman crouched down and pulled the needle from his grip. Dimly he wondered who she was and why she'd shot him.

The killer stared back at Jayant, favouring the dying man

with a cold smile. Jayant thought she had too many teeth in her face. It was his last thought before he sank into the darkness.

Darkness evaporated as coruscating whorls of warp-light blazed into brilliance. The prismatic illumination pulsated from the sockets of gilded skulls soldered to titanium walls, as though drawing sustenance from the spirits of the vanquished dead.

The cold, deathly light revealed a space as macabre as the lamps themselves. Ghoulish talismans cut from the corpses of men, beasts and aliens dangled from cords of wire, chain and sinew. The horned scalp of a monster floated in a cauldron of blood, its essence maintained by the grisly runes etched into the sides of the vessel. A tapestry stitched together from the flayed skins of a dozen psykers stretched across one of the metal walls, every centimetre of the hideous hanging covered in bilious sigils of arcane potency. Upon a dais cut from a single immense gemstone, a chalice of ceramite rested, a cup hammered out of the armour of an infamous marauder whose very name was reckoned a blasphemy among those in the Imperium's Ordo Hereticus who remembered it.

At the centre of the sinister chamber, poised in such manner that it stood at the very convergence of the blazing warp-light, was a morbid column of gold. Impressed up the front of the column was a shape, the body of a veritable giant. Jewels sparkled from the sculpted features of a cruelly handsome face, rings and circlets glittered from the arms folded across the figure's broad chest, hands clasped about its shoulders. Tiny beads of bloodstone coursed down the sculpture's breast, shifting about like crawling insects to create a succession of cabalistic symbols.

As the light fell upon the column, the crawling line of bloodstone became more agitated, the pattern of symbols they created changing faster and faster until at last the little beads winked out, consumed by their own frantic energy. Lustreless they fell from the golden column to clatter upon the plasteel floor.

An expectant silence brooded over the room. The wait wasn't long. A tremendous agitation passed through the golden column. Like melting wax, the brilliant metal began to drip away, splashing to the floor in molten sheets. The image of the cruel giant didn't vanish with the flowing gold, but instead stood exposed as a thing of flesh. The mighty chest expanded, a flicker of motion passed across the pale flesh of the face. Slowly the powerful hands relaxed their grip upon the broad shoulders.

Eyes colder than the warp-light that shone upon them snapped open. A grim smile lent a still more vicious quality to the cruel features. With the column melting away around him, the giant stepped away from his disintegrating sarcophagus.

Cornak advanced to the ceramite chalice. He dipped a finger into the cup, drawing from its depths a measure of ash, which he touched to each of his eyes. The sapphire hue of his pupils faded, retreating into a milky white. The limited vision of biology withdrew with the colour, supplanted by an ethereal telemetry that surpassed the frailties of flesh.

Cornak no longer gazed upon the macabre accoutrements of his sanctum or the walls of the ship that now housed them. His awareness had transcended such surroundings. The greater part of him had been drawn away, hurtling through the mysteries of the warp, projected into the presence of the Circle.

It was no physical place, this realm in which the Circle conferred, but a shard of eternity itself, a fissure through which light and darkness merged to become nothingness. His senses were simultaneously beset by a blinding inundation of sights and a deafening thunder of sounds, while his mind shuddered from the perfect absence of all sight and sound. The paradox of infinity, which was at once everything and nothing. Even for a sorcerer of the Circle, it was an experience that threatened madness unless it was quickly restrained. Eldritch exercises, magical calculations fabricated by beings ancient before the first ancestors of man crawled from the slime of prehistoric seas, now became the focus of Cornak's consciousness. He fixated upon the arcane passes, narrowing his awareness until it was distilled and restrained, funnelled towards a single moment and a single thought.

The shades of the other adepts of the Circle were all around him. There was nothing to see, nothing to hear, but they were there all the same. The connection that bound them together was such that it went beyond either flesh or spirit; through the nexus of the immaterium they'd melded themselves into something greater than their disparate parts. Individuality existed only as a facet, a component of the Circle, and when it was extinguished, that essence passed into the extant adepts, heightening their powers and faculties.

Future, past and present were all as one in this gathering place. Cornak saw scenes and images play across his mind. The scenes were always shifting, always in motion.

They represented the experiences of the Circle, a record of what had happened, was happening, and what would happen. All events were in a state of flux, even the past wasn't immutable, yet to the discerning mind there were patterns. From the confusion, portents and prophecies could be sifted. Clues of tomorrow and yesterday.

Cornak found a pattern amidst the bedlam of eternity. It was always difficult to distinguish the pattern that applied to a lone facet of the Circle, such was the mixture of their beings as they delved into the nexus. Here, however, he'd found a key. It was the name of a world.

Lubentina.

When he felt other adepts of the Circle clutch at that name, trying to take it from him, the knowledge only sank deeper into his mind. It was meant for him. It was the answer to the question he'd invoked when he sent his spirit hurtling into this place of eternity and oblivion. Greedily Cornak held it close, denying the others more than a glimpse of what he'd seized. They would all reap the benefits of his discovery, but the glory would belong to him alone.

Lubentina. Not simply a world, but *the* world. The place where Cornak would find the treasure he'd been seeking for so long. Now, however, a complication had arisen. A cry for help, an entreaty cast upon the winds of the warp. Time had suddenly become a critical factor in his plans.

When Cornak's consciousness withdrew back into his body, when his eyes regained their colour and the spell lost its power, the sorcerer regained his sense of existence beyond the Circle. Ambition pulsed through his hearts as he turned away from the chalice and marched to the tapestry of skin. Drawing it aside, he exposed a rack of bones from which hung the segments of an ancient suit of power armour.

An instant of confusion gripped Cornak as he looked upon the armour. It took him a moment to understand why it was coloured in shades of silver and gold, why it bore the striping and iconography of the IV Legion. Out of the shifting confusion of the Circle's communal memories and predictions, he fixed upon this facet. Whether he truly belonged to the Legion, whether it was their gene-seed buried within his towering frame, these details were inconsequential. All that mattered was the utility of the moment, a means to an end.

The sorcerer lifted the silver helm from the stand, running his fingers across the sharp rows of spikes that marched away from the gold-coloured visor. He was Cornak, Sorcerer-Adept of the Circle, but he was also Cornak of the Iron Warriors, Hexmaster of the Third Grand Company.

Cornak closed his eyes and focused again upon the portents he'd witnessed with the Circle. They'd drawn him to the battered fortress world of Castellax, moved him to swear his services to Warsmith Rhodaan. Now they bore him towards Lubentina on an Iron Warriors warship. Promises and prophecies had drawn Rhodaan this far, manipulations of both ambition and malice. It had been easy enough to appeal to Rhodaan's martial pride, to harness it to the desires of the Circle.

What wouldn't be so easy, Cornak reflected as he began removing pieces of armour from the stand, would be maintaining control over the warsmith once they reached Lubentina. He wondered if he should tell Rhodaan what he'd just learned, if he should alert the Iron Warriors that the planet had dispatched a cry for help.

Would the urgency to accomplish their task before the forces of the Imperium arrived make the warsmith more or less pliable to the sorcerer's purposes?

CHAPTER V

The boom of artillery rolled across Tharsis, an apocalyptic thunder that made the very air shiver. Thick plumes of smoke billowed from districts abandoned by the local militia, fires racing unchecked through fabrication-plants and hab-blocks. Explosions rocked the region around the incense factories as caustic chemical stocks boiled in their storage tanks and stocks of prayer sticks were ignited by flying embers. Rioting mobs of the most degenerate and abandoned of the city's inhabitants ransacked the palaces of the merchant elite, looting grand manors even as the Cult of the Cataclysm advanced upon them.

Guided by the mental impulses of their magus, the cultists had accomplished much in the days since they'd emerged from their subterranean lairs. Through the old mines and the tunnels of the Cloisterfells, they'd managed to stage attacks against every quarter of the city. Some of the assaults had been mere feints, distractions to draw the militia away from Bakasur's real objectives or force the Imperials to commit more forces to defensive positions instead of mobilising them for counter-attacks in genuinely contested areas of Tharsis. Deception had brought the mansions of the Pythian Hills under the control of the Great Father's children. Believing the cult would advance from the scholarium to encircle the avenues of the low temples, the local militia had left only a token force to guard the palaces. They hadn't suspected that Bakasur's followers would strike from the hidden shafts beneath the hills, the tunnels they'd dug and kept in readiness for several months before the uprising. Loss of the Pythian Hills put a third of the city under the cult's control, but it was the psychological impact that appealed to the magus. The wealthy merchants and ministers might have left their residences to take shelter with the Cardinal-Governor, but they would certainly be outraged that their homes had been lost. Their ire would trickle down to the officers of the militia, further demoralising them and lessening their ability to combat the cult.

Confusion, Bakasur mused, was the great failing of mankind. Even with a common purpose or a common threat, there was no real unity. Each human, no matter how he tried to claim otherwise, was a selfish creature. The illusion of community was created through deceit. A human had to be coerced into setting aside his own individual needs and desires. Whether that coercion was created by direct threat or subtle manipulation of the psyche, they ultimately served only their own identity. The mobs of looters, free from the threat of authority, sated their sense of identity upon immediate and physical plunder. The soldiers and militia who stubbornly struggled against the cultists did so because their sense of identity was bound into the idea of community, that by sacrificing themselves they endowed their individuality with a greater meaning. They had no real conception of what it was to deny the self, to actually become one with a unified mentality, to be subsumed into a communal consciousness.

As he watched a pack of Inheritors stalking through the rubble of a stretch-car corral, Bakasur felt a profound regret. The mammalian taint in his biology meant he would never fully experience the oneness with the Great Father that the Inheritors enjoyed. There would always be the residue of 'self', the human stain denying him that ultimate adoration of the Beast. Only when the cult was triumphant, only when he ascended into the stars to be reborn could that blight be lifted from him and he could truly enter into the glories of the Great Father.

The magus followed behind his aberrant bodyguards as they prowled through the ruined corral. The hulking cultists probed into every shadow, inspected every doorway and window. It was a commendable exhibition of vigilance, but one that was pointless. The Inheritors wouldn't have left anyone behind. The star-children were most thorough when they went through a building. Any possible threat to Bakasur would have been shredded by their claws before they left.

Through the shattered walls Bakasur could see the slopes of Mount Rama and the leaning bulk of the Warmason's Cathedral. Every street and concourse that wound its way up the mountain was a seething mass of refugees. Each moment bedraggled groups of survivors came creeping out from the dying city to join that surging flood of flesh and fear. The ones that did so now were too late, however.

As they came prowling out of the ruins, lasguns flashed from the soldiers posted all around the base of the mountain. Mount Rama was one of three sections within the city that the local militia absolutely refused to concede to the cultists. To secure these bulwarks, it became necessary to close them off to the outside.

Bakasur shared the sense of loathing his fellow hybrids had for their human lineage, but he urged them to restraint. As much as possible they would herd non-combatants towards the perimeter, driving them into the cordon established by the militia. Whipped to the heights of desperation and terror, the panicked mobs needed more than barked commands and shouted pleas to make them turn away from the only sanctuary they could reach. Again and again, the soldiers at the perimeter were forced to fire into the refugees to keep them from charging the barricades. With each shot, the resolve of those soldiers was shaken, eaten away by self-loathing and disgust. Again, the identity of the individual overcame the necessity of action and the pragmatic truth that there were limits to how many people could be sustained within the confines of Mount Rama.

Shot by shot, the perimeter was eating itself alive. The soldiers were losing their efficiency as their senses lost focus. Some numbed themselves to their actions by slipping into a calloused and brutish mindset. Others sank deeper and deeper into a mire of guilt and recrimination. Bakasur could feel the limitations of their discipline stretching. When the crisis came, these men would break.

Then the slaughter would truly begin.

The thunder of artillery drew closer. Some of the nearby buildings were rocked by explosions as shells came ploughing into them. Bakasur detached a segment of his awareness, concentrating it upon producing a psychic shell around himself to spare him the hazard of flying shrapnel. The militia had withdrawn their artillery outside the city, rotating it along the outskirts to target those districts where the cult had supremacy. The barrages had been providential to Bakasur, smashing bridges, blocking streets and reducing the orderly patterns of construction to jumbled mounds of rubble where it needed only a few determined defenders to transform them into fortresses. The artillery campaign served the cult more than it did the militia. While the movement of soldiers was blocked by the destruction, the cult continued to use the tunnels underneath to manoeuvre.

Bakasur stirred the minds of the closest of the cult leaders, advising them to pull their followers back into the Cloisterfells until the distant artillerists could be induced to direct their fire elsewhere. He started to issue a more direct note of caution to the Inheritors themselves, but hesitated when he discovered their intentions. The four-armed star-children were moving ahead of the campaign Bakasur had planned. They'd bypassed the cordon, slipping around the embattled soldiers by climbing directly up the sheer cliff beneath the long stairway that wound around Mount Rama.

Crouched low, scuttling along using all six of their limbs, the Inheritors were ascending the Ladder. The few refugees desperate enough to climb the stairway to reach the cathedral were swiftly exterminated by the rapidly advancing creatures, their mangled bodies left to bleed on the ancient steps.

The magus rejected the impulse to call the Inheritors back.

It would be a profanation of his powers, a blasphemous violation of beings superior to him in every way. If the star-children had rejected his plans, then it wasn't his place to question their choice. He was to accept it and amend his strategy so that he might best serve their intentions.

The narthex was like a lake of weeping, whining humanity. The stink of smoke, sweat, blood and fear was almost overwhelming, the babble of distraught voices not unlike the roar of a storm. The hall was packed from wall to wall with refugees, filling faster than the acolytes and frateris militia could usher them away to inner chambers and passageways. Try as they might, such order as the Sisters were able to impose on the crowds as they passed through the enormous doors swiftly collapsed once they were inside.

Trishala felt her frustration mounting every time she saw some vacant-eyed hab-serf or befuddled prayer-wright frozen in place, oblivious to his blockage of the ranks of refugees behind him. The lines would disintegrate as people strove to get around the human obstacle, pressing upon the crowds around them and breaking the coherence of the other formations. The ripple effect would quickly pass through the whole narthex. Each time it took the Battle Sisters to restore order, their power armour endowing them with both the strength and mass to push their way through the crowds without being swept away by them.

Prelate Azad was doing his best to find room for those seeking safety within the cathedral, opening long-disused annexes and half-forgotten storerooms for their use. His acolytes had recruited work-gangs from the refugees to barricade the lesser doorways and many windows that opened on the building's lower levels. They'd sealed off the exterior balconies and walkways, leaving open only those being used by the Sisters as vantage points. The prelate had even come down to the narthex several times to confer with Trishala directly. Even in such a crisis as they now faced, there were certain strictures and rites that had to be maintained, but such flexibility as Azad could condone was made available to the Adepta Sororitas.

Trishala watched as some of Azad's acolytes inspected the latest group of refugees passing through the gate. In accordance with the stricture she'd given the crowd in the plaza, they had divested themselves of cloaks, coats and any other garment bulky enough to conceal the disfigurements of a cultist. Trishala had seen for herself on her home world that some of them could pass for a full human, but she was hoping such creatures weren't plentiful.

The support of the acolytes and frateris militia was essential. The Order of the Sombre Vow was already stretched thin. Only two hundred of the Battle Sisters had been assigned to the convent on Lubentina. Guarding the relics housed within the Warmason's Cathedral was the principal duty charged to them, and the masses of terrified laity filling the chambers and halls weren't making that task easier. Because of the nature of the cathedral's construction, its comparatively narrow rooms with their tall ceilings and the overall slanted arrangement of floors and walls, the refugees were being piled into every available space. Even some of the lesser shrines had been given over to the survivors, their artefacts removed for safekeeping. Even so, there were some relics too impractical or too sacred to be moved, and these required a constant guard. None more so than the Warmason's Casket and the Shroud of Singh in the Palladion. There was one sanctuary where the refugees hadn't been allowed to settle themselves.

There were ten Sisters always on guard in the Palladion, the largest deployment of her warriors outside the narthex itself. Accounting for the other sacred places, treasures and artefacts meant detailing another twenty to watch over them. Patrols sweeping through the cathedral to both maintain order among the masses of refugees and ferret out any hybrids still nestled among the crowds consumed still more of her resources. Then there were the Sisters posted to the gatehouse and the ponderous mechanisms that controlled the immense gate, the sentinels arrayed about the various balconies and porticos to keep watch over the plaza and the slopes of Mount Rama. There were even a few warriors up on the Curate's Leap with powerful magnoculars so they might report on the fighting in the rest of Tharsis.

Lastly there was the reserve. Thirty-six Sisters that Trishala could use to rotate with the others or draw upon should a crisis develop. It wasn't much, especially when she had to factor the panic of several thousand untrained, undisciplined civilians into her plans. If sending four Sisters away from the gate twice an hour was any indicator, should it be necessary to quell a panic she'd need not only the reserve but warriors assigned to other duties as well.

Trishala's attention narrowed when she saw Kashibai conducting Azad through the narthex. The prelate's expression was severe. 'We have been in communication with the militia. They will establish a cordon around the base of Mount Rama and constrain the flow of refugees.'

'It is what must be done,' Trishala said. 'The cathedral cannot hold them all.'

Azad's jaw tightened as he looked towards the doors. 'We can still bring more in. We can still find room for more of them.'

'You'll have to order the Great Gate closed soon,' Trishala stated. 'While the entrance is open everyone inside remains vulnerable. We have been charged with protecting this holy place and the relics housed here. Even our own convent has been abandoned that every Sister may be available towards fulfilling this obligation. We must not permit anything to jeopardise the cathedral's defence.'

'If I order the gate shut, I am abandoning all those outside these walls,' Azad said. 'Until the last possible moment, we must keep the way open. It is the God-Emperor's will that we save as many as we can.'

'It is also the God-Emperor's will that we keep any more infiltrators from getting in here,' Trishala said.

'We can do no good, prelate, if we let the wolves in with the flock,' Kashibai explained, her tone grim. 'We killed many innocents dealing with the cultists who tried to slip inside before.'

'There must be a way.' Azad touched his fingers to the jewelled aquila he wore. 'If I could impress on the local militia the gravity of our need, perhaps they would lend us aid. Soldiers to help share your burden.'

'Your acolytes have spoken with them over the vox,' Trishala said. 'Do you think they have any men to spare? The militia has been stretched thin already. As much as we could benefit from their aid, they are depending on us to hold the Warmason's Cathedral on our own.'

'Where there is faith in the Emperor's grace, all things become possible,' Azad replied.

'Then we will pray for your success, prelate,' Kashibai assured him. The two Battle Sisters saluted Azad as he made his way back across the narthex.

'If he is successful it would improve the situation,' Trishala told Kashibai, 'but we cannot build our strategy upon hope. Have you inspected the machinery of the Great Gate?'

Kashibai cast her gaze up at the ceiling and the control room above their heads. 'Prelate Azad wishes to keep the doors open, but that hasn't kept him from sending acolytes to rouse the cogitators and feed the motors. It will need a few hours to build up a sufficient reserve of energy, but they are doing their best to have everything in readiness.'

'We should have had them ready some time ago,' Trishala mused. 'When the first infiltrators tried to get inside, we should have stopped the intake.'

'You can understand the prelate's reluctance.' Kashibai gestured at the ragged crowds around them.

Trishala closed her hand around the icon that hung about her neck. 'I only pray that we can afford such mercy.' She turned towards the entrance of the narthex. 'Come, we'll see if there isn't something more we can do to ready things on the outside when we close the Great Gate. There's certain to be a rush once the crowds discover what we're doing.'

A squad of Battle Sisters were posted both within and just outside the entrance, their armoured presence doing much to quiet the column of refugees slowly moving into the cathedral. They saluted Trishala as she approached, opening a path for her and Kashibai as they moved out into the square. Standing on the broad steps outside the doors, they surveyed the scene.

The plaza was a sea of anguished faces, rolling relentlessly forwards. Vox-amplifiers fastened to the columns just outside the gate crackled and popped, the white hiss of their over-worked machine-spirit voicing its annoyance. Soon another voice droned over that of the unquiet spirit. In firm tones, one of the priests called out to the crowds, repeating the strictures Trishala had imposed. Because of the constant flow of new refugees into the plaza, the instructions were repeated every fifteen minutes, an endless litany that was forgotten by the crowd the moment they came close to the doors and saw sanctuary within their reach.

'So many of them,' Kashibai said. 'How can we shelter all these people, let alone care for them?'

'Prelate Azad has taken that burden onto himself,' Trishala said. 'The cathedral's stores of water and victuals have been supplemented by such supplies as the frateris militia could collect from the shops and homes on Mount Rama. Feeding and ministering to these people is the task the prelate has given himself. Ours is to make sure they are safe long enough to get hungry.' She glanced back into the narthex, pleased when she saw Sister Virika and her comrades moving towards the gate. They only managed a few steps before the lines behind them became snagged again. With a curt wave of her hand, she sent Virika back to restore order.

'If we only had–' Before Trishala could finish her statement, Kashibai lunged at her, dragging her to the ground. The next instant the edge of the gateway exploded in a burst of searing light, slivers of stone raking the nearest of the refugees.

The plaza erupted in screams. Even without Kashibai pointing to him, Trishala wouldn't have had any problem spotting her attacker. Refugees were fairly crawling over one another to get away from the shooter. He was a grisly-looking creature draped in a black dust-slicker and ash-hood, his gloved hands wrapped about the grip of a lascannon. The cultist was of such incredible strength that he hefted the cumbersome weapon up to his shoulder and took aim again.

'Down!' Trishala shouted at the terrified crowd in the plaza. She tried to aim for the cultist, but the confusion of the crowd made a mockery of her efforts. If she could be certain of hitting her attacker she'd risk a burst, but to fire blindly into the throng was another thing.

The cultists suffered from no such pangs of conscience. Autoguns and stubbers tore into the refugees as a dozen more cultists revealed themselves and moved to support the hybrid with the lascannon. Again the heavy weapon sent a beam of annihilating light searing into the gateway, burning away still more of its facade, exposing the thick layers of armoured metal beneath.

'Get inside!' Kashibai shouted to the nearest of the refugees.

Trishala turned from her foe to bark a hurried command to the Sisters at the gate. 'No one gets in!' she told Virika as the Sisters came running out from the narthex. 'Keep them out!' Trishala ignored the look Kashibai gave her. Kashibai was letting her revulsion at the refugees being shot down in the plaza cloud her judgement. She was forgetting all the people inside the cathedral and how an attack such as this was just the sort of thing to provide cover for more cultists to slip inside. If not for Prelate Azad, she'd order the Great Gate closed at once and remove the threat entirely.

From up above the gate, the bark of boltguns now sounded. The Sisters deployed on the balconies were taking a hand now, pelting the enemy with quick bursts from their weapons. One cultist with an autogun was sent spinning by a shell that fairly evaporated his head. Another was blown back by a round that exploded in his chest, crashing into the refugees trying to flee from him.

The fire raking the doorway slackened as the Sisters on the balconies took their toll. The instant there was a respite, Trishala was on her feet, plunging down the steps into the plaza. The ground was strewn with the bodies of refugees gunned down in the fighting. The viciousness of the enemy had betrayed them. They'd killed their own best protection. Once she was clear of those survivors streaming towards the gate there was no one between the Sister Superior and her prey.

Trishala's bolt pistol snarled, loosing a devastating burst into the cultists. She saw one fall, his belly ripped open and one leg severed at the hip. Another was thrashing on the ground, the left side of his chest blown apart. Only a single shell came close to hitting the creature with the lascannon, however, tearing through the foeman beside him. The hulking cultist cackled with shrill laughter as he swung his monstrous weapon in her direction.

Before the lascannon could fire, the enemy holding it was torn in half by a blast of bolter-fire. Kashibai rushed past Trishala, emptying the rest of her clip into the remaining cultists. The violence of her assault saw the last of the enemy turn to flee, even several that had stayed hidden among the crowds now exposing themselves to join the escape route. A good half a dozen of them raced towards the Chastened Road, shoving and shooting anyone in their way.

Trishala and Kashibai pursued the cultists, trying to close the distance with them so there would be no chance of their shots going astray. Before they could, however, the crack of lasguns sounded from the end of the plaza. The cultists had reached the road only to discover that their retreat was at an end.

Advancing up the road, scattering the crowds before them, was a company of local militia. The tan-uniformed soldiers spread out to form a line across the entrance to the plaza, snapping off shots from their lasguns as the cultists moved towards them. The searing beams of light stabbed into the enemy mob, burning through their coveralls and mining fatigues, ripping through the pale flesh beneath. An officer wearing the peaked cap of a captain raised his chainsword overhead. With the signal came a concerted volley from the front rank of troopers. Those cultists still on their feet collapsed under the scorching fusillade.

When the Battle Sisters reached the scene, a sergeant was moving among the fallen cultists, sending a slug from his shotgun into the skull of any he found that had only been wounded by the lasguns. Trishala left the man to his gory labour and marched towards the sword-bearing captain. The officer was relaying commands to his troops, waving a pair of lumbering Leman Russ battle tanks up into the plaza. At Trishala's approach, he directed a crisp salute to the Sister Superior.

'Captain Debdan, late of Colonel Hafiz's staff,' he introduced himself. He straightened somewhat and added with a touch of pride, 'Now field commander of the Three Hundred and Thirty-Fourth Composite Battalion.'

'What orders have you been issued, captain?' Trishala asked. She turned her gaze to the troops moving out into the plaza. Their uniforms were grubby from dirt and smoke, and several of them sported bloodied bandages. 'It looks like you've seen some fighting even before reaching the top of Mount Rama.'

Debdan nodded. 'We encountered a pocket of resistance entrenched along the prayer-wrights' row. Our losses were more severe than originally anticipated. Even after securing the site we lacked the strength to hold it. That's why we've been reassigned to reinforce you here at the cathedral.'

'Praise the God-Emperor,' Trishala said, thinking of Prelate Azad and his appeal to the militia for help.

The captain looked past Trishala, a puzzled expression on his face. She followed the direction of his gaze, seeing Kashibai walking towards them. With the fleeing cultists dealt with, she'd gone back to secure the lascannon the hybrids had been using.

'The cultists were using that?' Debdan asked.

'They were taking shots at the gate with it,' Kashibai said. She held the weapon out to Trishala. 'This isn't some scratch-built knock-together. They must have looted it off soldiers they killed.'

Debdan stepped forwards and took the weapon from Kashibai. After a brief inspection, he shook his head. 'This weapon was never issued,' he declared. He set the lascannon leaning against his leg and reached to his pistol holster. Holding the gun out to the two Sisters, he indicated a number branded into the side of the grip. 'When a weapon is taken from the stocks, the identity number of the trooper who receives it is marked on it. This lascannon has no such marking. Not even a blemish where such a mark might have been removed.'

'Then these mutants are able to make these weapons on their own,' Kashibai hissed. The thought that the cultists could manufacture armaments as sophisticated and deadly as a lascannon was a far from pleasant one.

'No, it is a regulation weapon,' Debdan stated, but his tone was too grim to draw any comfort from.

Trishala understood the implication and why it was even worse than Kashibai's initial suspicion. 'A traitor has been smuggling weapons to the cultists.'

'Right from the arsenal itself,' Debdan said. 'It would have to be someone of high rank to both move the weapons and conceal the theft.'

'And who's to say how long they've been arming the cult,' Trishala observed.

Captain Debdan nodded. 'There's no knowing how many guns have been handed over to the cultists. It would help explain why they've been able to mount such a vicious resistance. But there's a bigger problem to consider. If this traitor has been arming the rebels, what other things might he have done to help them?'

Trishala felt her gorge rise. A traitor, a human in league with these monsters. 'It isn't just the things the traitor has done,' she said. 'What about the things he may be doing right now?'

Colonel Hafiz felt distinctly uncomfortable sitting in his chair at the near-deserted council table. With Tharsis ablaze with insurrection and reports of other uprisings from a score of smaller settlements across each of Lubentina's continents, his place was out there, contributing to the fight. There were things he needed to be doing, things more productive than this conference with the Cardinal-Governor.

Adding to Hafiz's uneasiness was the tension he sensed whenever Murdan stirred in his throne and glanced at Palatine Yadav. Officially the decision to have the astropath send a distress call four days previously had been made by the Cardinal-Governor alone as he reconsidered the scope of the cult uprising. He was putting a good deal more credence in the rumours that it had been Yadav who forced Murdan into the action against the governor's will. If the Cardinal-Governor reprimanded Yadav it would be an admission that his authority had been defied. Hafiz could well imagine Murdan biding his time until he could retaliate from a position of strength rather than weakness.

'Certainly I sympathise with the difficulty of these choices. None of them are ideal, or even palatable, but that doesn't make them any less necessary.' The speaker was Minister Kargil, one of the very few councillors in attendance. Since the crisis began, Kargil had lost a tremendous amount of weight, the folds of skin drooping from his cheeks somehow giving him a shrivelled aspect despite his still considerable paunch. When he raised a finger to emphasise the point he was trying to make, the rings he wore slid and clattered against each other. 'Of course we should all like to save as many of the people as possible, but the simple practicality of the situation means sacrifices must be made.'

'So long as those sacrifices aren't demanded of yourself,'

one of the other councillors scoffed. The respect of his peers had dwindled almost in tandem with Kargil's weight.

Hafiz shook his head. For the better part of an hour now Kargil had been trying to sway the rest of the council. Thus far he'd met only revulsion and disgust. The sort of men who would have been swayed were the ones not at the table, the men who'd already fled the city, striking out for other parts of Lubentina. Kargil was proposing something almost incredible in its audacity – using one of the transports at the spaceport to leave the planet. With two-thirds of Tharsis either destroyed or in the control of the rebels, he argued the situation was beyond recovery. It might be years before there was any answer to the distress call Rakesh had sent. By then Lubentina would be lost.

'There is turmoil enough at the spaceport already,' Hafiz pointed out. 'We still have transports bringing thousands of pilgrims to Lubentina, unaware of what is happening here. Each ship that arrives and tries to unload its passengers is immediately beset by thousands of terrified pilgrims trying to get away. The soldiers posted at the spaceport already have problems enough trying to maintain order and control the crowds. Can you imagine the panic if we made any move to take over the ships? It would destroy whatever faith the people have in us to protect them.'

'One transport,' Kargil retorted, excitement in his tone. 'That's all I'm asking for. One ship. We're going to need more than survivors to rebuild. It will take money.'

'Your money,' another of the councillors snarled.

Kargil spun around, appealing to the men who had once acceded to every whim the minister expressed. Now that he no longer intimidated them the other councillors were bold. 'Does it matter where the money comes from? We'll still need it to rebuild once the rebels have been exterminated.'

'One transport would mean four thousand pilgrims,' Yadav said.

The minister slammed his fist against the table. 'And how many have already been abandoned? The militia has withdrawn from three-quarters of Tharsis and are still in retreat! They're already shooting anyone who tries to get into the spaceport without authorisation and I've seen for myself that the perimeter around the Sovereign Spire is being enforced with firepower.'

Hafiz glowered at Kargil. 'To prevent the rebels from overwhelming us completely, the strategy has been to concentrate our resources in three key areas – the government complex, Mount Rama, and the spaceport. To maintain our control over these sites, it has been necessary to restrict how many survivors we take in. Too many and order will break down. If that happens, we're lost before we've even started.

'There is also the realistic issue of supplies,' Hafiz continued. 'We have no way of knowing when relief will come. We could be looking at months, even years of protracted siege. The supplies here in the Sovereign Spire are assessed at a level to provide rations for ten thousand for a year.'

Murdan shifted forwards on his throne. 'Coordinate with the outlying settlements and secure whatever stores they possess,' he told the colonel. 'Arrange to bring supplies in by air, and let us thank the God-Emperor that these mutants haven't threatened that avenue of operation.' There was just a hint of a smile when Murdan looked towards Kargil. 'As for removing resources from

Lubentina, I forbid it. The wealth of Lubentina remains on Lubentina. Nothing will proclaim louder to the Imperium that we will not abandon our world than leaving our treasure here.'

The fatalistic note in Murdan's words sent a chill through Hafiz's flesh. If Lubentina was to be saved, the Cardinal-Governor demanded it be saved on his terms.

If the astropath's message had been heard, if help was coming, then it couldn't come fast enough.

When tech-savants in the control-turret first detected the craft descending towards the spaceport, Major Ranj voxed the operator to signal the vessel to slow its approach. The haste with which the spaceport was trying to get ships off Lubentina was taking its toll on everyone. The pilots of the ships, the controllers in the turret, the ground personnel waiting to fuel and supply the ships when they landed. Most of all there was the strain being felt by the militia officers trying to impose some kind of discipline on the proceedings. Major Ranj and his staff had been made responsible for keeping the spaceport under control. His troops had to hold the perimeter against not only probing cultist attacks, but from mobs of panicked survivors trying to batter their way through the barricades and reach the ships. It was a hard thing to shoot other Lubentines, but it was essential that order was maintained.

Ranj looked across the airfield through one of the armourglass windows of the observation tower, watching as a platoon of soldiers forced a crowd of pilgrims away from one of the landing pads and to one of the empty hangars that lined the field. Each of the hangars had been repurposed into temporary shelters for thousands of civilians, holding areas to house them while the local militia tried to wrest back control of Tharsis. Another platoon was posted about the base of the control tower, securing it in the event the crowds became unmanageable.

'The ship isn't responding,' an exasperated controller voxed Ranj. 'I've redirected those transports that were going to make their ascent so they shift around this ship. Those on approach have been told to retard their descent and wait.'

The controller's tone became even more agitated. 'That ship isn't a pilgrim transport. I don't know what it is.'

Ranj was silent for a moment, staring up at the observation tower's vid-feed. The strange vessel was drawing closer. Rapidly he considered possibilities, discarding most of them. The ship was a massive vessel, savage in its outline, festooned with an array of vicious guns. It was clearly no civilian ship, that much was certain.

'Keep trying to raise them,' Ranj told the controller. Even as he gave the order, cries of horror rose from the personnel in the control tower. Communication over the vox collapsed into a whir of white noise.

Major Ranj gazed at the vid-feed in horror. The upper section of the control tower was a smouldering ruin. Even as he watched, the strange vessel sent another salvo slamming into the structure, bringing it down in a cascade of ferrocrete and armourglass. Ranj whipped around, hurrying to the walkway that circled the outside of the observation tower. He looked up, staring at the mysterious attacker.

The ship that had destroyed the control tower was blocky, almost box-like in its outline. The bifurcated tail was sharp and angular, arching back from the main body like the stinger of a scorpion. Two nubby wings jutted out from its sides, each laden with bulbous weapons pods. The nose of the craft had a wart-like protrusion to one side, a wart that had the muzzles of heavy bolters projecting from it like ugly black hairs. It was unlike any ship Ranj had ever seen, but there was no question of its purpose. It was a military vessel.

The craft crunched down onto the surface of a landing pad. Heavy skids on the underside of the ship jostled as their pneumatic compensators absorbed the impact of the landing. For a time, the strange ship was silent, resting on the field like some great silver spider. The numerals and heraldry painted onto the sides of the craft were both archaic and unsettling. The soldiers on the field scrambled to bring weapons to bear on the unknown attacker while pilgrims fled from its vicinity, pressing the troops guarding the transports even more desperately than they had before.

Major Ranj hurried down from the observation tower. Whoever was inside the warship was obviously hostile. He wondered if it could be some subterfuge of the rebels, if they'd somehow made contact with sympathisers from off-world. Whatever they were, he intended to receive them in kind. Barking orders to his men as he sprinted towards the landing pad, he commanded them to hold fire until the attackers exposed themselves.

After several anxious minutes, the ship exhibited signs of activity. A loud hiss sounded from just behind where the tail joined the main body of the craft. Dark steam jetted into the air, expelled from the windlasses that lowered an armaplas ramp onto the ferrocrete pad. A black, cave-like bay within the ship was revealed as the ramp slammed down. Ranj could feel the change that swept through his men. Apprehension quickly turned to terror. The major felt his own heart racing as he looked at what was emerging from the ship. Striding out from the darkness, descending the lowered ramp, was a colossal figure. Nearly three metres tall, encased in an immense suit of power armour, the giant strode out onto the landing pad, indifferent to the fear of the onlookers.

Those soldiers who'd drawn close to the landing zone to confront the destroyers of the control tower were beset not simply by fear but also confusion. Ranj shared their distress. There wasn't any mistaking what kind of warrior they were looking at. He was one of the holy Space Marines, the revered defenders of humanity. The mighty protectors of the Imperium.

Yet this ship had only moments ago obliterated the control tower.

The Space Marine stepped out from beneath the shadow of his ship, making room for his brethren to descend the ramp. As he did, Ranj could see more clearly the dull silver armour bordered and accented in gold, the black pauldrons that covered his shoulders and the yellow slashes painted across his vambraces. A chainsword nearly as tall as a normal man hung at the Space Marine's hip and in one of his gauntlets he held a savage-looking bolt pistol adorned with disquieting symbols and barbarous flourishes of bone. The helm that enclosed his head was a still darker shade of silver than his armour and the face was pulled out into a long beak, the sides of which were etched to resemble the fangs of some reptilian horror. A pair of horns rose from the back of the helm, curling back from the mask.

The Space Marine looked across the landing field, raising his head as he stared off in the direction of Mount Rama. For a moment the mountain and the cathedral perched atop it held his attention, then he turned his gaze upon the soldiers and labourers watching him. Ranj felt a thrill of horror rush down his spine when the Space Marine's gaze fixed upon him, aware that he was the ranking officer among those near the landing pad.

'I am Rhodaan, warsmith of the Third Grand Company of the Iron Warriors Legion,' the Space Marine's voice rumbled through the speakers inside his helm. 'I will suffer no obstruction of my mission here.' He gestured at the rubble of the control tower. 'If you are wise, you'll tell your minions to stay out of our way.'

CHAPTER VI

Rhodaan turned away from the frightened soldiers and civilians watching the Iron Warriors disembark. They were only flesh, of little concern to a Space Marine. What was of more concern to him were his surroundings. Lubentina was a world the Third Grand Company had raided several millennia before. Rhodaan had been there. What he looked at now was almost unrecognisable. There had been no sprawling city or bustling spaceport then, only scattered mineral outposts and the camps of explorators.

'They've been busy since we were last here,' Captain Uzraal commented as he marched out from under the gunship's wing.

'They're still busy,' Rhodaan said. He indicated the plumes of smoke rising from the skyscape of Tharsis. When the gunship's augur had scanned the city on their descent, the signs of turmoil had been evident. Now that he looked on the scene for himself, Rhodaan dismissed possibilities of industrial accident or natural disaster. No Iron Warrior could mistake the signs of combat for anything else. Who the opponents were, what was in contest, were of less concern to the warsmith than how he could use this to accomplish his mission.

'Unless the flesh provides provocation, take no action against them,' Rhodaan voxed to his followers.

'Mercy for the flesh?' The question crackled across the vox. Rhodaan swung around to face the Space Marine who'd said it.

Periphetes was a recent initiate of the Third Grand Company, a renegade from the Steel Brethren who'd made his way to Castellax on a pirate raider some little time after the invasion of Waaagh Biglug. His armour still bore elements of his old allegiance. Not of his own choice, but on Rhodaan's order. He wanted Periphetes never to forget that his comrades in the Steel Brethren had splintered off from the Legion, and by doing so had forsaken their share in the legacy of the Iron Warriors.

'You are here to reclaim something for the Legion,' Rhodaan said. 'Anything that distracts from that mission will be avoided.'

Rhodaan turned from the chastened Periphetes, letting his gaze linger on the other Space Marines of his retinue. Brother Gaos and the lethal bulk of his autocannon. Brother Morak, a veteran of the former warsmith's bodyguard. Brother Turu, his pauldrons adorned with the skulls of enemies. Brother Mahar, who'd fought his way across a hundred kilometres of ork-infested desert to rejoin the Iron Warriors at Aboro.

'All of you will do what is expected of you,' Rhodaan told them. 'Any failure will be considered defiance and there are none who defy me twice.' He looked aside to Uzraal. 'We march as soon as I confer with the sorcerer.'

'It would seem he heard you,' Uzraal said as the sorcerer emerged from the ship.

'Good. There is much I would have him hear,' Rhodaan said.

Cornak of Ouroboros stalked out from beneath the gunship's fuselage, yet even when he stood in the open, his aspect seemed dulled by shadows. The cabbalistic emblems woven into the black robes he wore over his armour exuded a pulsating glow, at once appearing to inhale and expel the darkness within which Cornak strode.

'I overheard you talking to your warriors,' Cornak told the warsmith. 'Most instructive.'

'It is a simple lesson to learn,' Rhodaan replied. 'Failing me is a dangerous mistake.' He stared into the yellowed lenses of Cornak's mask. 'It is a simple lesson but there is always one who refuses to learn it.'

Cornak bowed his head. 'I stand to gain nothing by defying you, Dread Lord.' He tapped an armoured finger against the side of his helm. 'My visions have guided me to you. The portents are clear. My future is bound into that of the Third Grand Company. Only through your triumph can I find my own.'

'I have invested no small effort to chase these visions of yours, sorcerer,' Rhodaan said. 'It will go ill for you if your warp sight has led us astray.'

'You may trust my divinations,' Cornak assured the warsmith.

Rhodaan laughed at the remark, the vox speakers in his helm turning the sound into a reptilian cackle. 'Things must be very different on Medrengard. Had you spent more time on Castellax you would understand that nothing and no one is to be trusted. Those who forget that wind up being fed to the flesh.'

The sorcerer bowed once more, acknowledging both the warsmith's threat and his authority to make it.

Rhodaan wasn't taken in by the display. Cornak had an unerring facility for alternating between a pose of dutiful subservience and one of cold indifference, depending on the mood of those around him. His appearance on Castellax after the ork invasion had been a complete mystery. No raider or transport had deposited him on the world. He'd simply shown up one day, requesting audience with the warsmith.

'Lubentina isn't the world I was familiar with,' Rhodaan stated. 'Much has changed. Before it was an isolated mining world. Now it is a den of the False Emperor's slaves. How is it that your visions failed to show this to you? Or did you simply forget to mention it?'

'My spells were directed at locating the relic,' Cornak explained. 'It was upon that purpose alone that I set my magic. And I have found it, Dread Lord.' He raised his grisly staff, a fossil rod that once had been the tooth of some alien leviathan, pointing it at the mountain that had arrested Rhodaan's attention before. 'They are keeping it there, within the temple on the summit.'

'Your magic can tell you precisely where the relic is, but fails to inform you that there's an entire city around it?' Rhodaan waved at the distant smoke billowing from Tharsis. 'Did your spells warn you this place was a battlefield?'

'It was more important to locate the relic,' Cornak said. 'When peering into the warp, the more one tries to see the less clear the picture becomes.'

'I will hold you to account,' Rhodaan promised. 'What the flesh calls the Warmason's Casket had best be where you say it will be.' The warsmith turned from Cornak and issued orders over the inter-squad vox. 'Captain Uzraal, get our brothers moving. I want to get what we came for and be gone before the dust of our landing has time to settle.'

The Iron Warriors marched away from their gunship, striking out across the spaceport. Eight armoured giants, they held the fascination of every eye with a view of the field. Soldiers kept away from their line of march, trying to do nothing that would provoke the Space Marines. Crowds of pilgrims fled in terror as the Iron Warriors passed them.

The Space Marines didn't encounter any resistance until they drew close to the gates at the perimeter of the spaceport. Here the soldiers didn't abandon their posts, but maintained their position with grim resignation. Even as the threat of the Iron Warriors poured fear into their minds, an awareness of what would happen if the barrier was left undefended instilled a stubborn determination in them to stay where they were.

Rhodaan stared across the defences. 'The Fourth Legion commands you to open your gates.' The order thundered from his helmet's vox-caster.

Uzraal glanced back at Rhodaan as they came closer to the gates. The soldiers had positioned several Chimeras and flamers to bolster their defence, but all of these heavy weapons were turned outwards to address the threat posed by the mobs trying to gain the comparative security of the spaceport. As yet, none of these weapons had been turned around to confront the advance of the Iron Warriors. The commander at the gates was still trying to walk the line between antagonising the Space Marines and defending the barrier.

Rhodaan wasn't going to wait for the men to reach a decision. Uzraal was an old comrade of Rhodaan's, last survivor of the Raptors the warsmith had once commanded. All it needed was a slight dip of his horned helm for Uzraal to understand his leader's intentions.

'Break them,' Uzraal cried out to his warriors. The instant the command was given, the hulking Space Marines erupted into action. Gaos set his autocannon raking across the Chimeras, high-velocity rounds sheering through the plasteel hulls to bounce about within the interiors and pulp the soldiers inside. Periphetes blasted troops from the barricade with his bolter. Turu stormed forwards with a shaped meltabomb, flinging it underneath the chassis of a Taurox assault vehicle.

The explosion as the meltabomb detonated lifted the Taurox into the air, hurling it several metres upwards before its armoured mass came slamming back down, crushing a huge part of the gates as it landed. A few dazed soldiers staggered about the site of the impact, but they were swiftly overwhelmed by the surging crush of humanity that came rushing into the breach. Held at bay so long by the threat of militia guns, the desperate pilgrims trapped within Tharsis had cowered in the buildings facing the spaceport, watching with envy as transports rose into the sky. Fear of being left behind was the single passion left to them. They didn't trouble themselves over the nature of what had happened behind the high walls of the barricade. All that spurred them on was the fact that the wall had come crashing down.

Decimated by the Iron Warriors, such troops as remained

fled when the crowd surged through the breach. The mob came rushing onwards, their impetus pushing those at the forefront ahead even as they stared in wonder at the towering Space Marines.

'Clear a path for us,' Rhodaan told Uzraal.

On the warsmith's command, Uzraal sent a blast from his meltagun searing into the pilgrims. The front of the crowd was vaporised instantly; those behind them screamed as their hair and clothes caught fire and their skin blistered. Desperately the burning victims tried to find escape, fleeing back through the gates. Those trying to force their way inside, refusing to give ground before, now broke and fled as these living firebrands came streaming at them. In a matter of moments the flood of pilgrims fell back, retreating from the gates that had moments before offered them hope and now presented them only with terror.

Across the scorched ruin, the Iron Warriors marched. They spared no notice for the devastation they'd inflicted. It was but a mote in the atrocities they'd already witnessed over the course of the Long War. After ten millennia, of what consequence were a few dozen flesh crushed underfoot?

When the Iron Warriors emerged onto the street beyond the gates they found thousands of stunned pilgrims watching them. Some fled as the Space Marines came forwards, but most simply observed them in shocked silence. With cold indifference, the Iron Warriors marched past the crowds. As they left the pilgrims behind, a dull roar rose from the throng, a desperate cry that betokened a renewed rush on the gates. With neither soldiers nor Space Marines to stop them, thousands of pilgrims swarmed into the spaceport.

The crack of lasguns as the remaining local militia tried to stem the tide was of less concern to the Iron Warriors than the boom of artillery and the chatter of gunfire they could hear in the distance. Some of the shots sounded only a few kilometres away while others were so faint they could be several times as far.

'This conflict will make things easier,' Cornak said. 'Rebellion or guild war, this turmoil will benefit us.'

'An opportune moment, as you said,' Rhodaan agreed. 'Whatever this unrest means it will keep the Imperial dogs busy while we attend to our business.'

Cornak tapped the butt of his staff against the charred ground. 'It is as my visions have shown me,' he said. He pointed upwards, past the buildings around them towards an immense structure that rose above the city on the peak of a small mountain.

'Captain Uzraal,' Rhodaan called across the vox. 'Check the auspex and tell me how far that is.' It was a petty, mundane task to set the captain. Just the sort of thing to remind him of his place.

'The mountain is just over forty-five hundred metres from our current position, warsmith,' Uzraal answered after a moment.

Rhodaan peered at the towering temple, scrutinising its leaning structure. His appraisal was one of disdain. The cathedral was almost childish in design, hardly built with an eye towards fortification. Certainly it wouldn't withstand a siege – not one executed by the Iron Warriors.

The pack of genestealers scrabbled up the winding stairs of the Ladder of Obeisance, circling round and round the slopes of Mount Rama. They kept close to the side of the mountain, their chitinous shells scraping against the intricate frescos carved into the rock. At regular intervals they came upon the cave-like stalls where vendors sought to tempt pilgrims with flasks of water and tubes of protein paste to sustain them on their arduous climb, their inhabitants now fled during the general exodus to the cathedral.

Less frequently the genestealers came upon small bands of humans struggling to ascend the Ladder. Pilgrims caught upon the stairs when the crisis began or refugees thinking the long route was a better prospect than the mobs filling the Chastened Road, the weary travellers were easy prey for the prowling aliens. By claw and fang each little band was brought down, their mangled bodies pushed close against the mountainside lest some observer from above spy their corpses.

In the rush to gain safety, in the desperate effort to control the crowds sweeping up the mountain, the Ladder had been forgotten by those above. The few pilgrims who entered the plaza from the top of the stairway were nothing when measured against the surge of refugees ascending the other approaches. No guard had been set upon the Ladder, no sentinel waited to receive the handful of people braving the stairs. When that trickle of pilgrims fell to nothing, there was no one paying attention to wonder why, to discover that the only creatures left on the Ladder weren't human.

Warily, the three-armed genestealer advanced up the stair, the blood of its last victims still dripping off its remaining claws. It glared out across the plaza, studying the mass of refugees packed into the square, struggling against one another in their efforts to reach the Great Gate of the cathedral. It could see the massive Leman

Russ battle tanks drawn up at either side of the square, the tan-uniformed soldiers trying to direct the crowds. On the steps of the cathedral and standing in the gigantic doorway it could see the black-armoured Sisters, their bolters at the ready. High above them, from balconies and platforms, local militia troopers kept watch.

The three-armed genestealer uttered a low hiss when it spotted Trishala walking through the gateway. It wasn't anger that provoked the creature's snarl, but rather warning. The others of its pack could feel its agitation and through that empathic bond they were aware of the menace this enemy posed. She was the one who had forced the Great Father to advance the cult's plans through her interference. She was the one who'd proven herself bold and resourceful enough to survive combat with a pure-strain. She represented a threat that had to be disposed of. Such were the impulses the maimed alien passed to its fellows.

Silently, the aliens crept forwards. The mental stimulus passed into their minds by Bakasur gave them a greater awareness of what they could expect. The cult had been active around the cathedral and only the most direct and overt of those activities had been discovered by the Sisters. Some of the obstacles that appeared before the genestealers could be safely bypassed. It was the Sisters themselves that would represent the biggest menace. Yet there were ways to blunt even their threat.

Once the pack was at the very edge of the plaza they lunged forwards in a shrieking mass. They charged onto the plaza, slashing a path through the masses of refugees. No opportunity was given them to escape the rushing genestealers. The creatures kept close to the crowds, weaving among the screaming humans. With the incredible precision of their shared consciousness, the genestealers guided the panicked mob, steering it towards the steps.

The efforts of the defenders were thwarted at every turn. The Leman Russ tanks rumbled into life, their crews trying to ready their weapons in case the genestealers tried to rush their vehicles. Suddenly the tank on the left side of the plaza burst open in a cloud of flames and shrapnel, ripped apart by an internal explosion. The right-hand tank fared better, only a plume of smoke billowing up from its engine. The fearsome machine shuddered and fell silent, its crew leaping out of its hatches as smoke began to fill their compartment. The infantry gazed at the burning tanks in disbelief – their heaviest weapons destroyed just when they were needed. Sabotage was a word that invoked anger and fear in equal measure.

The soldiers in the plaza had no time to consider sabotage as they were trampled by the panicked crowd, dragged under by the sheer numbers of crazed humanity that stampeded towards them. Some few spared themselves by forsaking any pretext of maintaining control and simply allowing themselves to be swept away by the terrified throng. The sentries high upon the walls refrained from firing down into the plaza, unable to pick friend from foe in the confusion.

On the steps outside the Great Gate, the Battle Sisters likewise hesitated, none of them favouring the idea of being the first to shoot into the swirling morass of refugees. Trishala rushed out from the gateway, shouting commands to her warriors. 'Open fire!' she cried, putting action to words as she sent a burst from her pistol down into the plaza. 'We can't let even one xenos get inside! Prelate Azad, you have to close the Great Gate now!'

Grimly the Sisters blazed away, dropping the panicked refugees being herded towards the steps. From behind the falling bodies, the aliens sprang at their attackers, rushing them in a blur of scything claws and gnashing fangs. Less resolute soldiers than the Order of the Sombre Vow would have broken before the xenos assault, overcome by horror of the creatures. Trishala and her warriors stood their ground, loosing bursts of bolter-fire into the oncoming pure-strains.

One of the genestealers staggered, its carapace shattered by the explosive shells. Then the rest of the pack was amongst the black-armoured women. Sharp claws lashed out, digging through ceramite to rip at flesh and bone. One genestealer, leaping up from the bottommost step, landed on one of the Sisters, knocking her to the ground. Before she could rise, the alien's jaw closed on her helm, crunching through the armour and burying its sharp fangs in her skull. A second and third warrior fell as the xenos tore through them and rushed the doorway. A volley from the Sisters inside drove the creatures back onto the steps.

'Close the gate! Close the gate!' Trishala shouted as a repulsed genestealer came at her. The last round from the clip in her pistol cracked against one of the creature's legs, its impact partly deflected by its carapace. It charged her, weaving around the flare of her power sword, trying to strike her from the side. Trishala met its rush by the merest margin. The energised field of the blade went crunching down through the thing's shoulder and into the organs buried deep beneath its exoskeleton.

Trishala kicked the mutilated alien off her blade. Around

her she could hear the screams of the crowd, the shrieks of the genestealers and the chatter of bolters. The one sound she expected, however, was absent. The thunderous rumble of the gate being closed.

She looked for the other xenos that had been driven away from the doorway, watching as the genestealer leaped at the cathedral's facade. With incredible speed the agile creature scrambled up towards the balcony overhead. The soldiers posted there fired away at the enemy, but their panicked shots were far from the mark. Snarling, the alien climbed onto the balcony and tore its way through the troopers as it rushed the door behind them. The portal was ripped from its mounting by the powerful claws and the next instant the creature was inside the cathedral.

Trishala shouted into her vox, alerting her Sisters to the enemy that was now inside. She raced towards the entrance to the narthex. As she did she was struck from the side, sent tumbling down the steps. In her fall, her sword was knocked from her grip, sliding away towards the plaza below. Above her she could see a genestealer racing after her. One of the alien's claws was missing, but from the other dangled shreds of black armour.

The xenos sprang at the fallen warrior, but as it pounced, Trishala brought both her legs kicking up. Strength enhanced by her power armour, the Sister Superior's kick propelled the beast backwards, hurling it back up the steps. She watched it only long enough to see it land in a tangle of thrashing limbs, then Trishala was scrambling down to the plaza to recover her sword.

At any moment Trishala expected to feel the genestealer's claw tearing into her, but the threatened attack never came. Instead, when she looked up from the foot of the steps, she saw Kashibai leading a pair of Battle Sisters towards her. There was no sign of the xenos she'd kicked away. Indeed, the only aliens that were visible were dead ones.

'Where are they?' Trishala demanded.

The expression on Kashibai's face was dour. 'The one you were fighting scrabbled back towards the Ladder after you kicked it. We don't know where it is now. We're still looking for the one that got in through the balcony.'

'The gate should have been closed,' Trishala said.

'Prelate Azad didn't approve the order, Sister Superior,' Kashibai said. 'The acolytes refused to act without his approval. Before you ask, no one has been able to raise him on the vox.'

Trishala shook her head. 'Then we have two searches to organise. One for the xenos and the other for the prelate.' She looked across the dead Battle Sisters lying on the steps. 'First, however, we're going to speak with the acolytes in the gatehouse. With or without the prelate's permission, we're closing the Great Gate.'

A grinding shudder passed through the narthex as the Great Gate rumbled closed. An armaplas sheet nearly as thick as the bronze doors themselves, the gate set a shiver through the cathedral walls as it sealed off the entrance. Faintly the pleas and cries of the crowds outside in the plaza could be heard. The reaction of refugees already inside was more subdued, a quiet and guilty kind of relief. They weren't without sympathy for those outside, but fear of the genestealers returning had a much stronger hold on them.

Only when the Great Gate was sealed did Trishala exit the narthex and withdraw to the antechamber that had become surrogate headquarters for the Order of the Sombre Vow. She bowed her head and whispered a solemn prayer when she saw the shrouded bodies lying against one wall. After a moment of quiet reflection on the sacrifice of her Sisters, she walked to where Kashibai waited for her.

'What were our own losses?' Trishala asked.

'Six dead,' Kashibai said. 'Perhaps seven given how grievous Sister Mohana's wounds are. There are three others with lesser wounds. Prelate Azad is still missing.'

'And one of these things is at large in the cathedral,' Trishala cursed.

'I've sent every available squad to hunt it down,' Kashibai reported. 'So far there hasn't been a trace of it.'

'The xenos is clever,' Trishala said. 'It is much worse than a mindless killer. There is some purpose to its actions. It hides because it is trying to accomplish something.'

'Perhaps it is simply wary of our bolters,' Kashibai suggested.

Trishala nodded to the dead Battle Sisters under the shrouds. 'Out there we were able to confront them at a distance and they still mauled us. In here, we'll have to come at them. Close quarters. Sword to claw.'

The Sister Superior pressed a hand against her side, feeling the rent in her armour, a series of scratches that were dug so deep she could feel the fabric of the shift she wore. A tiny bit deeper and the xenos would have ripped into her flesh.

'We take no chances,' Trishala ordered. 'The squads looking for these xenos are to be called back and issued flamers. When they find them, we burn them out. I don't care who or what is in the way.

'Understand, anyone around one of these things may already be infected with their taint, degenerating into one of those hybrid cultists. We'll need to use the acolytes, have them check for anyone who has been injured by a genestealer. Anyone they find will need to be quarantined, confined in one of the under-cellars.' Trishala pressed her hand to the rent in her armour, reassuring herself that the attack hadn't reached her.

Kashibai pointed to Trishala's gouged armour. 'What of the Sisters who weren't so fortunate as you? What about Sister Mohana and the others?'

'There can't be any exceptions,' Trishala declared. 'Our Sisters must be confined and observed for any sign of corruption. Just like anyone else. It is better to perish in the Emperor's grace than exist as something beyond His light.

'Carry out my orders, Sister,' Trishala said. 'Believe me when I say it is the best way.'

Cornak could feel the psychic vibrations of a powerful intellect observing him as he strode down the rubble-choked avenues of the prayer-wrights' district. It was cautious, this invisible spy. Rather than setting telepathic probes directly against the sorcerer, the unseen psyker was only brushing against his consciousness, trying to draw out impressions in the most unobtrusive fashion.

The talismans dangling from Cornak's staff acted not merely to focus and magnify his powers, but also to surround him in a perpetual shell of psychic energy. The telepathic emanations of the spy could only scratch against that shell, unable to reach into the mind guarded by it. Perhaps, with a more direct effort, the spy could have forced an entry.

Cornak decided to discover for himself the nature of the psychic intruder. Deliberately he opened a gap in the shell that enclosed him. Like some lurking predator, he waited for the telepath to discover the opening. When he felt the outsider's awareness reaching into his own, the sorcerer pounced, seizing hold of the mental vibration in an arcane trap.

The sorcerer hadn't anticipated the kind of mind with which he now contested. Cornak had considered the intruder to be some psyker enslaved by the Imperial authorities, perhaps even the same astropath that had issued the distress call. Some renegade mutant with psychic abilities serving a rebel force that was trying to gain control of Tharsis was another possibility. He hadn't been prepared for something so utterly alien.

The probing mind was an insane admixture of human understanding and xenos comprehension, a riotous discord of sensation and impulse. This alone wasn't enough to discomfit Cornak. His eldritch powers had burned their way into the brains of eldar and loxatl, even the spectral essence of daemons, without any disruption of his own faculties. This was something beyond anything he'd encountered before.

The individual consciousness of the telepath was more veneer than actuality, independent in the sense that an organ was independent of the body around it. The intruding mind had purpose, function, even desire – but it was only a component of a larger whole. The trap Cornak had raised to seize hold of the probing mentality now turned itself upon the sorcerer. He felt himself being drawn out, his mind fracturing into dozens of shards, sinking into a labyrinth of awarenesses. The sorcerer's consciousness fragmented still further, draining down into hundreds of alien minds. He could feel himself being pulled even farther, towards a precipice that would break him into thousands of tiny motes amongst xenos brains.

Hurriedly, gasping with the last essence of his diminishing self, Cornak closed the gap he'd created in the psychic shell. Instantly the connection was severed. His mind recoiled back into his corporeal frame, blazing through his brain with the rage of a dying star. The sorcerer clutched at his staff to keep himself standing.

Dimly, Cornak was aware of the Iron Warriors around him. He heard Turu shout, alerting Rhodaan to the sudden distress of the warband's sorcerer.

The Iron Warriors had been marching for nearly an hour through the desolate, darkened streets of Tharsis, the warsmith maintaining the pace from near the front of the column. Rhodaan arrested the advance when Turu's shout sounded over the vox. Immediately he sent his warriors to cover the rubble that littered the avenue, calling on them to watch for enemies. While the Space Marines took position, their commander drew back to the sorcerer.

'What happened?' Rhodaan asked, his eyes roving across the empty windows of the buildings above them.

'I heard nothing, Dread Lord,' Turu replied. 'The sorcerer suddenly staggered.'

'The flesh know they cannot fight us in the open,' Rhodaan told the Iron Warrior. 'Their only chance is to strike at us from the shadows and slip away before we find them.' The motors of his gauntlet growled as he clenched his fist. 'But we will find them.'

Cornak reached to his helm, unlocking it and lifting it away from his head. The sorcerer's ashen features were now mottled by splotches of bruised skin. Blood trickled from nose, eyes and ears. Rhodaan grabbed hold of his chin, forcing his face upwards.

'What's happened to you?' Rhodaan demanded.

The sorcerer drew back, trying to summon whatever dignity he could from the circumstances. Cornak could sense the scorn rolling off Rhodaan's mind. The Iron Warriors had no patience for any sign of weakness, especially from those they were already uncertain of.

Cornak forced any hint of pain from his voice before answering the warsmith. 'I was subjected to a psychic attack. I was able to fend it off with my sorcery and vanquish my assailant, but there may be others capable of launching a similar assault.' The lies dripped from the sorcerer's tongue more easily than the truth would have. If there was one thing he'd learned over the millennia it was the trepidation with which those uninitiated in the black arts regarded anything that threatened to give them a glimpse into the methodology of sorcery.

'I would advise greater caution as we advance,' Cornak continued. 'When he attacked my mind, I was afforded a glimpse into his. The psyker that assailed me belongs to the rebel cult faction that has rampaged through the city. It is likely that the attack on me was but a prelude to a more direct attack against your warriors.'

'Then they will learn they should have kept to spells and witchery,' Rhodaan snarled. The warsmith strode back to relay new orders to his Space Marines.

Cornak drew his helm back down over his bruised features. His dubious warning would serve its purpose.

The Iron Warriors would be ready when the attack came. There was no need to tell Rhodaan that the sorcerer's prediction was more than speculation or prophecy, but a certainty.

As he pondered the impressions he'd taken from the xenos, a troubling thought occurred to Cornak. He knew what he'd learned from that brief contact between his mind and the xenos. But what might the xenos have learned during that exchange?

CHAPTER VII

Screams of horror echoed through the sacred halls of the Warmason's Cathedral. Trishala raced towards the grisly sounds, a squad of Battle Sisters close on her heels. The tilted corridors of the cathedral were swarming with refugees, a tide of panicked humanity that rolled against the Sisters as they tried to advance. Such was the terror that gripped the crowd that their usual reserve was forgotten. Only the enhanced strength and durability afforded by their power armour enabled Trishala and her followers to gain any ground.

'Make way!' Trishala raged at the crowds. 'Let us through!' She was certain only one thing could have provoked such terror. The genestealer that had forced its way onto the balcony and then vanished into the labyrinthine passageways of the cathedral. Somewhere beyond this stampede of fear, they would find the alien. At least, if they moved fast enough.

Pressed close against one of the supports that jutted out from the corridor wall, an ashen-faced sacristan looked desperately in Trishala's direction. He cupped his hand to his mouth, calling to the Sister Superior. It took some time before the Battle Sisters were near enough to hear him over the rumble of the crowd.

'Sister Superior!' the sacristan cried. 'The xenos is in Gauntlet's Retreat!'

The report set a conflict of emotion coursing through Trishala. Elation, for the Retreat had only a single exit, meaning the genestealer would be trapped if the way were barred quickly. Revulsion when she considered that the priests had opened the room to refugees when the Warmason's Gauntlet was removed to the Palladion. A score or more could have been crammed into that space, helpless as the xenos burst in upon them with razored teeth and ripping claws.

'Captain Debdan,' Trishala called across the vox. 'The xenos has been spotted in the Gauntlet's Retreat. We are approaching the site from below. Bring your men down through the hallway connecting to the shrine of Vadok the Architect. If you're fast, we may catch it between us.'

'We're moving now, Sister Superior,' Debdan's response came back to her. The captain had already lost some of his men on the balcony when the genestealer forced its way inside, but Trishala wondered if he understood the devastating strength and speed of the xenos. By itself the creature had the potential to slaughter Trishala's squad. The twenty soldiers in Debdan's patrol would stand even less chance against the thing, even if they did have a flamer. It was some caprice of fate that it was the militia rather than one of the other Adepta Sororitas patrols that was in a position to support Trishala's squad.

Soon after passing the sacristan, the Sisters suddenly found themselves at the back of the frightened throng. The last refugees streamed past them, leaving the way ahead open. Evidence of the unthinking nature of their retreat lay strewn about the corridor. Precious flagons of water and packets of hardtack taken from the cathedral stores to minister to the supplicants were littered about, trampled underfoot. Here and there the broken body of a hapless civilian who'd slipped beneath the rushing tide lay crumpled in a bloodied heap.

The Battle Sisters marched through the steeply angled halls to confront the xenos infiltrator. Boltguns were readied on the advance, Sister Archana moving up to join Trishala at the head of the squad. Archana was a stout, powerfully built woman and didn't break stride with the others despite the bulk of the heavy flamer she carried.

'Would this xenos be smart enough to take hostages?' Archana asked the Sister Superior.

Trishala thought again of the shelter on Primorus. 'Even if it has, there can be no hesitation. The genestealer threatens more than whoever is trapped with it in the Retreat. Everyone seeking sanctuary in the cathedral is at risk. The instant you see the creature you have to attack. Don't underestimate how fast it can move. Is that understood?'

'Yes, Sister Superior,' Archana said in a chastened tone. The other Sisters echoed her, reaffirming their understanding.

Trishala knew the Battle Sisters would obey. Their discipline was too great to allow for anything less. What concerned her was them not reacting quickly enough when they found the xenos. The genestealer was swift enough to seize even the slightest delay and use it to its advantage – whether to escape or fall upon the Sisters with its rending claws. She had only to glance down at the white chestpiece that had replaced the one torn in the fight outside the narthex to remind her that even power armour wasn't proof against those claws. She hoped that the mismatched section of ceremonial armour would act as a reminder to the rest of her priory that the least mistake could be deadly.

The screams ringing out from above swelled to a piteous crescendo, then were muffled by a loud whooshing sound. Trishala quickened her pace as the nauseating smell of promethium and burning flesh came spilling down the corridor. She'd endured such a stench before, down in the Cloisterfells.

A last turn in the corridor where the walls suddenly became much thicker and the way far narrower, brought the Sisters to the Gauntlet's Retreat. Foul black smoke was spilling out of the door, streaming away into the miscellany of vents and ducts that pitted the high ceilings. Beyond the smoke, Trishala could see a soot-covered man in the uniform of Lubentina's militia. Arrayed along the corridor were twenty of his comrades.

'Here, Sister Superior,' Captain Debdan's voice called out. 'Keep watching the door. Sergeant Kalidas, give it another blast.' On his order, one of the troopers moved into the doorway, thrusting the blackened muzzle of a heavy flamer into the vestry. An instant later a stream of blazing fire was rushing into the room, sweeping it from side to side as the sergeant manipulated his weapon.

'We cornered it in the Gauntlet's Retreat,' Debdan reported to Trishala. 'I moved the flamer up before it could try to slip out.'

Another plume of smoke rushed out into the corridor as the sergeant cut off the blast of fire spilling from his flamer. The stink of burning flesh intensified, making Trishala's eyes water. She kept any display of revulsion off her face, unwilling to indulge even so slight an expression of weakness.

'What happened here, captain?' Trishala asked.

'We caught the xenos,' Debdan reported. He tried to make his words sound bold and proud, but there was a tremble of fear behind them that undermined the effort. 'Rather than engage us, it withdrew back into the Gauntlet's Retreat.'

Trishala looked at the smoke-filled doorway. 'You are certain it went inside?'

Debdan shuddered. 'That much I am sure of. Otherwise we wouldn't have acted as quickly as we did. I saw what it did to my men on the balcony.' He pointed at the heavy flamer Sergeant Kalidas carried. 'The schematics for this section showed no other way out. We had to act before it found that out for itself and turned back.'

'Did any of the refugees in there make it out?' Though the question came from Archana, Trishala thought it was just the kind of concern Kashibai would express, regardless of protocol. It was a pointless thing to ask. Trishala knew the answer even before Debdan gave it.

'I couldn't risk the xenos getting out, and escaping again,' he said. 'We had to act fast.'

'You've done what needed to be done,' Trishala told him. 'You can leave the rest to us. Once the room cools down, we'll go in and verify it's dead.'

Debdan shook his head. 'We saw it go in there. By the God-Emperor, I wouldn't have given the command if I wasn't sure.'

'But *I* have to be sure,' Trishala told him. 'Before I call off the hunt, I have to know.' The smell of the slaughter filling her nose, Trishala looked back at the other Battle Sisters. Their expressions were pensive, their gaze grim. It was a gruesome task ahead of them.

The great archway that spanned across the boulevard, uniting the fresco-covered facades of two monolithic municipal buildings, came smashing earthwards. It shattered against the road-bed, disintegrating into a burst of rockcrete and plaster. Elaborate designs cut into the archway were reduced to jumbled wreckage, puzzles of limbs and bodies that no longer bore any semblance of their original shapes. The same could be said of the clutch of marksmen who'd taken position on the bridge, raining shots on the street twenty metres below until their vantage was rocked by the sustained impact of Gaos' autocannon rounds. Supports blasted to dust by the brutal fire, the span broke free and hurtled downwards with its shrieking occupants.

For good measure, Rhodaan lobbed a grenade into the pile of wreckage. The explosion cast up fragments of rubble and organic debris. The Iron Warrior waited for a moment, watching the nearby windows and doorways. Such viciousness often provoked the False Emperor's slaves into some foolhardy and reckless effort at retaliation. Spurred by some pathetic hunger for retribution, they'd expose themselves and soon join the very carrion they were trying to avenge.

As though flesh had any comprehension of what revenge truly was. They would never understand the Long War, how revenge could become the only thing that still gave life purpose. To have loyalty and service exploited and betrayed by the False Emperor. Only those like Rhodaan, who had been there, who had seen and heard and felt, only they could ever really know.

The retaliation Rhodaan expected failed to appear. Either the ambushers up on the archway had been alone or their comrades were too crafty to expose themselves. Fear could do that, but so too could discipline. He didn't think the local defence forces would be of high calibre, but where training was lacking a fanatical zealotry could endow flesh with a degree of fortitude.

Rhodaan turned his gaze towards the gap between the municipal buildings. Beyond he could see the slopes of Mount Rama and the cathedral that was their objective. The peak was at once close and frustratingly far away.

'Periphetes, advance,' Rhodaan heard Captain Uzraal growl into the vox. Out of the corner of his eye he could see the warrior from the Steel Brethren stalking forwards. Periphetes was coming to understand his position in the Third Grand Company. He was a utility to be harnessed and used, nothing more. He was twice a traitor, leaving the Legion with the other apostates of the Steel Brethren, then abandoning the other renegades. There was no reconciliation waiting for the prodigal Space Marine. He was a dog running with wolves and the least mistake would see the pack turn on him.

'Brother Turu, provide cover for Periphetes,' Uzraal ordered. 'The rest of you form up on me.'

Following Periphetes' lead, the Iron Warriors continued down the devastated boulevard. Rhodaan looked back and watched as Cornak followed behind the other Space Marines. Though the sorcerer maintained a good pace

Rhodaan still noticed the way he used his staff to support himself. A pretence of infirmity or actual injury? If the former, then to what purpose? If the latter, then from what cause? The psychic assault? Cornak had boasted of his arcane powers often enough on Castellax, displayed abilities that even Rhodaan grudgingly had to concede as being impressive. If there was some enemy psyker who could inflict such a wound on the sorcerer then their mission here might pose some actual risk.

Rhodaan was still uncertain of Cornak. Sorcerers were rare enough among the Space Marines of the IV Legion, and Cornak was even more of an enigma. He had all the traits of an Iron Warrior, all the knowledge of one who had fought the Long War. He spoke of Olympia only as one who'd walked the ground of their home world could and vividly he described the great tank battles of Tallarn. Yet still there was something there that provoked Rhodaan, something he felt but couldn't describe. Perhaps it was the way Cornak always knew the right thing to say to allay the warsmith's doubts, just enough prophecy to show the path ahead but not what lay around the corner.

The rattle of a heavy bolter rumbled down the street followed by the snarl of petrochem engines. Periphetes snarled an alert to the Iron Warriors across the vox. 'Warsmith, the intersection ahead contested. Soldiers against some manner of irregulars.'

'If they're in our way, it matters little who they are,' Rhodaan voxed back. At his command the other Iron Warriors advanced to the corner beyond which the sounds of gunfire emanated. Ahead was a broad intersection, slabs of rockcrete from the buildings around it strewn about the roadway. Between the debris was the damaged bulk of a tan-coloured Taurox, one of its wheels shorn from its axle. A second Taurox was nearby, partly protected by a jumbled pile of rubble. Around the two transports, a number of flesh in the same uniforms as those he'd seen at the spaceport were trying to fend off the attentions of the 'irregulars' Periphetes had cited.

Screaming down the boulevard were a number of stretch-cars. The civilian machines had been crudely adapted to a more martial role with sheets of metal bolted to their chassis, covering windshield and wheel-wells. Cultists stood upon the running boards, their purple robes and crimson coveralls snapping in the wind as the vehicles roared down the street. Shots poured out from the motorcade at the embattled soldiers. Slug-throwers, shotguns, lasrifles, even the glowing discharge of a plasma pistol were fired at the troopers, felling several of them. The heavy bolter mounted to the top of the undamaged Taurox blasted away, pitting the side of one of the vehicles and sending it crashing into one of the piles of rubble.

The loss of one of their comrades wasn't enough to fend off the motorcade. The surviving machines were soon turning about to make another pass against the trapped soldiers.

'Engage the irregulars first,' Rhodaan ordered his warriors. Gangers or rebels, they were the more mobile of the two forces and therefore required the more immediate attention.

As the motorcade came screeching towards the intersection, the Iron Warriors opened fire on the stretch-cars. Periphetes peppered the lead car with his bolter, punching holes through the improvised armour and pitching the shooters from the running boards. Gaos raked another with his autocannon, smashing the hood of the vehicle and causing it to flip over onto its roof. Turu shredded the scattered gunmen before they could recover from their violent discharge from the hurtling car.

'Iron within! Iron without!' The war cry thundered from the speakers in Uzraal's helm as he joined the attack. The blast of his meltagun spilled across one of the oncoming stretch-cars, immolating it. The shooters clinging to the machine's sides were vaporised, the car itself now a charred hulk that slammed into the vehicle Gaos had upset. The collision turned the blackened mass into a shower of slag that sprayed across the street.

Rhodaan added his own fire to that of his warriors, spraying the hostile motorcade with his bolt pistol, felling the gunmen on the running boards. He noted their distorted aspect, the deformities many of them sported. Rebels then. Some mutant cult that had risen up against the Imperial custodians and plunged Lubentina into a state of riot and confusion.

Against the pathetic flesh of Lubentina's defenders, the mutants would have prevailed. Against Space Marines they amounted to little more than an annoyance. In less than a minute, the intersection was choked with the wreckage of seven vehicles and over fifty cultists.

The embattled soldiers added their fire to that of the Iron Warriors, trying to extricate themselves from the trap that had snared them. When the last of the stretch-cars was turned into a smouldering wreck and only dead mutants littered the street, the men emerged from the cover they'd taken. Cheers of awed gratitude rose from many of them as they thanked their deliverers.

Rhodaan didn't allow them the opportunity to learn

their mistake. A burst from his pistol tore open the officer who commanded the bedraggled force, hurling his body against the side of the immobile Taurox. Rounds from Gaos' autocannon ripped through the other Taurox, demolishing its heavy bolter before the weapon could be turned on the Iron Warriors. The brutally efficient fire of the other Space Marines finished most of the soldiers before they could even think of diving to cover. The few who did only delayed the inevitable by a handful of seconds.

'Uzraal, auspex,' Rhodaan snapped the order.

Uzraal drew away from the smouldering mess of a human soldier and pulled the auspex from its holster. 'Our current position is twenty-three hundred metres from the objective.'

'Then your warriors should be moving,' Rhodaan stated, 'not dawdling over carrion.'

As the Iron Warriors started to march away the growl of massive engines and the rumble of heavy machinery announced a new threat. Roaring down the left branch of the intersection, a huge truck charged into view. A heavy stubber mounted in the armoured cab chugged away as the giant vehicle plunged straight into the twisted wreckage of the stretch-cars. The axe-like dozer blade riveted to the truck's hood smashed into the destroyed vehicles, knocking them aside as though they were toys.

A few of the Iron Warriors opened up on the Goliath Rockgrinder, trying to smash the engine or kill the driver with their bolters. The slabs of ferrocrete and metal plates with which the huge mining truck's chassis had been reinforced were too thick to penetrate from any great distance. Even a blast from Uzraal's meltagun only slowed the machine, forcing it to drag the disfigured residue left by the immolating beam.

Rhodaan rushed straight towards the oncoming Goliath. Uzraal's shot had done more than slow the truck. The melted armour had washed across the heavy bolter, locking the weapon in a fixed position and restricting its angle of attack. There was a blind spot, a weakness that the warsmith seized. He might be commander of the Third Grand Company now, but the habits of millennia serving as captain of a Raptor assault company were never far from his calculations.

Rhodaan sprang at the Goliath, leaping up onto its still smoking hood. The magnetic clamps in the boots of his power armour took hold, maintaining his footing as he stood on top of the speeding truck. He holstered his bolt pistol and drew the fat-bladed chainsword from his belt. The saw-blade churned into murderous life as he activated it. Leaning down towards the melted confusion of armour and chassis Rhodaan brought the weapon slashing across the Goliath's cab. The shriek of tortured metal rang out as the chainsword bit into the Goliath, sparks and shreds of armour flying as he worried the blade back and forth, gouging a hole in the armour.

The Goliath lurched violently as Rhodaan's attack caused a section of the melted armour to shear off, reducing the drag upon the truck. The Space Marine scarcely noted the change in momentum, the clamps in his boots keeping him securely fixed to the chassis. A final twist of his chainsword and he was rewarded by a dim electrical glow, the red luminance of the truck's instrumentation panel. A brutish visage with oversized mouth stared up at him with an expression that had both rage and horror in it.

Before the cultist could decide which impulse to embrace, Rhodaan took the decision away from him, dropping a krak grenade into the hole he'd made.

Disengaging the magnetic clamps, Rhodaan dived off the Goliath's hood an instant before the grenade detonated. Flame and shrapnel exploded from the cab. The now driverless truck turned sharply to the right, glancing off the facade of a building before crashing against a rockcrete pylon and slamming down on its side in a cloud of dust.

Rhodaan gave only a brief glance at the crashed machine. A second Goliath was roaring down the intersection, blasting away with a lascannon mounted to its roof.

'Brother Gaos,' Rhodaan spoke into the vox, 'put an end to this nuisance.'

At the warsmith's command, Gaos swung around, aiming his autocannon not at the oncoming trucks but at one of the huge columns that flanked the intersection. A burst from the Iron Warrior's weapon ripped into the base of the obelisk, disintegrating its carefully constructed balance. With a rumbling shudder, the column frayed away from its base, pitching downwards into the street. Tonnes of stone slammed down into the leading Goliath, flattening much of the truck.

'Kill them all,' Captain Uzraal commanded, his meltagun bathing one of the flattened trucks in a disintegrating blast of light. The machine's fuel detonated under the intense heat, incinerating any rebels that had survived inside.

'Behind us!' Cornak's alarm brought Rhodaan's attention away from the slaughter at the intersection. Instinctively his eyes went to the first Goliath lying on its side. The truck's undercarriage was heaving, bulging outwards from some terrible violence unfolding within. He saw a ragged tear appear and swiftly widen.

Instantly the scene was enveloped in a coruscation of green fire. Rhodaan could feel the eerie chill of the warp crawling across his skin even inside his armour. He didn't need to look towards Cornak to know he was turning his sorcery against whatever menace lurked within the crashed Goliath. On Castellax he'd seen Cornak use this fire against rebel janissaries and ork stragglers, burning the meat off their very bones in the blink of an eye.

This foe was of a different calibre. Loathsome shapes came leaping out from the smashed truck, plunging through the sorcerer's flame. The green fire washed across their multi-armed bodies, gnawing at their purple-hued carapaces, pitting and scouring the chitinous plates until they resembled rusted iron. But it wasn't enough to stop them, or even to slow them down. A trio of xenos creatures came charging towards the Space Marines.

'Genestealers,' Rhodaan gave name to the creatures. Many centuries ago he'd fought the monstrous creations of the tyranid hive fleets. One lesson he'd taken away from those battles was always to keep the beasts at arm's length.

'All fire to the rear,' Rhodaan commanded across the vox. A burst from his bolt pistol ripped across one of the monsters, cracking its carapace in a spurt of scintillating fluids. Fire from Mahar and Turu raked the injured alien, leaving it sprawled on the ground.

Unlike the xenos Rhodaan had fought before, these genestealers exhibited a startling independence of action. The surviving pair of aliens didn't remain together but rushed at the Iron Warriors from either flank like the pincers of some murderous claw. One of the creatures fell upon Brother Morak, bearing him to the ground and tearing into him in a frenzied burst of ferocity. A blast of searing energy from Uzraal's meltagun evaporated the creature's bulbous skull, but not before the street was littered with Morak's organs.

The second flanker rushed for Rhodaan. The warsmith's pistol was knocked from his grasp as the thing smashed him to the ground. Before its claws could start gouging his power armour, he brought his gauntlet cracking against its head. One of Rhodaan's armoured fingers gouged into the genestealer's eye, bursting it. The thing reeled back in pain, something else that wasn't quite in keeping with the tyranid monsters he'd fought before. He was quick to seize upon the creature's distress, driving his ceramite helm up into its throat. He could feel the genestealer's neck snap under the impact. With a shove he pitched the beast onto its side. Recovering his bolt pistol, he pumped a few shots into the alien's twitching body.

Rhodaan looked across the battlefield. The alien he'd dispatched was the last of the genestealers that had been hiding inside the Goliath. It seemed the monsters had been the last layer of the trap the rebels had laid for the Iron Warriors.

'Captain Uzraal, report.' Rhodaan turned away from the dead aliens and moved towards the intersection as he listened to Uzraal's voice across the vox.

'One casualty,' Uzraal said. 'If Brother Morak's gene-seed was viable, the xenos claws have ruined it now.'

Rhodaan climbed up onto the toppled obelisk, staring down at the wreckage and the rebel bodies strewn about the street. Despite the magnitude of the injuries they'd been dealt by the Iron Warriors, there were variances and deformities to the bodies that made it clear that even before death they'd been an unpleasant sight. There was a horrible suggestiveness about their physiognomy that made Rhodaan wonder about their provenance. It was something beyond mere mutation. Taken in concert with the unexpected behaviour of the genestealers, a suspicion began to take form in his mind.

'Periphetes,' Rhodaan called out. He pointed down at one of the more deformed of the bodies, a corpse that had a third arm sprouting from its shoulder. 'I want a closer look at that carrion. Fetch it for me.' He dropped down off the obelisk, leaving Periphetes to attend to his task.

'Why linger over dead flesh, Dread Lord?' Cornak asked Rhodaan.

'Because I want to know what manner of enemy stands between us and our objective,' Rhodaan said. 'The deluded slaves of the False Emperor I anticipated, but your divinations didn't warn me to expect xenos,' he pointed at the carcasses of the genestealers. 'Forewarned is forearmed. I will not be taken by surprise again. It may be that this mission won't be the simple affair you told me of back on Castellax.'

'Divination is an art, not a science,' Cornak protested. 'The future is always in motion, always uncertain.'

Rhodaan glared at Cornak. 'You told me once that you'd had a vision of the moment of your own death. If I learn you have dealt false with me, you will discover just how uncertain even a sorcerer's future can be.'

The telepathic reverberations of each Inheritor's death were like a hot iron stabbing into Bakasur's skull. Singly, the pain was something the magus could suppress through exertion of his powerful will. This was different; the agonising feedback was compounded by the rapidity with which one death followed upon another. Such was the debilitation inflicted by the psychic screams that for nearly an hour it was all Bakasur could do to keep from dashing his brains out against the wall of the crematorium near the base of Mount Rama that he'd adopted as a temporary sanctum.

The loss of hybrids was inconsequential to the Cult of the Cataclysm. Their purpose was to work towards the time of ascension. Death was simply a means to achieve that purpose. Each cultist could envision no greater display of his fervour than to perish for the Great Father.

The Inheritors were different. They were cast in the sacred design of the Great Father, kindred of the holy pure-strains that had descended from the stars with the cult's primogenitor. They were living representations of the ascension, wondrous and inviolate. Any hurt visited upon them was a cause for lamentation and reprisal.

Reprisal? Bakasur tried to slough the weak human impulse. Concepts of anger and revenge were base, emotional appeals. Primitive, and unworthy of his exalted station. He, whose mind communed directly with the wisdom of the Great Father, had to rise to a clarity of thought that had no place for illogical sentiment. His sight must always be upon the grand scheme, the design laid out by the master. Anything that did not serve to further that plan was to be discarded.

Bakasur stirred from his tortured daze, meeting the anxious stares of his bodyguards and attendants. A large throng of hybrids had gathered in the crematorium, flocking to the magus in his moment of debility. To many of them, he was an extension of the Great Father, the voice and prophet of their faith. Bakasur would have felt shame at such mislaid devotion had his half-alien mind been capable of the sensation.

Instead, the magus gestured to his followers, waving his wormy fingers as though in benediction. Through words and telepathic impulses, he gave them their orders. Those with him in the crematorium would hasten through the Cloisterfells, gathering the cult reserves yet lurking in the tunnels. The time had come to commit them to the battle. They had a part to play, and the scene for their role would be Mount Rama.

His brush with the mind of Cornak had revealed things to Bakasur. When the Iron Warriors arrived on Lubentina, it had been natural for the cult to believe they were the answer to Palatine Yadav's call for help. The Great Father had been troubled by such development. Regiments of Astra Militarum could have been infected and infiltrated, but the enhanced biology of Space Marines offered no such possibilities. They were threat without profit. That being the case, the magus had thought to eliminate them as quickly as possible.

It was there that Bakasur had made a grave error in judgement. He'd grossly underestimated the nature of his enemy. He hadn't counted upon the fearsome abilities of the Space Marines or believed there could exist such warriors as these. Outnumbered by several orders of magnitude, the Iron Warriors not only survived but triumphed. Now even the sacred Inheritors were falling prey to them.

Yes, Bakasur had failed to appreciate the abilities of the Iron Warriors. Now that he did, that knowledge passed from him into the Great Father. Again, where the magus saw an obstacle the patriarch discerned an opportunity.

The Iron Warriors were as much the enemy of the planetary authorities as the cult itself. They might prove a useful distraction when the cult moved against the Warmason's Cathedral. From their route of march it was clear the Space Marines were making for Mount Rama, doubtless the cathedral itself.

Mobilising the reserves waiting in the Cloisterfells, the cult would besiege the cathedral, accomplishing two tasks in one action. There would be an entire army between the Iron Warriors and their goal, odds even the Space Marines must be hesitant to confront headlong. They would also capture the attention of Trishala and her Sisters inside the cathedral, occupying them with repelling the attackers. And while the Order of the Sombre Vow was occupied with the danger outside, they would be less vigilant towards the menace already inside their walls.

The Warmason's Cathedral would fall to the Cult of the Cataclysm. Its loss would break the spirit of the Imperials, leave them shattered and broken. A ripe harvest to be gathered into the Great Father's brood.

CHAPTER VIII

The bellow of explosions thundered down the battered streets of the psalmists' quarter. A few frag grenades brought the purple-garbed hybrids stumbling out from their improvised fortification, blood and an inhuman treacle dripping from their battered bodies. Periphetes wasted no time in raking the cultists with his bolter, cutting them down at the knees as they emerged from the ferrocrete blockhouse. The vicious renegade brought his boltgun scything back around as he dropped the last of the survivors, ensuring none of them would crawl off to carry word back to their leaders. The blockhouse itself, the reinforced facade of an air-recycler's shelter, exploded outwards as Captain Uzraal threw a krak grenade through the vent-like window.

Cornak could feel the mind of the magus focusing on him. It was too cautious to test the sorcerer's psychic defences and arcane wards, but it wasn't so timid as to keep away entirely. He had the impression that it was studying them, evaluating them like a magos biologis. It was trying to see how they worked and what use might be made of them.

Such was the impression that had reached Cornak's consciousness. If that had been the only intelligence he distilled from the hybrid's psychic presence, he would have felt rage. Though he was a sorcerer, he was foremost a Space Marine, the pinnacle of human perfection. He was no specimen to be ogled by a curious alien.

Yet there was more. A chilling familiarity that slowly stirred his hearts. Cornak had 'seen' this being before. He'd witnessed it in that confusion of prophecy shared by the Circle in the warp. He could give it a name, Bakasur, and he could give it a twisted sort of face. He could see it in a place of hellfire and shadow, leering and triumphant. At its feet, one of the Circle lay sprawled in death.

Cornak had seen many deathly visions over the centuries, witnessed the unfolding of prophecies that had taken others of the Circle. Always there'd been the concern that the doom might be his own, but never had the concern grown into a certainty. He was here and Bakasur was here. The temptation was there to try to escape the vision, to leave Lubentina and forget the ambition that had brought him here. Such timidity was for the merely human, the wretches Rhodaan and his warriors disdained as 'flesh'. A daemon had once told Cornak that those who seek to escape their doom will find it while those who embrace their doom may find they instead have escaped it. The sorcerer had always found that the more enigmatic and vexing a daemon's words the more truth there was within them.

'The xenos are persistent,' Rhodaan's voice crackled

across the vox. Cornak shifted his awareness from the psychic shadow of Bakasur to the forbidding presence of the warsmith. Rhodaan was looking across the demolished blockhouse and the hybrids Periphetes had slaughtered.

Captain Uzraal kicked one of the dead cultists. 'Half human but all fool if they think they can stop us with such pathetic opposition.'

'Uzraal, auspex,' Rhodaan told him.

The Iron Warriors captain consulted the device. The only exhibition of annoyance he didn't quite suppress was the surly way he returned it to its holster when he'd relayed the details.

Cornak advanced towards the two officers, the butt of his staff tapping against the scarred street. 'They don't think to stop us, only delay us.'

'More visions, brother?' Uzraal grumbled. His wasn't the most complex mentality among the Iron Warriors of the Third Grand Company. His distrust of Cornak's powers was something he didn't bother to conceal. The sorcerer rather suspected it was loyalty more than capability that had caused Rhodaan to elevate Uzraal to his position.

'One doesn't need sorcery to make that determination,' Rhodaan said. 'The rebels haven't made a serious effort against us since we killed the genestealers.' He turned towards Cornak. 'The question is why they are only content with these half measures. These creatures don't shun a fight and seem to have absorbed some of the ferocity of the genestealers in their tainted blood. You say they want only to delay us. Why?'

Cornak was careful in his answer. 'They think we've come to aid the Imperials,' he said. 'The xenos are trying to get at the flesh hiding inside the cathedral. That is where they have concentrated their strength.'

'The xenos are right to worry,' Rhodaan declared. He looked away, lifting his horned head and peering between the burned-out buildings lining the street, staring up at Mount Rama and the Warmason's Cathedral. 'They've put themselves in my way. They will find that a costly mistake.'

Lieutenant Manat watched the desolate streets around the base of Mount Rama from the turret of his Leman Russ. It was an eerie, almost surreal scene to see these avenues that had once been packed with pilgrims and acolytes now utterly deserted. The sensation was even more pronounced when he considered the combat raging elsewhere in Tharsis. Fierce fighting along the Netjali overlooking the scholarium that had seen an entire division of infantry and a brigade of armour committed against the enemy. A gun battle that was entering its fourth day among the hab-stacks of the Illuminators' Guild. Riots at the spaceport that pitted thousands of desperate pilgrims against the defence forces.

Here at the mouth of the Redeemer's Road the only conflict was in keeping the refugees away from the barricades. It was an inglorious assignment, even cruel in its way, but Manat had impressed on his men the importance of their duty. Too many refugees were already on the slopes of Mount Rama, more than could possibly take shelter in the Warmason's Cathedral. Preventing more from swarming up the mountain increased the chances of survival for the ones already there. Even for the ones who weren't, if they would only see reason and seek safety elsewhere. After hours of trying to get them to disperse, Manat had stopped trying to reason with the frightened mob. It was enough that they respected the guns of the local militia and didn't try to force the issue by rushing the barricades.

The whine of a hatch door opening drew Manat's attention from the refugees and the streets. He looked down to see his vox-operator Ganak motioning to him.

'Lieutenant, we have an alert from the Adepta Sororitas,' he said, handing the headset up to his commander.

The Battle Sisters had observers posted around the top of the cathedral, affording them a bird's-eye view of the districts around Mount Rama. Manat had heard them vox reports to various militia units and to Colonel Hafiz's headquarters in the Sovereign Spire, relaying the enemy movements they spotted.

Now what the Sisters had seen was of much more immediate concern to Manat and his men. Concentrations of enemy vehicles had been seen moving towards the base of Mount Rama, rushing straight towards the barricades.

Manat hurriedly barked orders to his men. Ganak issued a last appeal to the refugees to disperse across the tank's vox-casters, refraining from telling them about the approaching enemy lest the information send them into complete panic. The Leman Russ' turret slowly rotated around, the battle cannon aiming towards the deserted streets. The gunners manning the heavy bolters of the two Taurox assault vehicles at the barricade elevated their weapons to direct their fire against more distant targets. The few dozen infantry took position along the top of the barricade.

As Manat listened to the Sororitas observers describe the enemy forces moving against not only his position, but all of the approaches to Mount Rama, he felt a chill rush through him. Knowing what was coming wouldn't make it any easier to face.

From the direction of the Chastened Road, Manat heard the crack of gunfire. A moment later he heard shots sound from near the barricade across the Pilgrims' Path. Then from the darkened buildings facing his own position, a motley array of ordnance opened up. Las-beams sizzled against the barricade, bullets clattered from the armaplas plating of the Leman Russ and the armour of the Taurox.

The hasty, imprecise gunfire inflicted no casualties among Manat's men, serving only to harass them and force their heads down. Among the refugees the effect was more direct. They rushed at the barricade, screaming in terror. While Manat's men tried to force them back, the rebels threw the next phase of their attack against the local militia.

The darkened streets disgorged an array of crudely armoured trucks and tracked labour-crawlers, each machine crewed by fanatics and armed with lasguns and stubbers. From the ruined buildings, a horde of purple-clad cultists charged towards the barricade. The aggression of the rebels accomplished something Manat's entreaties couldn't. With the cultists rushing towards them, the refugees scattered, fleeing in every direction.

Manat's troops sent a withering salvo into the oncoming cultists. Heavy bolters and lasrifles chewed up the purple-clad infantry, lascannons and missile launchers wrought a grisly toll against the scavenged motorcade that barrelled towards them with zealous abandon. Heaps of twisted, smouldering wreckage were thrown into the air as shells from the battle cannon met civilian machinery.

More warnings were being issued by the Sisters watching

from the cathedral. Manat passed the alarm along to his command. The rebels had two of their Goliath trucks and a large mass of infantry assembling behind the cover of the deserted buildings. It was clear they were readying another assault. The first attack had been to draw their fire and gauge the strength of their position. The real effort would come next.

Throwing open the turret hatch, Manat pulled himself up to get a better view than what he could see from inside the tank. As he did, his attention was caught by motion along the Redeemer's Road. Most of the refugees already on the slopes of Mount Rama had fled higher up the ascent the moment the fighting started, but there were three tatterdemalion figures rushing back *towards* the perimeter.

Shouting to alert his men, Manat drew his laspistol and demanded the trio stop where they were. No sooner had the words left his mouth than one of the refugees sent a blocky, angular object skittering across the pavement. Manat's shot caught the infiltrator before he could turn to flee, but even as the cultist fell a blinding roar exploded across the lieutenant's senses.

Looking down on the slopes of Mount Rama from the vantage afforded by the Curate's Leap, Trishala could see the cultists as they pressed their attack. The militia barricades at the base of the mountain were besieged, swarmed by the tremendous numbers the cult was throwing at them. Sister Reshma, still impaired by her injuries, had been posted as a sentinel on the balcony. It was her alarm that had drawn the Sister Superior to the observation post.

Intervening terrain obstructed the view at the base of

much of the mountain. The exception was the area around the Redeemer's Road. The cathedral's angular tilt permitted someone on the Curate's Leap to look almost directly down on the road and the barricade that now closed it off.

Reshma had been able to see the cultists readying their attacks against the barricade, passing warning to the militia. The soldiers had fought off the first wave, but Reshma feared it had been nothing more than a probing attack.

'I pray that I'm wrong, Sister Superior,' Reshma said, her fingers pressed to the purity seal affixed to her breastplate.

'The wise never underestimate an enemy,' Trishala told her.

A sudden explosion from the barricade closing the Redeemer's Road flared into grisly brilliance. The detonation was of sufficient force that the Battle Sisters on the Curate's Leap could feel it as a dull vibration that swept through the railing under their hands. Through the smoke and flame, Trishala could see the mangled wreckage of a Taurox and a Leman Russ pitched onto their sides, a second Taurox shoved through a wall. The shapes of dead soldiers were strewn everywhere. The refugees that still packed the lower regions of the approach had been flattened by the explosion, slashed and cut by debris and shrapnel. Worse was to befall them, however.

Close on the explosion, a fresh surge of cultists rushed out from the streets, making straight for the Redeemer's Road. A pair of huge Goliath trucks led their way, the immense dozer blades mounted at their noses swatting aside the burning wrecks that blocked their path. The soldiers at the other barricades, still dealing with their own attackers, couldn't divert sufficient fire to stop the rush of cultists. There was nothing that could be done to stop the slaughter that would soon make the Redeemer's Road run red with Lubentine blood.

Trishala felt a cold fury as she noted the peculiarities of the blast that had opened the Redeemer's Road. The buildings just beyond the barricade had suffered minimal damage while those behind it were blackened and crumbling. The reason was obvious. The detonation that had obliterated Lieutenant Manat's position had come from within, not without.

Trishala snapped a warning into the vox-bead she wore. 'Commanders of all barricades! This is Sister Superior Trishala! Be alert for an attack from the rear! I repeat, watch for enemies already inside the perimeter! The explosion on the Redeemer's Road was the work of infiltrators!'

One after another, the commanders at the barricades acknowledged Trishala's alert. All except Captain Harshal at the base of the Pilgrim's Path. A violent roar and a blinding flash from that direction exhibited why he failed to make contact.

'They must be using high-yield blasting charges if we can feel the vibrations all the way up here,' Reshma said.

It was a sound theory given the cult's affinity for turning mining equipment into armaments, and one that provoked a new worry for Trishala. The Warmason's Cathedral had been constructed with strength and durability in mind, built to withstand the worst of Lubentina's earthquakes and sandstorms. But a high-yield blasting charge was designed to break the very bedrock of the planet. One of those pressed against the Great Gate by a cultist could rip it open. What such an explosive could do against the less protected doors and windows of the cathedral was an even grimmer prospect.

'Captain Debdan,' Trishala called into the vox. 'I want you to take your men down to the gatehouse. You will support Sister Kashibai.' After their reluctance to close the Great Gate without Prelate Azad's authority, Trishala was certain the acolytes would balk at the next order she wanted implemented. It was why she switched to a private channel when she issued it to Kashibai.

'Implement total lockdown,' Trishala ordered. It was a command to drop siege plates down across every door and window in the structure, thick slabs of armaplas that would seal off each opening. Once they were in place, those within the cathedral would be cut off from the outside. Though a single command issued to the cogitators would lower all the plates automatically, to raise them again required employing manual force against each one.

'The acolytes are certain to protest,' Kashibai voxed back.

'You'll have Captain Debdan to enforce the command,' Trishala said. 'The local militia isn't under the Ecclesiarchy's authority. That might give the acolytes pause.'

A dull, mechanical groan drowned out Kashibai's reply. It was a sound that Trishala had become only too familiar with. It was the sound of the Great Gate in motion. She peered down towards the base of the cathedral, her suspicions confirmed when she saw the refugees outside in the plaza rush up the steps and towards the entrance that should have been closed to them.

'Sister Superior!' Kashibai shouted to be heard over the reverberations of the machinery. 'The Great Gate's opening.'

'Stay there and keep anyone from getting in,' Trishala ordered. She shifted channels and raised Sister Virika, commanding her to link up with Captain Debdan's troops. 'We have to get that gate closed again.' She turned to Reshma. 'Maintain your watch here. Alert me if there are developments.'

'You cannot suppress this information!' Colonel Hafiz's voice boomed through the Sovereign Spire's council chamber. The great hall was all but deserted now; even the cybernetic cherubim had been dismissed. It was the first time any of the remaining councillors could recall the room being without their pious chanting.

Cardinal-Governor Murdan appeared even leaner than usual, the administrations of his servants unequal to the ordeal of hiding the strain he was under. It spoke volumes to the governor's agitation that he'd dispensed with the sanctimonious trappings of his office. Psalms and incense were things that provided him no solace in present circumstances. The reports from the spaceport had upset his equilibrium. For the first time there was doubt in his voice and a gleam of fear in his eyes. The xenos cult had been a menace he was prepared to confront, but the incursion of traitors from the Heresy on his world was something that shook him to the very core of his being.

'It will not be spoken of,' Murdan said, clinging to the jade aquila that he'd removed from the altar in his private chapel. 'No one will speak of this... affront. This profanation of Lubentina! That it should come to this. Just when it seemed we were turning back the rebels.'

Hafiz's troops had managed to reclaim several districts already ravaged by the cultists. The uprising had been prevented from spreading across the Netjali and the fight for the Illuminators' Guild had finally been won. Units had moved into the missal-works and even advanced into the scholarium. Yet, while on a map it seemed the Imperial forces were reclaiming Tharsis, Hafiz knew the reality was very different. The militia hadn't beaten the rebels. There had been no decisive confrontation and victory. All there'd been was a slow push across ruined districts, hunting down the remnants the cult had left behind to harass the soldiers. The real strength of the rebels had been withdrawn, pulled back to strike elsewhere. From all indications, they were moving on Mount Rama.

Hafiz had tried to explain as much to the Cardinal-Governor, but Murdan was too focused on the Space Marines to listen.

Minister Kargil extrapolated upon Murdan's position, though with far less emotional reasons. 'Lubentina exists, thrives as a shrine world. A suggestion of corruption... could be our downfall. There are opportunists even in the Ecclesiarchy and they would be quick to seize upon any excuse to turn the faithful away from Lubentina and towards shrine worlds more conducive to their own aspirations.'

'The xenos can be purged,' Murdan declared. 'Chaos is corruption incarnate.'

The last member of the conclave spoke up. Palatine Yadav had listened to reports of Traitor Space Marines with horror. He shared Murdan's sentiment that it was preferable to fight the xenos cult than have their planet defiled by these heretics. At the same time he appreciated that it wasn't something they could choose. The Chaos Space Marines were on Lubentina. They were already killing people, slaughtering loyalists and rebels with equal savagery.

'After all your men have endured, after all our people

have suffered, can we treat them with such disdain?' Yadav asked. 'I understand your disgust, Cardinal-Governor, though I have less sympathy for Kargil's financial worries. The very knowledge that beings such as these could ever have existed is an affront to the God-Emperor,' Yadav touched his fingers to his heart. 'In here I know there is no enemy more vile and loathsome than a traitor and no traitor more accursed than those who betrayed the God-Emperor. Yet as one who serves the Emperor I know there is no more noble an act to prove my devotion than to stand against such an enemy. Courage is the mark of my faith. So too will it be with our people.'

A dry hiss of laughter rasped from Murdan's drawn lips. 'You would shame me for my uncertainty.' His skeletal hand emerged from the folds of his robe to stifle the palatine's protest. 'Your oratory does you favour, but I wonder how much valour there is behind those fine words. You think if I tell my people that instead of the help... I requested... our troubles have been magnified a thousandfold that they will steel themselves and become fighting tigers? You think they will rush to fight monsters that have defied even the holy Adeptus Astartes?' Again, the governor laughed. 'They will run, Yadav. Terror will blot out all other considerations. Tell Hafiz's soldiers that Chaos marches on Tharsis and they will abandon their positions. They'll scatter and leave this complex and the spaceport undefended.'

'I say that they will fight to defend what they believe in,' Yadav insisted.

Kargil sneered at the palatine's assurance. 'Could it be because the heretics seem intent on gaining the Warmason's Cathedral that you want to believe what you say? From their route of march since leaving the spaceport there can be little question that the cathedral is their objective.'

'Which is why warning must be relayed to Sister Superior Trishala and those guarding the cathedral,' Yadav insisted. 'They must be made aware of this new threat.'

Murdan looked towards Hafiz. 'Tell us, colonel, do you think there is anything more Trishala and her Sisters could do to defend the cathedral that they aren't already doing?'

'Not being there to assess the situation, I should not like to commit myself to any theory,' Hafiz said. He shifted uneasily as he felt Murdan's eyes lingering on him. 'It is true that the cultists have thrown immense numbers at Mount Rama and have overwhelmed parts of the perimeter my troops established.'

'Then she will already be doing everything she can to defend the cathedral,' Murdan concluded. 'It can only serve to worsen her situation to inform her of the Traitor Space Marines. Should that knowledge slip out among the refugees packed into the cathedral there would be riotous panic.'

'There is a left-handed benefit to be had,' Kargil opined. 'With the cultists focusing on the cathedral and the Traitor Space Marines sharing that objective perhaps they will be obliging enough to kill one another.'

'You would gamble the sacred relics of Vadok Singh on such a conceit?' Yadav glared at the minister. 'Whichever side prevailed, the lives of all those within the cathedral would still be forfeit.'

'They will become martyrs,' Murdan declared, raising the jade aquila to his lips. 'They will die so that Lubentina might live. By their deaths they shall purify the taint of Chaos and the filth of the xenos. Their sacrifice will shine as a new beacon to the faithful, a glorious pyre to act as testament to the glory of Vadok Singh. Though the Warmason's relics pass, the martyrdom of those devoted to him will be eternal.'

Murdan's zealous inspiration quickly had Kargil calculating ways in which the expected tragedy could be turned to advantage. Yadav listened to them confer, unable to decide which he found more disturbing, the governor's zealotry or the minister's opportunism. Sickened, he turned to leave the council chamber.

Hafiz caught the palatine by the arm as he passed. 'Murdan may be right about the danger of passing a warning across the vox. I have confidence my soldiers would stand firm, but there's no saying the effect on civilians.'

'What would you do?' Yadav asked.

Hafiz raised his voice. 'I would pray for them, palatine.' Leaning closer to the priest he continued in a whisper. 'I'd do my praying with the Three Hundred and Forty-Fifth Division, bivouacked in the West Garden. They can be ready to move in less than an hour.'

Yadav fell silent, stunned by the offer Hafiz was making. They would both be circumventing Murdan's orders and it was doubtful Yadav would escape punishment for defying the governor a second time. That is, if he even survived long enough for that to be a concern. He'd be leading the local militia troops right into the worst of the crisis and at the heart of the conflict they would find monsters of almost unspeakable power. Now that the reality was right in front of him, he wondered if faith alone was enough to confront the horror of Chaos.

Balanced against his uncertainty was the knowledge that Trishala and the Order of the Sombre Vow, all the monks and priests who tended the cathedral, all the multitudes of faithful who'd sought sanctuary within its walls, all of them were in peril. So too were the relics of Vadok Singh. Could it be that was what they'd come for? To steal the Shroud of Singh and the Phylactery of Dreams, the Star of Knossos and the Warmason's Casket, the most revered of them all.

The choice was to abandon everything, to sit back like Murdan and Kargil and simply watch, or to sally forth on an errand of almost certain death. Even as he weighed the two, Yadav knew it was no choice at all.

The plasteel door burst from its hinges as Periphetes drove his armoured bulk against it, propelling himself into a broad foyer with the remains of a registration cubicle littered about the floor and a flight of stairs snaking its way upwards. Whatever other appointments the room might have once possessed had been dragged off and piled up around the windows at the far end of the room. A gang of fifteen cultists firing through windows from behind their improvised fortification swung around when Periphetes made his entrance. Mahar and Turu were close behind, storming through the denuded doorway and raking the group of rebels they'd taken by surprise. The purple-robed hybrids crumpled under the bolter-fire, smashed back against the antechamber's side wall. If the sounds of violence hadn't alerted their comrades on the floors above, the dead hybrids that were knocked through the front windows would.

The first cultist that came running down the stairs was cut down by a burst from Rhodaan's pistol as the warsmith made his entrance. 'Captain Uzraal, secure this structure,' he ordered across the vox.

Uzraal swept past the warsmith, leading the other Iron Warriors up the stairs. A moment later Rhodaan saw the white-hot flare of his meltagun as the captain immolated whatever enemies had been waiting above. The chatter of bolters soon followed, settling whatever rebels had escaped Uzraal's attack.

'I thought you weren't going to allow the enemy to delay us?' The question was uttered by Cornak of Ouroboros as the sorcerer stepped into the foyer. He glanced over at the litter of cultists Mahar and Turu had gunned down. A burst from his pistol stamped out such life as remained in one of the wounded creatures.

Rhodaan nodded at the jumble of bodies. 'They've been making a feeble effort at keeping us back, but have refused to commit any large force to oppose us. That means they're concentrating their strength towards another objective. One that interferes with our mission here.'

Overhead, the sounds of fighting drifted down to the Iron Warriors. When the Space Marines had neared the base of Mount Rama, they'd noted the gunfire streaming from this building, harassing the Imperials at the blockade they'd raised across the path ascending the mountain. The Iron Warriors had been of a mind simply to ignore the cultists and force their own way through the Imperials when a tremendous explosion shook the district. A cloud of flame and smoke rose from somewhere beyond the press of buildings nuzzled against the mountain, suggestive of some assault against Mount Rama itself. Less than a minute later, a second blast roared up from the opposite side of the slope.

It was then that Rhodaan determined they would see

what the rebels were up to before starting their ascent. One of the buildings the cult had seized as a strongpoint overlooking the barricade was the place the warsmith decided would be ideal to look over the battlefield.

A signal from Uzraal across the vox proclaimed the building to be clear. 'Assemble the warband on the roof. Periphetes will stay below and discourage any rebels curious about their comrades here.' Rhodaan looked over at Cornak. 'We'll inspect the situation for ourselves before engaging. Unless you'd prefer to use your magic?' He took a deep satisfaction when Cornak's fingers curled tighter around the heft of his staff. The sorcerer was always quick to boast of his powers, but he was also quick to explain their limitations.

'It is dangerous to draw upon the arcane too often,' Cornak said. 'Magic isn't something to be drawn upon for matters of small import.'

'Those explosions we heard would be of some consequence if they were caused by the Imperials trying to keep invaders off their mountain,' Rhodaan said. Turning from the sorcerer, he climbed the stairs, marching through the carnage unleashed by his Iron Warriors. When he reached the roof, he found Uzraal and the others gazing down on the barricade and the swarms of purple-clad infantry trying to overrun it.

'They've tenacity,' Uzraal stated, pointing to the sprawl of bodies strewn around the barricade. The Imperials behind the barrier were blazing away with lasguns and heavy bolters, flamers and cannon. Each rush the cultists made, the Imperials left scores of them stacked on the ground.

'The flesh expect trouble from the rear,' Rhodaan

observed, gesturing to a squad of soldiers who took no part in the fighting at the barricade but instead kept their guns aimed at the road they were protecting. Several hundred metres up the ascent, a huge press of refugees could be seen, struggling in their panicked climb. Between the Imperial rearguard and the refugees, several bodies lay strewn on the ground. Civilians that had been trampled by the mob, or something in league with the rebels outside?

Rhodaan soon had his answer. From a darkened structure a hundred metres behind the barricade, a large group of cultists charged into view, hundreds strong. The soldiers of the rearguard started firing away at the enemies inside their perimeter. The cultists returned fire, but it appeared their more important concern was getting hold of the bodies lying in the road. Or more particularly, the bulky bundles each of the corpses held.

'This should be interesting,' Rhodaan said.

The Imperials sent shot after shot into the rebels at their rear, dropping several. Their alarm at having such a large force flank their position and come at them from behind had unnerved the soldiers, reducing their efficiency. Even so, had their enemy possessed any degree of self-concern they might have driven off the attack. Instead the rest of the rebels returned the Imperial fire, and three of the cultists rushed at the barricade, their arms wrapped around the bundles they'd taken from the bodies. One of the charging hybrids was felled but the others endured the shower of las-blasts. As they neared the vehicles behind the perimeter, the saboteurs threw their burdens at the barricade. They didn't bother to run away – knowing they couldn't outrun the destruction they'd just unleashed.

The charges the cultists had activated went sliding down

the approach straight at the tanks and armoured transports. One of them slipped under a Leman Russ before detonating, the other exploded a little less than a metre from the barricade itself. The result was a blinding flare of violence. The Leman Russ was sent flying, somersaulting through the air before slamming down into the street twenty metres away, its turret flattened as the wreck rolled onto its back. Smoke billowed from the jagged rent in its belly, sparks and flashes of fire licking out from the gaps in its hull.

The rest of the barricade was likewise demolished. The other vehicles were knocked around like toys, squashing soldiers as they were sent spinning away from the blasts. One side of a building collapsed into the road, dumping tonnes of rockcrete onto the approach and pulping the ragged carcasses of the saboteurs. Debris and shrapnel slashed into the rebels, killing some of the cultists and leaving the rest bloodied and shaken. The refugee column was too far up the approach to be directly affected by the explosion, but as the rolling cloud of dust kicked up by the demolished building shot towards them the crowd descended into abject panic.

The lenses of Rhodaan's helmet blazed with a dull glow as the optics compensated for the thick pall of dust that billowed across the rooftop. Through the grit, he could see another surge of cultists pouring in from the outlying district. A Goliath with a massive dozer blade fitted to its nose barrelled towards the demolished barricade, ready to smash aside the wrecked vehicles and clear a path for the infantry following behind.

'We must thank the xenos for opening the door for us,' Rhodaan said, aiming his bolt pistol.

Focused upon the breach their comrades had opened for them, the cultists were taken utterly by surprise when the Iron Warriors began decimating their ranks.

After watching their ploy against the Imperials, it struck Rhodaan as quite fitting to use the same trick against the rebels.

CHAPTER IX

'Controlled bursts! Be certain of your targets!' Sister Kashibai's admonition rang out across the vox, carrying to the Battle Sisters assembled with her in the narthex. The position had been reinforced by Sisters detached from other duties within the cathedral so that Kashibai now had upwards of thirty warriors to defend the Great Gate.

Looking out into the plaza from the gateway, Kashibai appreciated how immense was the task set before them. The square was fairly crawling with refugees, a panicked morass of humanity that was trying to force its way into the cathedral. Clawing, kicking, trampling, the mob was lost to reason now. All that was left was the fear that hammered in their hearts and the prospect of safety that goaded them on.

Sister Superior Trishala had given the order and Kashibai could do nothing but obey. No more people were to be admitted into the cathedral. She would pray for their souls when the fighting was done. For now, she had to forget them. It was the crowds already inside who demanded her protection.

Las-bolts caught Sister Rachna in the throat when a clutch of supposed refugees drew weapons from beneath their coats. More cultists revealed themselves in a blast of fiery plasma as they charged the gate, Sister Shanta's left side reduced to a mess of melted armour and vaporised flesh. The enemy rush was silenced in a hail of bolter-fire, but the damage was already done. Far more than the loss of two Battle Sisters, the attack had demolished the discipline of the crowd. Already on the edge from the breaching of the perimeter, the civilians lost all restraint.

The fusillade the Battle Sisters loosed into the crowd saw no less than two score hurled back in a welter of blood and dying flesh. The deafening salvo for a brief instant accomplished a miracle. The wave of maddened humanity drew back, stunned by the menacing display. For an instant, silence brooded above the square. Kashibai looked towards the Great Gate, wondering why she couldn't hear the portal growling its way back into its hidden recess to leave the doorway and the cathedral exposed to the masses in the plaza. The immense gate had stopped, freezing in place midpoint in its journey.

The silence was broken by a rumbling mechanical shriek. Up from the crowd rose cries of protest and horror, screams both terrifying and piteous. The sound that had broken the silence was that of the Great Gate's mammoth door shuddering into motion. Plaster and masonry crumbled as the huge portal began to creep out from its hidden recess, its tremulous momentum sending a shudder through the mountain itself.

The Great Gate was closing again! The sanctuary those in the plaza had so desperately hoped to gain was being cut off, denied to them when they stood upon its very doorstep, when safety had so abruptly re-entered their hopes. Now it was being snatched away from them again. That realisation whipped the fires of fear into a conflagration. An inflamed horde rose up, charging the steps, rushing for the doorway before it could be closed to them.

'Hold them!' Kashibai gave the command to her warriors. Again, the sheer assault on the senses provoked by the salvo caused the mob to draw back, slipping and stumbling down the steps.

'God-Emperor forgive me,' Kashibai whispered as she looked down on the wretched crowd.

'We can't keep them back long,' Sister Pranjal cautioned Kashibai. 'Sheer numbers will make it impossible to hold them off.'

Kashibai nodded. 'We only need to hold them until the gate closes.' She looked askance at the groaning portal of thick metal. She prayed that the door's long-slumbering machine-spirit would rouse itself to greater effort. Otherwise she knew she'd be forced to a decision that would persecute her the rest of her days.

Slowly, much too slowly, the Great Gate lumbered outwards. With each groan and rumble, Kashibai could see the agitation of the crowd rebuilding itself. Subduing them wasn't enough, she had to regain control. She had to turn hope against fear. To do that would mean violating the letter of Trishala's orders.

'Listen to me!' Kashibai shouted to the crowd. 'The cathedral must be closed! The gate cannot be open when the enemy comes! There isn't time to get everyone inside!'

A bold idea came to her, one that would at once salvage something from the crisis and remind the panicked masses that they were humans, not animals. 'The children! Bring the children forwards. There's still time to save them.'

The declaration sent a murmur through the crowd. While some voices still shouted in protest, many more were raised in gratitude. Out from the crowd, the youngest of the refugees were brought forwards, sent scurrying up the steps. Kashibai felt a pang of guilt as she watched families torn apart, tearful parents pushing their children towards a sanctuary they knew they wouldn't share. She felt shame as the crowd piled onto those who tried to flee with the children, to seize this last chance at safety. She'd intended the crowd to police itself once they had something to fight for, but to see it executed with such savagery gave her pause. She felt as though she'd set a rabid animal loose.

'Your plan may work, Sister,' Pranjal said as the first of the children hurried past her into the narthex. 'So long as the gate closes before anything more happens to agitate them.'

Even as Pranjal spoke the words, a grinding shudder swept through the Great Gate. Kashibai looked aside, horrified to see the monolithic portal start to withdraw back into its recess. Instead of closing, the gate was being flung open once more. The reversal of the narrative she'd given the crowd was just the sort of thing that Kashibai dreaded. Resigned to their fate only a moment before, the retreat of the hulking metal barrier fanned the fading hopes of the mob.

'We have to hold them,' Kashibai told Pranjal. 'As long as we can, we have to keep them out.'

The peculiar tilt that marked the architecture of the Warmason's Cathedral was more pronounced within the forty-metre stretch of the gatehouse's narrow operating centre. The ceiling was comparatively low when balanced against the discordant symmetry of its upended floor. The windows set into the far wall looked down upon the plaza rather than out across the cityscape of Tharsis, the translucent armourglass material of such a thickness that only the barest impression of motion and shape could be seen through them. The metal walls were pitted with banks of machinery, many of them winking and sparkling with a deranged confusion of lights. Projecting up from the floor were banks of workstations, the awkwardness of their angle making them almost parallel with the firmament.

Here among this riot of machinery were the controls for the Great Gate. Generations of acolytes had acted as gatekeepers, sworn to silence and seclusion, instructed in the rituals and prayers by which the truculent cogitators could be coaxed into activity. The litanies of operation had been disseminated over millennia without once being put into practice, for to rouse the Great Gate without cause was deemed an act of blasphemy. Trishala's worry as she entered the gatehouse was that the gatekeepers had been too timid in their ministrations and the door had suffered some fault that had caused it to open. She'd almost convinced herself that the reason she couldn't raise the acolytes, Captain Debdan or Sister Virika was because of some discharge within the gatehouse that was disrupting vox traffic.

One look across the room changed Trishala's mind.

Sister Virika lay slumped on the floor a dozen metres from the entrance, a smoking hole drilled into her forehead by a lasweapon, the shot inflicted from extremely close range. The dozen acolytes had been drawn away from their usual stations and were clustered about a nest of machinery near the centre of the room facing towards the windows. Many of them had pale, trembling faces, gazing in fright at Virika's body. Others kept directing confused looks towards the raised terminal where a few of their number continued to operate machinery under the watchful supervision of their new overseers. Ranged across the hall were thirty soldiers in the uniform of local militia.

'Sister Superior,' Captain Debdan greeted her as she entered the room. He turned away from the troops surrounding the acolytes and walked towards her. 'Cultists were trying to seize control of the gatehouse. They shot Sister Virika. We have just put them down. The location is secure now.'

Trishala's bolt pistol was in her hand. The instant he noted her weapon, the captain arrested his approach. 'I see no cultists,' she told Debdan, her tone both tense and suspicious.

The captain pointed to the acolytes. 'There,' he declared. 'The xenos that got into the cathedral must have infected the clergy with its corruption.' He continued to walk towards Trishala. 'It is to be regretted that we weren't able to stop it from corrupting these men, but at least their treachery has been uncovered before they could do further damage.' Debdan pointed to the terminals still in operation. 'My men are forcing them to close the Great Gate. When they're finished we'll make them initiate the lockdown.'

Trishala shook her head. She was thinking of the shot that had killed Virika and how close her murderer must have been. Too close to be anyone she didn't trust. 'How is it that Sister Virika was killed but none of your men look as though they've even been hurt?' She raised her pistol, arresting Debdan's advance. The captain's expression turned anxious. He made a placating gesture with his hands. At the same time, Trishala saw a few of the soldiers starting to move. 'If anything happens, I promise you die first,' she warned Debdan.

'Please, there has been too much violence already!' Out from the doorway of an antechamber that branched off from the control room, a familiar figure appeared. Prelate Azad was dressed in the finery of his office, looking as regal and collected as if he were about to conduct the Rites of Singh in veneration of the God-Emperor's Warmason. As Trishala watched him walk into the control room, there was no sign of distress or compulsion in his manner, no wariness in his demeanour as he passed Debdan's troops. The confused, even alarmed expressions of the acolytes told Trishala all she needed to know.

'You've been missing several days, Reverence,' Trishala told the prelate. 'You caused us a great deal of worry. You were needed here.'

Prelate Azad bowed his head in apology. 'This crisis demanded utmost clarity of thought,' he said. 'I removed myself in contemplation, to pray to the God-Emperor for His guidance, to appeal to Him for the wisdom that can save His people.' He looked over at Debdan, frowning when he saw the captain's hand slipping towards his holstered pistol. 'There's already been enough killing,' he repeated. 'Let me do this my way.'

Trishala's mind raced, trying to deny the magnitude of what she was hearing. A cold sensation shivered through her as she realised that not only Debdan but also Prelate Azad were traitors. She looked across the room, evaluating the odds against her. She saw clearly how Virika had been killed without the chance to fight. The traitors wouldn't find her so easy to put down.

'You've violated every sacred oath you've taken,' Trishala accused. 'Forsaken the God-Emperor! Why?'

The accusation brought a sneer to Debdan's face, but on Azad's there was a look of actual pain. He held his hands out to Trishala in appeal. 'You don't understand,' he said. 'I haven't betrayed the God-Emperor. If anything, I have been drawn into an even greater understanding of His divine plan. I have been blessed to be granted a knowledge of things hidden from even the Ecclesiarchy.' A smile so rapturous as to be beatific gripped his features. 'I have seen the destiny the God-Emperor intended for all His children! The purpose towards which He led us across the stars! I have seen the means by which all the faults and weaknesses of mankind may be burned away. I have been shown how the mortal soul may be inoculated against all corruption.' Where Debdan had stopped, Azad now came towards Trishala, his arms outstretched. 'I have discovered the secret of a physical ascension.'

Trishala felt disgust as she gazed on Azad. 'You've been infected by the xenos,' she told him. 'Your mind has warped the corruption of your flesh and made you believe it to be some kind of holy revelation.' She raised her pistol, aiming at the prelate's smiling face. 'What you think is wisdom is nothing but madness.'

Contempt and horror at the defiled state of the prelate

caused Trishala's attention to focus entirely on him for an instant. In that moment, Captain Debdan ripped his pistol from his holster and fired at her. 'Kill the defiler!' he shouted to his men.

Trishala swung around as Debdan fired, his shot scorching past her head. Las-bolts from some of his soldiers came flashing towards her, cracking harmlessly against her armour. The same couldn't be said for Prelate Azad. Still advancing towards the Battle Sister, the priest was caught by stray shots from the traitors' guns. Trishala watched him pitch to the floor, his vestments scorched by several hits. As he died, she saw that terrible expression of rapture freeze on his features, his mind lost in the end to the delusions provoked by the xenos contamination. The monstrousness of it made a cold rage blaze within her. The next instant her bolter was barking away. Had Debdan hesitated, waited to snap off a second shot, he would have been caught in that burst of fire. As it was he managed the cover of a workstation, sheltering behind it as the explosive shells raked across its metal casing.

'Kill the infidel!' Debdan raged. 'Make of her an offering to the Great Father!'

At their captain's command, the rest of the soldiers sprang into action, sweeping across the gatehouse to encircle Trishala's position. An angry rebuke from Debdan explained why the traitors had taken such risks and chosen this moment to reveal their corruption. 'Not all of you! Lochan! Watch the acolytes! We must keep control of the gate!'

Trishala blazed away as las-bolts sizzled against the ceramite plates that encased her body. Sending a burst at one of Debdan's treacherous command, she put a shell through his chest and sent his carcass tumbling into the ranks of his fellows. A second traitor went down with his leg severed at the knee, his wails of pain ringing through the gatehouse. A third soldier, trying to creep around behind a projecting stanchion, made the mistake of exposing the top of his helmet. Trishala's shot burned through the armaplas covering and pitted the skull inside.

Trishala dropped back behind a workstation, hastily reporting the situation in the gatehouse across the vox. She had to alert her Sisters to Debdan's treachery. There was no knowing how far his treason went, or what other sabotage his men had inflicted within the cathedral. The only response to her hails was a crackle of static. Somewhere, somehow, the brood brothers were jamming communications within the gatehouse.

A fusillade of las-beams came cracking back at Trishala, scorching the tilted workstation she'd ducked behind to such a degree that it broke from its moorings and went spinning away, reclaimed by the gravity it had so long defied. She rushed out from her compromised position, plunging in the one direction she felt her enemy wouldn't expect. She lunged forwards, straight towards the gunfire.

Her ruse proved warranted. Caught off guard, the cultists were tardy in responding to Trishala's charge. When she rounded a cogitator's terminal and found a soldier crouching behind it, the man was so startled that he didn't even finish putting a fresh cell into his weapon. Instead he swung the lasgun around, thrusting it at her like a club.

Trishala caught the improvised bludgeon in her armoured fist and wrenched the gun from the soldier's grasp. Unarmed, he sprang at her, clawing for her throat with his hands. Trishala struck back, smashing the side of his head against the terminal with such force that both the console and his skull were dented by the impact. The traitor collapsed in a heap, his corrupt life oozing onto the floor in a mess of brains and blood.

'Defiler!' Debdan's voice raged. 'You are unfit for the ascension! Rush her together! She is but one infidel!'

Trishala looked at the grenade dispenser on her belt. She could even the odds quite quickly with those, but even more quickly she rejected the idea. The cultists had refrained from using krak grenades to penetrate her armour and she could easily guess why. The danger of damaging the Great Gate's machinery was too pronounced. She didn't understand why the cultists wanted the gate intact rather than simply disabling it, but she knew what would happen if she couldn't get it closed.

Trishala slapped a fresh clip into her bolter and prepared to meet the charging cultists. Perhaps she couldn't fend off all of these traitors by herself, but such was the situation into which she'd been thrust.

With bestial, subhuman cries, the soldiers converged on Trishala's position. Even as they started their charge, however, the attack was broken. From the far end of the gatehouse shots rang out, slamming into the cultists and sending half a dozen of them sprawling to the floor. Trishala turned her head to see Sister Kashibai and a squad of Battle Sisters rushing into the room. Heartened by the unexpected intervention, she added her own shots to the barrage.

From the overwhelming force that was set on drowning Trishala in sheer numbers, Debdan's traitors were swiftly reduced to a handful. Mangled by bolter shells, the ragged remains of the cultists were scattered about the gatehouse, strewn across the stanchions and workstations. The last few who rushed Trishala fell in gory heaps at her feet, ripped open by the impact of her fire.

'You will not prevail, defiler!' Debdan raged at Trishala. The Sister Superior motioned Kashibai's squad to settle the rest of the traitors. The captain was an enemy she'd deal with on her own.

'You were clever, Debdan,' Trishala conceded as she sent a burst from her bolt pistol slamming into his cover. 'No traitor hides himself half so well as when he warns others to be vigilant for traitors.'

'All of it will burn, defiler,' Debdan snarled. 'The Great Father will cleanse this world and only those who bear his blessing will be permitted to ascend!' Again he risked a shot at Trishala before moving back into cover.

From her position, Trishala could see Kashibai closing on the brood brothers. She could also see the acolytes frantically waving, trying to draw the Sister Superior's attention. She knew the reason why. The soldiers Debdan had sent back to guard the prisoners were gone. The acolytes were pointing to the doorway Prelate Azad had emerged from, a portal set halfway up the curiously angled wall. The doorway was parallel to where the brood brothers had withdrawn. Kashibai wasn't coming to grips with the traitors, she was being drawn into their trap.

'Kashibai! On your left!' Trishala shouted as she leapt over the las-bolt-scarred terminal and dashed towards the doorway. She fired into the darkened passage. A traitor soldier cried out as he toppled back into the gatehouse, his chest a crimson ruin. A second man fell beyond the threshold, coughing as life fled from him.

Trishala was just thinking she'd ended the threat of

ambush when the true import of the soldiers' diversion rushed into the gatehouse. Utterly inhuman, its jaws open in a bestial shriek, the genestealer was through the doorway and lunging at her almost before she was aware of its presence. The xenos slammed into her, its hooves grinding her down against the floor. She felt its claw rake across her back, shearing into her armour. Armour that had resisted the force of las-bolts parted under the genestealer's talon.

Prostrate upon the floor, Trishala couldn't see her attacker. All she could do was aim her bolter upwards and fire. She felt the sickening wash of xenos ichor splash down on her as the shells ripped into the alien. The genestealer's shriek was deafening. She could feel its pressure against her back increase, braced herself to feel those sharp claws tear into her body.

Suddenly the weight on her back was gone. Trishala heard the genestealer slam down a few metres away, carried away by its own tremendous lunge. She could see the horrible work her bolter had made of the thing, the exposed organs that dangled from its shattered carapace. The monster snarled and shrieked for a moment, then was blown apart by a barrage from Kashibai's squad.

The genestealer's destruction threw the last brood brothers into a frenzy. Like madmen they rushed the Battle Sisters, snapping off wild shots that failed to hit their intended targets. The response from the Sisters was far more effectual and final.

'Infidels and desecraters!' Captain Debdan howled as he stepped out from cover. 'The Great Father will not forgive this blasphemy against his children.'

He charged at Trishala, his shots searing the floor as he tried to put a las-bolt into her face. From the ground,

Trishala sent a burst that withered the officer and threw his body against the thick window behind him.

Trishala rose from the floor, casting her gaze towards the genestealer Kashibai's squad had finished. She didn't feel any pain where the genestealer's claws had struck her and a quick inspection with her fingers told her that the alien's talons had pierced but not quite penetrated the ceramite plate. As before, it was a narrow margin, but within it was the difference between life and death. She gave praise to the God-Emperor for extending to her such mercy.

'I grew concerned that the Great Gate was still open and detached a few Sisters to investigate when I couldn't reach you,' Kashibai reported.

'Praise the God-Emperor for your intervention.' Trishala turned to the surviving acolytes. 'Close the gate,' she told them, holding them under her commanding gaze until they had the door grinding its way shut once more.

'Debdan was a clever traitor,' Kashibai said. 'He kept the gate's movement erratic so we would think it malfunction rather than treachery.' She pointed at the genestealer sprawled on the floor. 'That must be the monster his men supposedly killed in the Gauntlet's Retreat.'

Trishala walked towards the dead creature. The similarity of the attack against her on the steps had provoked an awful suspicion. With the toe of her boot, she turned the carcass over. The xenos had been mangled by the many bolter shells that had killed it, but the injury to one of its arms was much older. An injury that had removed one of its claws and, in some way, reduced the overall strength of the creature.

'This isn't the one that got in by the balcony,' Trishala said, a chill in her voice. 'This is the one I fought on the steps, the same one I wounded in the Cloisterfells.'

'But how did it get in?' Kashibai wondered. 'And what became of the one Debdan's men claimed to have killed? We found no trace of it in the Retreat.'

'Doubtless the other genestealer is still prowling the cathedral,' Trishala said. 'It or Debdan must have let this one in somewhere. Our task is to find out where and how... and discover how many more may have been admitted with this one.' She pointed to where Prelate Azad's corpse lay. 'The xenos infected the prelate,' she declared. 'With his collusion there's no secret of this cathedral that may not have been disclosed to them.

'They wanted to keep the Great Gate open,' Trishala explained. 'But they were also intent on keeping it intact. If they simply wanted to let their filthy cult inside, why would they be worried about being able to close the gate again?' She shook her head. 'It was my decision to initiate the lockdown that forced Debdan to reveal himself, but if the cult simply wanted to prevent the lockdown, Azad would have known which litanies to invoke and which rites to perform so that the cogitators would remain dormant.'

'They wanted everything intact,' Kashibai stated, a horrible suspicion coming to her mind. 'They don't simply want to force their way inside the cathedral. They intend to capture it, to hold it as their own.'

Trishala nodded in grim agreement. 'We must vox our suspicions to Palatine Yadav and have him communicate them to the rest of the council. They must know of Captain Debdan's treachery and be aware that other officers and officials may have been corrupted.' She turned again to the dead genestealer. 'The moment the Great Gate is closed, leave the frateris militia in charge of the narthex.

We'll need every Sister we can spare to go through this cathedral all over again. Room by room, hall by hall, looking for any of Debdan's traitors that may still be around and for any trace of any xenos they let inside.'

The snarl of bolters echoed down the Chastened Road, drowning out the screams of the dead and dying. Flames licked at the darkening sky, billowing out from buildings unfortunate enough to present an obstacle to those who now ascended the Chastened Road. Smoke, thick as mud and black as night, spilled through the avenue, fanned ever onwards by the fires that produced it. Terror had claimed Mount Rama before the Iron Warriors set their boots upon its streets, but it was only under the malignancy of the Third Grand Company that terror became an all-consuming force, as elemental as fire and wind and death.

'Periphetes, report,' Rhodaan growled into his vox. The optics of his helm pierced the thick smoke as keenly as a knife; only the hottest of the flames provoked even the slightest distortion of the image conveyed to him. He could see the renegade Steel Brother ahead of the other Space Marines. It was a further sign of how far the Steel Brethren had fallen from the standards of the Iron Warriors that Periphetes would vent his hatred on the broken flesh strewn about him. Hate was a tool, an instrument to be harnessed and used, not an addiction to be sated on even the most insignificant prey.

'No resistance, warsmith,' Periphetes' reply came back. 'These rebels have no fight in them.'

Perhaps that was true, by the standards of the Iron Warriors, but Rhodaan considered that there was no scarcity of cultists to oppose them. Every dozen metres another batch of the rebels would appear, firing from the buildings flanking the road or swarming en masse onto the street to block the path. They were dealt with quickly enough, but even so they cost the Iron Warriors time. After watching the demolition of the barricade, Rhodaan knew the cultists had done the same at other approaches and were even now sending their forces climbing towards the cathedral on parallel tracks. The mobs that harassed Rhodaan's retinue were splinters of those invading forces, diverting from the main advance to attack the Space Marines while their comrades stormed the summit.

Behind him, Rhodaan could hear the distinctive tapping of Cornak's staff on the street surface. The sorcerer had demurred at performing a magical divination, insisting he had to keep his mind entirely devoted to blotting out the psychic inveiglement of the xenos magus. Only by complete concentration could the Iron Warriors hope to slip beneath the enemy's awareness. Rhodaan cared little about the xenos or their awareness; what did concern him was getting to the cathedral before them. The more foes that stood between the Third Grand Company and his prize, the longer it would take to seize it and claim the power and prestige it offered.

'Well, sorcerer, any sign of your xenos witch?' Rhodaan demanded.

Cornak slowly shook his head. 'No, not even a hint of his mentality. That alarms me, warsmith. He is aware we were making for Mount Rama. Why has he so abruptly lost interest in us?'

'You have a theory?' Rhodaan asked.

'I believe he is trying to lull me into a false sense of

security,' Cornak said. 'Tempt me into letting my defences down so I may use my powers to benefit my brothers.'

'The opponents we've met during our ascent have been random and disconnected. Isolated pockets, not concentrated ambushes. Rearguards left to watch the road and deny it to flesh... not iron. You've said yourself that this magus has gained an appreciation of what kind of enemy he faces in the Third Grand Company. No, he wouldn't hope to stop us with such nuisances. Mark me, Cornak, the reason you don't feel his presence now is because he's focused on something bigger than a lone sorcerer from Medrengard.'

Rhodaan didn't need to be psychic to tell that his own theory rattled Cornak. With his faculties not wearied by his efforts against the magus, perhaps he would have had the composure to conceal that reaction, but as things stood, the warsmith could see it clear as day. Had his speculation struck a bit too close, or had he simply voiced a possibility that Cornak hadn't foreseen? If the cult's resources were being devoted to some other enterprise, then what might that be?

Again the snarl of bolters came from up ahead. This time, it seemed, Periphetes had encountered something stiffer than a rabble of frightened flesh. Whatever it was, Rhodaan wasn't going to be delayed by it. 'Captain Uzraal, Gaos and Mahar with you. Brother Turu and myself will draw fire, the rest of you silence it the moment it reveals itself.'

Leaving Cornak behind, Rhodaan marched ahead. The lane had been blocked off by the wreckage of a demolished building that had toppled across the street. A litter of dead refugees lay strewn about the rubble, pilgrims caught in the path of the collapsing structure.

Periphetes was in a small alcove between two doorways, leaning out to direct shots at the mound of rubble. Answering fire sounded from the big stub gun stationed atop the rubble and by a motley array of small arms arrayed amidst the debris.

'Brother Turu, Periphetes, keep their attention away from me,' Rhodaan voxed.

Orders given, Rhodaan advanced to an alcove across from the one occupied by Periphetes. Gunfire peppered the street around him, a few las-bolts glancing off his power armour. It was better marksmanship than he'd expected, given the heavy smoke. Then again, these cultists were only partly human. Their xenos taint may have altered their senses as well as their bodies.

'These ones decided to shoot back,' Periphetes told Rhodaan, a smug quality to his voice.

'Their accuracy leaves much to be desired,' Rhodaan answered. He was tempted to order Periphetes to do what he now had in mind, but the renegade's pride had rankled him. He needed a reminder of why Rhodaan was his commander.

'Suppress the stubber,' Rhodaan told Periphetes, nodding at the weapons team. 'I will show you how a true Iron Warrior removes an obstacle.'

When he heard the autocannon of Brother Gaos growling from Uzraal's advancing group, Rhodaan decided it was time to move. The cultists would be momentarily distracted by the reinforcements and that lapse of vigilance was the opening he needed. Emerging from the alcove, the warsmith charged towards the debris pile, his pistol rattling away at the heavy stubber. One of the crew pitched and fell, his body sliding down the rubble.

Another purple-clad cultist rushed to take his place, only to suffer the same fate.

Before Rhodaan could send another burst up at the weapons crew, enemies sprang at him from the building on his left. He swung around, his shots felling several snarling hybrids. One managed to weather the murderous storm, flinging itself on the huge Space Marine. Rhodaan found himself in the grip of an enormous, semi-human beast. It was at once the most debased and the most formidable of the hybrids he'd yet seen. The brute brought its fist cracking down against his horned helm, while a third arm pawed at the chainsword fastened to his belt.

The warsmith didn't try to pull free of the hybrid's grip. What he did instead was press the barrel of his pistol into its gut and empty the clip. As the creature's body went slack, he threw it contemptuously at the pile of debris.

Foolishly, the cultists poised along the mound of rubble had held their fire while Rhodaan was in the grip of their malformed comrade. There was a pause while they took aim again, a pause that the warsmith used to the utmost. His bolt pistol cracked away again, this time smashing into the stubber itself and knocking the gun from its perch.

'Iron within! Iron without!' Rhodaan bellowed as he reached the rubble and climbed the heap of broken rockcrete. His chainsword was in his hand now, lashing out at the rebels who tried to contest his ascent. Their maimed bodies went sprawling to the road below.

Roaring their own war cries, the other Iron Warriors followed Rhodaan's lead, butchering their way through any rebel that tried to stand against them.

Rhodaan reached the top of the obstruction, hurling aside the bloodied husk of the last cultist to fall on the whirring blade of his sword. He gazed across the havoc he'd unleashed, then turned his attention to the road ahead. What he saw had him snarling orders to Uzraal and the others to join him. Ahead he could see a wide plaza that terminated in a series of broad steps that rose to the cathedral.

The Warmason's Cathedral was a titanic edifice, redolent of the pomp and decadence of the False Emperor's slaves. Elaborate flourishes of adornment and lavish excesses of ornamentation were in abundance everywhere. A riotous proliferation of windows and balconies opened across its upper reaches, presenting a hundred points of entry to disperse the building's defenders and stretch their strength. The immense gateway that stood at the end of the steps leading down into the plaza looked to be the most formidable feature on display. A strongpoint those inside would be depending on to keep them safe.

The crack of lasguns and the snarl of bolters rang out from the plaza. Rhodaan could see masses of rebels dressed in purple and crimson laying siege to the building. Their attentions were returned with vigour by warriors encased in black armour poised on the balconies above. The plaza was something of an abattoir, the dead strewn deep upon the ground, a stream of blood trickling off down the various approaches. Rhodaan focused on the massive door that sealed off the entrance to the cathedral, a door the cultists were striving to gain control over and which the cathedral's defenders were just as determined to deny them.

'It seems we aren't the only ones trying to get inside,' Rhodaan declared across the inter-squad vox. 'Our objective is also of interest to the xenos,' he added, just a hint of accusation for Cornak's benefit.

'Your orders, warsmith?' came Uzraal's response.

Rhodaan could appreciate the irony of the plan that had occurred to him, inspired by the confusion at the spaceport. The Imperials inside the cathedral might mistake the Iron Warriors for allies if provided with a little encouragement. With the city in such confusion, it was possible those inside the cathedral lacked lines of communication to the outside. They might be unaware of who it was that had landed on their world. Would they be recognised as invaders or celebrated as liberators? True, if it was the latter, the deception would be brief, but the fools inside the cathedral would have even less time to rue their mistake.

'Fighting the rebels and the defenders will delay us,' Rhodaan voxed to his retinue. 'Fire only on the xenos. Take no action against the flesh inside the cathedral. Let us see if they won't open the doors for us and spare us the effort of smashing them down.'

CHAPTER X

The throng of deformed cultists swarmed across the plaza, rushing the Great Gate from every direction. As they charged the steps they mercilessly raked the remaining refugees with their clawed hands and gunned down the crowds with a motley array of arms. No longer did these subhuman hybrids value the refugees as living shields. Now the panicked masses of humanity were nothing more than an obstacle to be swatted aside with heinous abandon.

The Great Gate was closed to the cultists, the gatehouse now under the watchful guard of the Adepta Sororitas. Battle Sisters stood upon the balconies overlooking the square, vengefully shooting into the purple-garbed cultists, trying to exact from them every drop of human blood they'd spilled in their push to the cathedral. Droves of the snarling hybrids were ripped apart by bolters or burned alive by sweeping bursts of flamers. Grenades lobbed down from the overlooking walkways and balconies exploded amidst the hybrid mob, mangling dozens of the degenerates. Yet still they came. With inhuman tenacity, they pressed the attack. The madness of the fanatic was upon them, a frenzy that paid small notice to the casualties inflicted upon their own. From the balcony above the statue of Vadok Singh, Trishala aimed her pistol at one of the hybrids carrying the cult's obscene banner. Her first round ripped through the standard, tearing a jagged hole in the painted wyrm that writhed across the purple cloth. Her second round turned the hairless head of the cultist carrying it into a red smear. Even as the standard bearer fell, another cultist scurried forwards to take up the flag, waving it defiantly as he shrieked obscenities at the Sisters.

'They won't break,' Kashibai called out in frustration, nearly tripping over the bloodied body sprawled at her feet. The frateris militia had taken it upon themselves to support the Battle Sisters, but unlike the female warriors they didn't have power armour to protect them from the cultist guns. The balconies and walkways were littered with their bodies.

'Kill them all,' Trishala sent her order across the vox. 'Don't let even one reach the Great Gate.'

Though Debdan and Azad had tried to seize the gatehouse intact, their failure might have caused the cult to change their plans. If one of the charges used on the barricades was brought against the cathedral, it would be the finish.

'We can't hold them,' Kashibai objected. 'We can't kill enough of them to keep them from overrunning us.'

The admonition broke through the cold fury that gripped Trishala. Was this revenge or duty? She could recognise the distinction. Her first responsibility was to protect the relics locked away within the cathedral, the Warmason's Casket, the Shroud of Singh and all the lesser artefacts. Her second was to protect the multitude of refugees that had already taken sanctuary within the cathedral.

Trishala looked over the balconies above the steps. She had twenty Sisters with twenty more posted at interior windows. Add another twenty up on the higher balconies and walkways. Arrayed against them were hundreds, perhaps thousands of cultists. Thus far there'd been little evidence of heavier weapons or full genestealers among the mob, but she knew it could only be a matter of time before the cultists brought these deadly assets into play. A plasma gun or heavy bolter would be capable of piercing the power armour the Battle Sisters wore. She'd seen for herself that the genestealers were able to climb the cathedral walls in a matter of heartbeats.

'We only have to hold them back until the lockdown sequence has been completed,' Trishala said. She looked aside at Kashibai. 'When the sequence is ready you will lead half the Sisters back inside.' She shook her head when she saw Kashibai wanted to protest. 'There has to be a rearguard to watch your back and I am the one to lead it.'

'The Order of the Sombre Vow needs you more than me,' Kashibai retorted. She punctuated her words with a burst that tore apart a four-armed hybrid rushing up the steps with a snarling power pick in each hand.

'Do as I command and listen for the alert from the gatehouse,' Trishala snapped. A shell from her pistol punched through the abdomen of a cultist trying to direct a flamer at their balcony. The round did more than rip through his body, it also exploded the fuel canister for his weapon, bathing the hybrids around him in searing promethium.

Trishala appreciated Kashibai's show of concern and loyalty, but now wasn't the time to express it. Trishala trusted the duty to no one else. If the rearguard was too weak, if the cult saw a chance to punch through and get inside then she expected they would call up the genestealers. The swift aliens could rush past a weakened rearguard and slip inside before the siege-plates closed off the cathedral. Trishala wouldn't risk that, not when the cult already had elements hiding somewhere within the cathedral.

'Sister Superior, look!' The cry came from Sister Archana. She pointed towards the street that connected one of the approaches to the plaza. Trishala watched in amazement as the cultists there began to draw back, retreating before something ascending the path. For an instant she expected to see one of the huge mining trucks the cult had transformed into weapons of war driving out into the square. Then she saw some of the hybrids dropping, heard the thunderous discharge of a bolter sounding from somewhere just beyond the path.

An instant later the cause for Archana's excitement marched into Trishala's view. She felt a sense of awe flood through her as her eyes set upon the lone warrior who advanced fearlessly into the xenos throng. He was a huge, superhuman figure, easily three metres in height and encased in power armour of immense, massive bulk. The ceramite was a dull colour, touched with sections of shiny metal and gilded ornamentation. The bolter he held was barking away, ripping into the cultists, driving them back with a maelstrom of violence.

All her life, Trishala had hoped to see such a being. Though she'd never set eyes upon one, there was no mistaking the exalted champions of the God-Emperor, the Adeptus Astartes, the mightiest of mankind's defenders. To see one now, to see him fighting against the cultists, could mean only one thing. The distress call had been answered! Amazing enough that the call had been answered only days after it was dispatched, but that it had been answered by no less than the Adeptus Astartes was miraculous! She closed her eyes, whispering a prayer of gratitude to the God-Emperor for extending to Lubentina such a miracle.

The rebels reeled at the sight of the Space Marine. Before they could recover from their surprise and confusion, the lone warrior was joined by comrades as mighty and imposing as he was. Eight armoured Space Marines marched out into the square, their guns ploughing a path through the xenos.

'Space Marines!' Kashibai gasped. 'We are saved!'

Trishala slapped a new clip into her pistol. 'They are still outnumbered!' she growled across the vox. 'Support them! Help the Adeptus Astartes clear a path to the cathedral!' She glanced down at the Great Gate and thought of the lockdown that would seal the cathedral off from the outside. It would close before the Space Marines could reach the cathedral. They'd be cut off, left among the surging masses of the cultists. Awesome and mighty as they were, Trishala feared even they could be overcome if the xenos brought enough numbers against them.

'Sister Jyoti!' Trishala voxed. 'The acolytes have to terminate the lockdown or they will cut off the Space Marines!' She waited anxiously for the reply, anticipated with dread the sound of the alert siren screaming from the top of the gatehouse as the siege-plates started coming down. When Jyoti replied, Trishala released the breath she'd been holding. She issued fresh orders, commanding the Sisters to remove the barricades from the abbot's door and be ready to open it at her word. The path was clear for the Space Marines and the Order of the Sombre Vow would keep it open for them if it meant fighting to the last round and the last drop of blood.

Even with the Sisters supporting them, the Space Marines were making slow progress across the plaza. The cultists had decided keeping them away from the cathedral was of more import than charging the gate themselves and their full fury was turned upon the giant warriors. Though they were decimated with bursts of bolter-fire, ravaged by chainswords and vaporised by the hideous energies of a meltagun, still the cult sought to overwhelm these liberators. Cutting a path through the hybrids threatened to slow the Space Marines' advance to a mere crawl.

Then from behind the Space Marines a new force appeared. Trishala saw hundreds of soldiers rushing up the Chastened Road and into the plaza. At first she thought they'd come to support the Space Marines, but soon it became clear that their intentions were anything but friendly. They formed firing lines and unleashed a fusillade into the armoured backs of the advancing giants. Trishala stood aghast. Despite the local militia uniforms the soldiers weren't loyalists, they were more traitors, like Captain Debdan!

Trishala was about to order her Sisters to open fire on the soldiers when a frantic voice came across the vox. It took her a second to recognise the panicked tones as belonging to Palatine Yadav.

'Sister Superior!' Yadav cried across the vox. 'You must close off the Warmason's Cathedral. The soldiers I've brought up the Chastened Road will only be able to distract the enemy for a little time. Use that time to protect the cathedral. "Epsilon Omega", input that sequence into the cogitators to revoke the safety rites and drop the siege-plates!'

'Your grace,' Trishala voxed back. 'We're ready to close off the cathedral, but we must give the Astartes time to...'

Horror was in Yadav's tone. 'Adeptus Astartes! I defy the Cardinal-Governor's order when I tell you this, but those aren't the Emperor's holy angels! They're an enemy worse than the xenos cult! They are Chaos Space Marines!'

'Chaos!' The word coursed through Trishala, chilling her to the very bone. The awed reverence of a moment before collapsed into horror and loathing. The Chaos Legions, the abominable traitors who'd turned upon the God-Emperor! The ancient monsters who had forsaken the Emperor's light for the madness of Chaos!

'Jyoti, resume the lockdown sequence!' Trishala countermanded her order. She waved the Sisters on the balcony to fall back inside. The cult was fixated upon the Chaos Space Marines, allowing the Sisters a chance to slip away. The Traitor Space Marines themselves were caught between two foes. Though the armoured giants had withstood the fusillade and everything the cult had thrown at them, the press of enemies had brought their advance to a halt. Until they butchered their way clear, they were caught.

As Trishala withdrew from the balcony, she wondered how long it would be before the Chaos Space Marines could cross the square. If even half the legends about them were true, there might not even be time to get the siege-plates dropped before they came charging up the steps.

The battle for Tharsis was favouring the militia at the moment. The cult was being driven from many of their earlier gains, though the rubble the Imperials recovered was hardly a cause for cheer. The Cloisterfells and tunnels below the city remained firmly in the grip of the rebels; any foray into the underworld saw the decimation of entire companies. Worse, entire platoons would expose themselves as traitors once their companies ventured into the tunnels, killing their loyal comrades before slipping away to join their xenos masters. Most of a division had been lost when a stretch of old mines a kilometre long had been demolished by the rebels and brought down on the heads of their pursuers.

Colonel Hafiz had better news from the spaceport to report to Cardinal-Governor Murdan in the Sovereign Spire's council room. The militia had retained control of the facility, though two landing pads had been compromised in the struggle with the rioting pilgrims trying to leave Lubentina. Strangely the rebels had made no move to attack the spaceport during the action, though there'd been ample opportunity to do so. Hafiz was concerned that the cult had some ulterior motive for this exhibition of restraint. With the revelation that many of his troops – even trusted officers like Captain Debdan – had been corrupted by the cult, Hafiz worried that some of the pilgrims had been infected and would carry that corruption with them if they got off-world.

Murdan, however, was focused on Lubentina's problems and destroying the rebels on his own world. He seized upon Hafiz's revelation that the cultists had massed considerable numbers for an assault on Mount Rama. It had prompted the Cardinal-Governor to issue a command that staggered the colonel.

'You have your orders,' Cardinal-Governor Murdan declared. He leaned back in his chair, sinking into the heavy folds of his robe. His eyes glittered with an almost reptilian intensity as he studied Colonel Hafiz.

The officer rose from his chair, his face grim. When he set his hand down against the table, a visible shiver swept through his arm. 'Palatine Yadav and the Three Hundred and Forty-Fifth are on Mount Rama. The Order of the Sombre Vow, Sister Superior Trishala and all those refugees inside the cathedral...'

Murdan bowed his head, his tone becoming solemn. 'They shall all be martyrs. Their blood shall consecrate the slopes of Mount Rama and purify it of the taint that has descended upon Lubentina.' He waved his thin hand towards Hafiz. 'The Traitor Space Marines are there. So too is this massed concentration of the xenos cultists. If it troubles you, then think on this. You will be annihilating the enemies of the Imperium when you attack. These Iron Warriors are a perversion of the mighty Adeptus Astartes, yet still they are a force of such power that no direct action by your militia could overcome them. Even the Battle Sisters are unequal to their menace. This is the only way to destroy them.'

Minister Kargil listened to the exchange with mounting unease. Murdan's mind was collapsing under the burden of his responsibilities, seeking refuge in the madness of zealotry. Hafiz had to see it, had to realise what was happening. If only the soldier would stand up to him, they might be able to restrain Murdan before he took his convictions too far. 'If we could delay, try at least to get the Order of the Sombre Vow out of there...' Kargil started to say.

The Cardinal-Governor laughed at Kargil's interruption. It was a bitter, cheerless humour. 'The Iron Warriors are monsters, but they aren't stupid. If they see anyone being extracted, then they will know something is coming.'

'I cannot execute these orders,' Hafiz stated. 'You want me to turn my artillery on Mount Rama. These orders are unjust. Unconscionable.'

Murdan returned his attention to Hafiz. 'You are the commander of Lubentina's militia, sworn by oaths of honour and loyalty to obey the orders of your Cardinal-Governor.' He pressed his hand to the jewelled pectoral he wore. 'You cannot disobey me while you command my army.'

Hafiz nodded, the tremble in his outstretched arm intensifying. 'I cannot issue this order. I beg Your Excellency to permit me to resign my commission. Major Darjit can assume my duties and responsibilities.'

Murdan sank deeper into the heavy robes. 'What of your honour, colonel?'

The officer pressed his hand against the holster of his laspistol and looked across the chamber to the door leading into Murdan's private chapel. 'If you will permit me to withdraw, I will see that honour is satisfied.'

The slightest of nods from the Cardinal-Governor dismissed Hafiz. Kargil watched in disbelief as the soldier marched off. He looked around the room at the other councillors. Each man wore the same expression of disbelief and shock. Long moments of silence passed, the quiet taking on an almost tangible atmosphere of despair. It was Kargil who stirred himself from the horror that oppressed them all. He turned back to Murdan, trying one last appeal to reach Lubentina's ruler. 'Palatine Yadav, surely you wouldn't abandon him.'

'Yadav should never have communicated with the astropath,' Murdan mused. 'His disobedience proves him an apostate, but when he becomes a martyr, all will be redeemed.' He looked over at Kargil. 'See that Major Darjit receives my orders. He is now commander of the militia. His first duty will be to reposition the Thirty-Eighth artillery.'

Shuddering, Kargil retreated from the council room. Before he had reached the outer door he heard the crack of Hafiz's laspistol sound from within the chapel. Kargil wouldn't risk Murdan's ire by disobeying his decree. He'd get word to Darjit. And once that was done, he'd see about getting himself as far from Murdan as possible.

Between the cultists, the Iron Warriors and the Cardinal-Governor, Kargil wasn't certain which posed the most danger to his own longevity. He didn't intend to remain to find out.

Bakasur's hulking bodyguards led the magus through the massed ranks of cultists swarming up the slopes of Mount Rama. They had no trouble with the hybrids, the mental vibrations of the magus clearing a path for them through the mob. Even the usual adoration with which the cultists regarded the Voice of the Beast was subdued by Bakasur's psychic influence. He had little time to spare, even to accept the worship of the Great Father's children.

The sound of combat drew Bakasur onwards. Uncertainty, that befuddlement of thinking that was so common to the weak minds of humans, came crawling back into his consciousness. The stubborn mammalian part of his brain dared to wonder if the Great Father had been mistaken to think the Space Marines could be used to any advantage. That they were a terrible, awesome force Bakasur couldn't deny. It was these very qualities that had awakened his concerns. Whatever obstacle he put before them, the Iron Warriors swatted it aside with abominable speed. Even simply trying to delay them had proven a costly endeavour.

Bakasur threw his consciousness forwards, entering the mind of a hybrid ahead of him on the plaza before the cathedral. With the cultist's borrowed flesh, Bakasur quickly assessed the situation. The plaza was an abattoir, filled with the torn remains of refugees and cultists. At one end of the square were the steps of the cathedral and the Great Gate. At the other were the Iron Warriors, armoured giants who butchered anyone who fell under their murderous gaze.

The Chaos sorcerer Cornak had erected a psychic wall around himself, a phantasmal shield Bakasur would expend too much energy trying to pierce. Only the most minor protection had been extended to guard the other Iron Warriors. The magus was able to glance at them with his psychic eye. What he found were grim, fearsome intelligences that cared for little beyond war and revenge. Some possessed more nuance in their thoughts, but ultimately their desires were the same, a twisted image of duty and service that absolved them of any atrocity they perpetrated. The most resolute of them all was their leader. Bakasur focused his powers on their commander, winding through the labyrinth of viciousness and bitterness that swirled in his mind. Like the others, this one clung to notions of honour and duty as a last ember of pride and purpose. But there was more here. Bakasur found a name and title, that of the Warsmith Rhodaan. In him, Bakasur found a monstrous fire of ambition.

Bakasur withdrew his mentality from the hybrid he'd possessed and poured his essence back into his own body. He pondered the things he'd observed. The Great Father was right. These Iron Warriors could be manipulated with care... but only at great cost.

Ahead, far up the street, Bakasur could see the cathedral. He raised his staff, thrusting it towards the structure, pointing its head at the Great Gate. 'Tear down the eidolons of the Golden Tyrant! Pull down the diseased tabernacle of the oppressors! Kill all that stand between you and the ascension that is your birthright!'

The cultists rallied to Bakasur's words and the psychic resonance that echoed through them. Hesitance evaporated, uneasiness was smothered as the religious fury of the cult was fanned into an inferno. Shouts of rage, cries of devotion, shrieks of bloodlust rang out from the more human of the hybrids, while those in whom the genestealer strain was strongest simply rushed ahead in deadly silence. The beleaguered forces in the plaza were bolstered by an inundation of cultists.

Bakasur followed behind the rush, his bodyguards keeping close to him. From the edge of the plaza he could see the swelling mass of cultists firing at the cathedral, firing at the Battle Sisters, firing at the Iron Warriors. He was surprised to see troops in the uniform of the militia just beyond the Chaos Space Marines. They weren't brood brothers, for they lacked the vibration that betokened kinship with the Great Father. Whoever they were, they courted destruction by seeking the attention of the Iron Warriors.

The magus lingered a moment to watch the Space Marines fight. Beset on all sides, attacked by the cultists and the militia, fired on by the Sisters behind the walls of the cathedral, still these giants were unstoppable. An Iron Warrior armed with an autocannon shattered a platoon of soldiers with a sustained burst. One of the invaders played the searing beam of his meltagun into an oncoming clutch of hybrids, transforming them into ash and steam. The horned Rhodaan fired his pistol with grisly precision, pulping the heads of militia squad leaders while using the snarling edge of his chainsword to savage the cultists who charged at him with power pick and shock maul.

It would need the Inheritors themselves to have a real chance of overcoming the Iron Warriors and Bakasur was loath to squander their sacred lives in such fashion. The hybrids would suffice to keep the Space Marines occupied. That was all he required for now.

Bakasur cast his gaze to the corner of the square that stood near the Ladder. A fitting place, indeed, for looming over one of the buildings was a scaffold, built to support the sagging roof of the structure. It seemed unremarkable but this one was special. The labourers who'd raised it had been cultists. Deliberately they'd stretched out the duration of their work, ensuring that the scaffold would be in a specific position.

'Leave them,' Bakasur admonished one of his bodyguards when he took a shot at the Iron Warriors. 'We have no part in this fight. Our place is up there.' He nodded to the scaffold. The aberrant bowed his misshapen head. The hybrid didn't need to understand, he only needed to obey. Urging his guards to haste, Bakasur circled the periphery of the square and advanced to the roof that would provide him entry to the cathedral.

They climbed through the deserted building to the roof

then ascended to the scaffold. From the framework, it was only a small stretch out to the funerary encrustations that bulged from the walls of the cathedral. A pair of cultist tomb-cutters were awaiting Bakasur's arrival, ready to lead the magus to the special crypts that would provide him ingress.

Long had Bakasur been preparing this violation of the cathedral's sanctuary, but with an eye to conquest and occupation. Seizing the cathedral, rededicating it to the Great Father, would have shaken the faith of every Imperial on Lubentina. The presence of the Space Marines put that objective into question. Bakasur would have to be content with a less monumental desecration of the Cult of the Warmason. If securing the cathedral itself was uncertain, then the magus would adjust his plans. There were other objectives he could pursue that would bring glory to the Great Father and sow despair in Imperial hearts. With the Sisters focused on the Iron Warriors and the mass of cultists on their doorstep, they wouldn't know about his trespass until it was already accomplished.

Rhodaan smashed the butt of his pistol into the subhuman cultist's shoulder, forcing the hybrid back onto the churning edge of his chainsword. The whirring teeth ripped into his foe's body, digging through it in a spray of shredded meat and shattered bone. He let the lower half of his bisected enemy slop to the ground but a vicious twist of his arm sent the cultist's torso careening into those who followed after him. The mangled body crashed into them like a boulder, knocking them in every direction. Before one of them could try to rise, Rhodaan plastered them with a burst from his bolt pistol. The explosive shells detonated inside their bodies, reducing them to gory heaps of quivering flesh.

'Iron within! Iron without!' The war cry boomed from the speakers fitted to Captain Uzraal's helm. He sent a beam from his meltagun scorching through the militia squad trying to manoeuvre around Rhodaan's back. The searing energy immolated three men and sent the rest fleeing back down the mountain. Bolter-fire from Brothers Turu and Mahar withered the retreating troops, hurling their carcasses into the ranks of their comrades.

The weak easily became lost to the call of combat. Rhodaan had seen many renegades who decayed into simple killers with no more thought than where they'd find their next victim. Such was not the way of the Iron Warriors. Battle was a tool, an instrument in their arsenal, a thing that was never wanton or directionless. Under Warsmith Andraaz, that distinction had become blurred and the Third Grand Company had become degenerate, several of its leaders becoming murderous sensationalists like Algol the Skintaker.

The weakness had been purged from the Third Grand Company during the Siege of Castellax. Rhodaan wouldn't see it regress while he was warsmith.

Satisfied that the militia advance had been broken, Rhodaan snarled commands to his warriors. 'The gate,' he said. 'Uzraal, Periphetes, blast us an opening in the wall. Brother Gaos, sweep those annoying viragos from the balconies that our comrades may place their charges undisturbed.'

With the other Iron Warriors raking the cultists with bursts from their bolters and the odd frag grenade, a path was opened for Uzraal and Periphetes to rush the steps.

Before either Space Marine could move, the voice of Cornak called out both across the vox and in their minds.

'Hold them back, warsmith,' Cornak advised. 'Something is coming!' The sorcerer was staring up into the sky, the psychic shell he'd raised around himself crackling as las-bolts and bullets sought to strike him. Abruptly he lowered his head and drew his staff close against his chest. The arcane shield flared into visibility, intensifying until it became a translucent dome around him.

Rhodaan's sharp ears caught the familiar whine that sounded overhead. 'Artillery,' he warned the Iron Warriors. The Space Marines braced themselves while keeping their weapons at the ready. Only such superhuman soldiers would be brazen enough to defy the coming barrage, looking to capitalise on the havoc it would wreak against their enemies. Running, hiding – these were things for lesser beings. The Iron Warriors would weather the storm right where they stood.

The shells came arcing down, smashing into the buildings surrounding the square, shearing into the plaza itself. Structures exploded under the impact, casting off great clouds of debris and smoke. The worst hit toppled against their neighbours, smashing down into a jumbled confusion of mangled architecture. Packs of hybrid cultists were buried beneath the collapsing structures while others were obliterated by the direct impact of the shells. Some of the ordnance even fell where the militia had taken position, exterminating entire squads in clouds of flame and dust. The carnage drove such refugees as had remained alive from their places of concealment. Confused and shocked by the bombardment, the cultists lashed out at the fleeing pilgrims.

The optics in Rhodaan's helmet compensated for the swirling smoke and dust, piercing the carnage with a battery of filters and visual enhancements. He could see some of the shots banging against the cathedral itself. Swathes of barnacle-like tombs were ripped from their moorings and sent crashing earthwards. Great sheets of masonry came sliding away, a cascade of broken statuary and savaged frescos that spilled into the streets beyond. The destruction surprised him. He knew the foolish reverence with which flesh regarded the False Emperor and those of his henchmen they'd made over into saints. Either the artillery had misjudged their aim or else they were unusually irreverent.

As the barrage intensified, Rhodaan was forced to reappraise his estimation. The amount of ordnance pelting the summit was too great, the rapidity of the barrage too intense. It was hitting in every direction, not focused upon one end of the plaza or one section of the peak. The artillery didn't care about the cathedral or any of their own people on Mount Rama. Their objective was simply to annihilate everything, be it friend or foe. It was a pragmatism that Rhodaan would have found admirable if it wasn't inconvenient to him. More so because he now understood how futile those charges would have been when it came to forcing an opening.

'Periphetes! On me,' Captain Uzraal shouted, his words standing clear across the vox as the audio dampeners in the helmets dulled the thunder of the artillery. 'We'll use the barrage to cover our approach.'

'The plan is aborted,' Rhodaan told Uzraal. 'Look at the cathedral again. Look at what the shells destroy and what they can't harm.'

'Warsmith, they've hit the building several times but they can't break through the walls,' Brother Gaos hissed, surprise in his tone.

Rhodaan could hear similar expressions from the rest of his Iron Warriors. All except Cornak. Perhaps the sorcerer had known something of the truth even before the barrage. It was another subject Rhodaan would discuss with him at a more auspicious time. For now he regarded the explosions that crumbled the facade but left the cathedral intact. The Cult of the Warmason, and a cathedral that might have been designed according to Vadok Singh's plans. The fortifications he'd built on Terra had defied everything the Chaos Legions could hurl against them. Small wonder then that something built to honour him could endure this barrage.

'How will we force the gate?' Uzraal wondered.

The barrage was intensifying. All but the most virulent of the cultists had gone to ground, sheltering amid the rubble or ducking into the craters, waiting for the artillery to relent. Others tried to pick their way through the bedlam. Their alien eyes made navigating through the smoke and dust an easy matter, but it availed them little. The Iron Warriors had lost none of their vigilance, even with shells raining down around them. Even as bits of shrapnel and debris glanced off their power armour, the Space Marines greeted the creeping hybrids with the chatter of bolters. Purple-clad cultists who'd come slinking out from the smoke were knocked down again by the punishing fire of the Iron Warriors.

It was in looking back at the militia soldiers that Rhodaan found an answer to Uzraal's question. One wall had spilled out into the square, affording the warsmith a view of stone steps leading down into the mountain.

'Forget the gate,' Rhodaan declared. The steps leading down made him think what could be below. He'd sacked enough temples devoted to the False Emperor over the course of the Long War to know they always had some sort of postern gate secreted away, a route by which cowardly priests could flee their doomed sanctuaries. An exit that could quickly be made into an entrance. All it needed was the right way to find it. He looked over at Cornak. It was time to use the sorcerer's arcane gifts, whatever toll they took on him. 'I expect to force a quicker way inside.'

Commanding his Iron Warriors to follow him, Rhodaan led them back across the square. The ground shook beneath their feet as the barrage continued its demolition of the area. Bands of cultists sprang up to impede their trek only to be crushed beneath a fusillade of fire. Some three-armed hybrid wearing the tatters of an acolyte's habit lunged at Cornak. The sorcerer's bolt pistol raked across the rebel's skull. An entire pack of gun-toting fanatics came afoul of Gaos' autocannon, their bodies left in a gory mash at the bottom of a crater.

Then the Iron Warriors were descending the steps. A few militia stragglers emerged from the gloom. One of them was cleft apart by Rhodaan's chainsword, the other crumpled as Periphetes exploded his belly with a bolter shell. The warsmith pointed his sword at the steps. 'Periphetes, lead the way. Uzraal, close the door behind us.'

As the Iron Warriors marched into the subterranean shadows, Captain Uzraal lingered near the opening. A blast from his meltagun brought the roof crashing down, sealing the entrance with a mass of fused rockcrete rubble.

Rhodaan drew Cornak aside. 'It is time to put your powers at my service, sorcerer.'

'What is your command, warsmith?' Cornak asked.

'The Imperial dogs will have a door hidden away, some secret route inside the cathedral. It will be buried somewhere in the mountain. Find it for me,' Rhodaan ordered.

Cornak clenched his staff tight, the talismans affixed to it vibrating as he invoked the dread forces that were at his call. 'This is a vast network of catacombs,' he said. 'It will need time to sift through this maze. It would be easier to find someone who knows the way already.'

Rhodaan glared at the sorcerer. 'Find them.'

'I already have,' Cornak reported. 'And he isn't far away.'

Trishala felt the walls of the Warmason's Cathedral shake as the artillery barrage rained down on it. The corridors and halls were filled with the screams of terrified refugees, convinced that the entire temple was going to be demolished around them. Trishala and the Sisters knew better, as did the acolytes who moved among the people and tried to ease their fears. The cathedral had been built to the standards of Vadok Singh. It could withstand any storm, even one hurled against it by man.

No, it wasn't concern that the cathedral would be destroyed that vexed Trishala. What bothered her was why Mount Rama had been targeted. Who'd ordered this attack and why? Certainly there'd been no warning voxed to them by Colonel Hafiz or Cardinal-Governor Murdan. If Palatine Yadav had been aware of such a plot then why should he have taken such pains to alert them to the Chaos Space Marines when a few moments later the barrage would begin?

Thinking of Yadav, Trishala considered the last vox communication from the palatine. The barrage had driven him and forty surviving soldiers down into the catacombs beneath Mount Rama. He was going to bring the survivors in through the underground Mourning Door. It was the only route into the cathedral that wouldn't be closed off by the siege-plates. Only a handful of the priesthood knew of the door's existence. Yadav was certain he could get inside without the enemy discovering his intentions.

As another artillery barrage set the walls shaking, Trishala prayed the palatine was right.

CHAPTER XI

The thunderous barrage unleashed by Lubentina's militia against Mount Rama continued to rain down on the summit, obliterating the surrounding structures and filling the cathedral with tremulous booms as shells slammed against the building's metal hull. Anxious prayers and quaking psalms rose from the masses of refugees as the cathedral's clergy strove to placate their fear. Sobs and screams echoed from those regions where there was no acolyte to appease the frightened laity.

Across the vox, Trishala and Kashibai could hear a sound that shook them far more than the artillery turned against them. Over the secured channel that only those of rank within the Order of the Sombre Vow had access to, came the voice of the man who was senior even to the Sister Superior.

'I have taken to the catacombs,' Palatine Yadav's tone was agitated, his words clipped and hurried. 'It is my fear that we've been followed down into the passageways. The soldiers with me report hearing the sound of something moving in the distance.'

Kashibai studied Trishala's face, read the grim expression in her eyes, the resolute set to her jaw. 'You don't mean to abandon the palatine?' she asked.

Trishala shook her head. 'Our duty, our sacred vow, is to guard the relics of Vadok Singh. We protect the Warmason's Casket and the Shroud of Singh.' She gestured at the Sisters around them in the narthex, weapons ready to defend the Great Gate should it somehow be breached. 'Holding the cathedral is a part of executing that duty. Detaching a squad of Battle Sisters for a reckless rescue mission isn't.'

'If not for the palatine, we would have welcomed Chaos itself into these halls,' Kashibai pointed out. 'He has risked much for the people of Lubentina. Even if you don't feel obligated to help him because he is your superior, surely you can't turn aside from one who has saved us all from disaster.' She could see just a hint of softening in Trishala's eyes. While that appeal to her sentiment was open, Kashibai pressed her cause. 'We have to at least try, or it will be a stain on the Order's honour, turning our backs on a palatine. Just a small force, warriors you can spare without weakening the perimeter.'

Trishala shook her head. 'Who can I spare? With Debdan's troops proving traitor, I need every Sister patrolling the corridors and seeking out any enemies they let slip inside. It is dire enough that I have only the frateris militia to watch the gate.'

'But every Sister isn't committed to that role,' Kashibai pointed out.

'We have no reserves left,' Trishala said. 'After Debdan's treachery, every patrol has had to be strengthened. We know at least one genestealer is unaccounted for, but there's no saying how many more the brood brothers let inside.'

'But you haven't,' Kashibai persisted. 'There are still the Sisters guarding the relics in the sanctuary.' She held up her hand, trying to forestall the dismissal she knew was on Trishala's tongue. 'You said it yourself. By holding the walls, keeping the enemy from entering the cathedral, we protect the relics. So long as you hold the perimeter then our duty is honoured. The guards can be withdrawn, committed to posts where they can be active...'

Trishala motioned for Kashibai to be quiet. She needed a moment to settle the turmoil in her mind. On the one hand there was the sacred obligation entrusted to her, to protect the Warmason's Casket. Against that had to be weighed her loyalty to Palatine Yadav, her duty to him as commander of the Adepta Sororitas convent. Kashibai's proposal was trying to let her have it both ways. To continue protecting the relics while also doing right by Yadav. It was a temptation Trishala found herself incapable of resisting. Even so, she was judicious about what resources she would commit to the endeavour.

'Try to reach the palatine,' Trishala said. 'You can take Sister Bashir's squad. If you head down through the crypts, you will find the tomb of Karim Das. Behind the casket there is a panel that can be opened and admit you to the catacombs. God-Emperor willing, you can be back in before the xenos learn you're outside.' She could see the uneasiness on Kashibai's face. It was no mystery why she was troubled. 'One squad is all I'm willing to detach from guarding the relics. They'll be enough. Your mission is one of rescue, not battle.'

'What if the enemy reaches the palatine before we do?' Kashibai asked.

Yadav's words crackled across the vox. 'If they have already found me you must count me as lost. I have only thirty-four men with me, not enough to resist more than a token force. There is a time for valour, and a time to recognise when a fight is hopeless.'

'If the enemies following you are cultists, my Sisters can still rescue you,' Trishala stated. 'But if your pursuers are Chaos Space Marines then it would need more Sisters than I can spare to overcome them.' She looked over at Kashibai. 'There is no shame in recognising the fact, unpalatable as it might be.'

Kashibai bowed her head. 'Understood, Sister Superior. If the Traitors reach the palatine before we do, then we are to withdraw.'

'I know you, Sister,' Trishala told Kashibai. 'Don't let your compassion move you to undue risk. Now hasten, gather Sister Bashir's warriors before I change my mind.'

As she watched Kashibai hurry away, Trishala reflected that it was even more important to keep the enemy from breaking through now that the guard in the sanctuary had been reduced. She prayed the Sisters left would be enough to deal with cultists or xenos they'd missed on their patrols.

The Battle Sisters simply couldn't afford to let any enemies get a foothold inside the cathedral.

It was mammalian weakness that provoked the sense of relief Bakasur felt when the interior wall of the tomb crumbled and exposed the round gash that had been torn from the roof of the catacombs. He knew that the psychic energies his brain projected would distort a stray artillery shell ever so slightly, such that its fury should descend where it wouldn't threaten the magus. Still, that impractical human residue felt a twinge of fear with every incoming shot. Logic was a thing that was simply at variance with the human mentality. Bakasur regretted the traces that blighted his biology even as he was thankful that the Great Father's bloodline had advanced him far beyond the limitations of such emotion-driven creatures.

As the magus and his bodyguards slipped through the hollowed tomb they encountered the Inheritors who'd laboured so long to prepare this entrance for them. The genestealers clustered about the bone-lined passageway beneath the cathedral. Beyond them could be dimly seen the glow of lights and the smooth walls of the crypts of the cathedral proper. Even the razored claws of Inheritors had found ripping through the reinforced ferrocrete of the crypt walls an arduous task. Persistence and complete obedience to the Great Father had kept them at their work. Aid from the genestealers already on the other side made the task much quicker. Just as the Inheritor Captain Debdan's men had allowed to slip inside had prepared the way for the pure-strains to enter, so had they prepared the way for Bakasur's arrival.

Stepping into the hall, Bakasur could feel the extreme age of the cathedral rushing down on him. The dust of millennia clinging to the walls had thickened into a stony concentration, a patina of neglect that caked the floor to a depth of several centimetres. Hidden behind the maze of chapels and hallways, the oldest catacombs had been forgotten by the acolytes. They had been sealed away, cut off from the cathedral's chambers. Isolated until they were rediscovered by the cultists, until the claws of genestealers dug through them to rejoin them to the crypts beneath the Warmason's Cathedral.

Bakasur brushed his hand across the encrustation, feeling it flake beneath his touch. As it crumbled away, the residue of a conduit was revealed, the petrified remains of a purity seal still clinging to it. Mankind had endured for so long, he reflected, yet in all that time they'd only become weaker and more decadent. They'd lost vibrancy and direction, allowed themselves to be consumed by distractions and deceits. Their ambitions had been shackled to monolithic traditions and cyclopean diktats. Humans had reached their limit. It was time for them to be swept aside, to vanish into the night and make way for those who would inherit.

The magus closed his eyes, reaching out with his mind, casting his mentality far from the confines of his body. Through the storm of artillery he could see the cultists persecuting the siege on the Great Gate. He could feel the Sisters of Battle and the desecrater Trishala concentrated on patrolling the corridors, ready to lash out at the first enemy they found. His psychic coils flowed out across the catacombs. He noted the presence of Palatine Yadav and a handful of soldiers trying to make their way to the cathedral from below. The Chaos Space Marines were close behind, soon to overtake the retreating cleric. The sorcerer Cornak kept his mind shielded from Bakasur's awareness, but the magus could read the determination of the others. Warsmith Rhodaan intended to force Yadav to expose the way into the cathedral. The intention was more than mere possibility – to the Iron Warriors it was a certainty.

The Inheritors drew aside as Bakasur entered the cathedral. From a side passage, several dishevelled refugees and acolytes stepped into view. All were in a weakened state, their bodies exhibiting injuries both new and old. In one respect, however, they were all alike. On each of them was the fresh brand left by a genestealer's ovipositor.

Raising his hand in a placating gesture, Bakasur reached out to one of the initiates. His palm hovered just above the acolyte's forehead. Deftly, with the delicacy only practice could instil, he drew from the man's mind the network of memories he needed to consult. He could see Trishala ordering all those injured by the cultists brought down into the crypts and sequestered. He felt the cold of the underground, the dark isolation. He heard that moment when the genestealers came and slaughtered the frateris militia guarding the crypts. He felt the stab of the ovipositor as the Inheritors broke down the doors and brought both freedom and enlightenment to the captives. Some tried to fight, the Sisters who'd been sequestered with the others among them. These found only the freedom within death.

Bakasur delved past the fresh surface memories. In exploring the deeper thought, the magus observed the maze of passages and chambers the acolyte had learned during his years of service in the cathedral. The direct perspective, unfiltered and undiminished, let Bakasur experience the familiarity of routine with a visceral intimacy.

A cold smile flickered on Bakasur's face. He knew now the route by which they would reach the sanctuary, unchallenged and unobserved.

* * *

The explosion ripped through the winding passageway, knocking bits of bone and ferrocrete from the walls. A gritty smog came billowing up the corridor, clattering against the ceramite of Rhodaan's power armour. The optics of his helm flickered as they adjusted the filters to compensate for the disturbance of his vision. The warsmith swung his horned head around, glancing over his Space Marines. The catacombs within Mount Rama had been built for the use of mortals, not the Iron Warriors. The bulk of the armoured giants filled the tunnel entirely, forcing them to advance in single file. Their pauldrons scraped against the morbid walls, sometimes ripping femurs and vertebrae from their settings. Their mass crushed the ribcages that were interlaced across the floor, pulverising them to jagged splinters. Their helms gouged the grinning skulls that stared down from the ceiling, stripping away teeth and jaws.

Tens of thousands of Lubentina's populace had been entombed just along the stretch Rhodaan had already traversed. There might be millions more, for there was no estimating the extent of the catacombs. Or how much of them the Iron Warriors would have to penetrate before the priest was in their hands. He would be the key, that slave of the False Emperor. He was the one who would lead Rhodaan to the door and set the Iron Warriors on the last leg of their hunt.

Periphetes came marching out of the gritty plume of dust and smoke. 'The way ahead is collapsed,' he reported. 'The barrage brought the roof down.' He pointed at the ceiling overhead. As he did, Rhodaan noted that Periphetes' armour had been cracked in places by the blast.

Rhodaan turned towards Cornak. 'Well, hexmaster, do your spells tell you of a way around the collapse?'

'Perhaps we're getting close to the priest, Dread Lord,' Gaos said. 'Flesh is cowardly when pressed too close. They may have voxed their artillerists to drop that salvo right on top of their position. The nearer we get, the more desperate they'll be to stop us.' He caressed the barrels of his autocannon. 'As though they can.'

Rhodaan shared Gaos' appreciation of the chances the priest and his entourage had once the Iron Warriors reached them. It wasn't a question of crushing them, only a matter of when, of how much effort they would need to invest in the enterprise. The delay was an annoyance to Rhodaan. He turned towards Cornak. 'This rat hunt becomes tiresome. I would see an end to it.'

'Caution, warsmith,' Cornak advised. 'Haste has collapsed many a victory into defeat.'

'Leave sermons to the Word Bearers,' Rhodaan snarled. 'It was you who brought this scheme to me, that the Third Grand Company should pay honour to Perturabo. My warriors have done their part, and now it is time for our sorcerer to do his.' He pointed his chainsword at the tunnel ahead. 'Draw upon your magic. Clear the way for us and sniff out this priest's hiding place.'

'You know the threat that hovers over me... over us all,' Cornak hastily corrected himself. 'The doom I have foreseen should this xenos psyker...'

Rhodaan glowered at the sorcerer. 'Iron within. Iron without,' he hissed. 'Have you forgotten the meaning of those words? There is no place for weakness among us. Are you weak, Brother Cornak? Does fear of this prophecy make you unfit to be among us?'

'It was I who told you of the relic,' Cornak said. 'My magic that brought you this far.'

Rhodaan activated his chainsword, letting the teeth whir into murderous life. 'What have you done for me lately?' he mused. 'I give you a choice, sorcerer. Use your sorcery for me or against me. Either way you will become vulnerable to this xenos witch you fear.'

Cornak's fingers curled more tightly around the staff he carried, but it was the only display of anger he allowed himself. When he spoke, it was in a respectful and resigned voice. 'As you will, warsmith.' The sorcerer fell to one knee, scratching a cabalistic sign in the floor. He held the head of his staff over the mark while slithering, inhuman words dripped off his tongue. A flare of bilious green light flashed, the sound of a roaring tempest bellowed, the stink of sulphur rose.

'The way is clear to the left,' Cornak declared, exhaustion now colouring his tone. 'A passage that circles around the cave-in and will intersect with the route the priest has taken.' He looked up from the still glowing mark he'd drawn upon the floor and stared at Rhodaan.

Rhodaan nodded and returned his chainsword to an idle setting. 'Lead the way, Brother Cornak. Trust is a luxury in short supply on Castellax.'

Cornak didn't protest as he took point and marched further into the gloom of the catacombs. He knew there was only so much defiance Rhodaan would tolerate before it could no longer be indulged. The warsmith's plans would be much easier with Cornak's magic to draw on, but that didn't mean he wasn't prepared to go on without the benefit of sorcery.

* * *

The black passages and corridors through which Cornak led the Iron Warriors opened into a larger, cavern-like chamber. Great pillars of fused bone supported the vaulted ceiling overhead while stone icons rested in niches cut into the walls. Doorways yawned in the face of the wall opposite the passage the Space Marines had been following, dark openings that each sported a golden plate above the lintel and a bronzed lantern bolted to the wall beside it. Across the stretch of the chamber, itself forty metres in length, there were no less than a dozen such doorways.

As the Iron Warriors stepped into the funerary chamber, their attention shifted from the darkened doorways to the tunnels that gaped at either end of the span. Rhodaan stared at the floor, noting that the dust had been disturbed, swept aside recently. Someone had been here and tried to obscure their presence. In that they'd failed, all they'd managed was to conceal their numbers.

'Did they go to the left or right?' Uzraal asked Rhodaan, noting the same signs.

Rhodaan's gaze shifted, looking towards the darkened doorways ahead. The optics in his helmet picked out the splotches of blood that stained the threshold of one opening. Someone hurt had come through here recently.

'Neither,' Rhodaan said. 'Though they mean us to think they have. Our prey is hiding in the rooms beyond those openings ahead of us.'

'The priest,' Cornak declared.

'Let's find out,' Rhodaan decided. He aimed his bolt pistol at one blood-stained doorway, sending a burst into the darkness. When there was no response, he shifted his aim to another opening. This time a cry of horror echoed from the room beyond as some lurker panicked or was hit. An instant later a stream of fire came blasting out from three of the openings. The Space Marines could see tan-uniformed soldiers leaning out from behind the doorways to loose shots at them.

The Iron Warriors surged forwards. Bolters snarled as they fired into the shadows, returning the shots levelled at them by Yadav's soldiers. A few screams rang out, grisly testament to the savagery of Rhodaan's Space Marines.

Suddenly the roar of boltguns intensified, the gunfire of the Space Marines returned in kind from the darkened doorways. Turu staggered back, one pauldron smoking where a shell had pierced it, one vambrace shattered where a high-impact round had splintered the ceramite. The other Iron Warriors spread out, wariness replacing contempt for their enemy. Rhodaan could see black-armoured shapes clustered about the marble doorway where he'd spotted the blood. It was from them that the heavy fire had come. Yadav had been reinforced, but his new protectors had been cagey enough to bide their time, to try to gull the Iron Warriors into thinking they faced only a rabble of common flesh.

Rhodaan looked aside at Cornak, recalling the sorcerer's prediction that the priest wasn't alone. The vagaries of his divinations were going to get someone killed. But perhaps that was the intention.

'Sororitas,' Uzraal spat, aiming his meltagun towards the marble doorway.

Rhodaan set a restraining hand on the captain's weapon.

'I still want the priest alive,' the warsmith warned. The admonition carried across the vox to every Iron Warrior in his command.

'And the others?' Uzraal asked.

Rhodaan peeled off a burst from his bolt pistol, the explosive rounds slamming into one of the black-armoured women as she leaned out from the edge of the doorway. Her body was flung back, hurled into the shadowy interior of the crypt.

'I only need the priest,' Rhodaan said. 'Kill everything else.'

The thunder of artillery slackened after half an hour. Trishala could only guess at the reason.

The lessening of the barrage brought such an influx of hybrids swarming out from the devastation of Mount Rama that Trishala found herself praying the guns would resume their earlier violence. Thousands of cultists draped in purple and crimson came rushing up the steps, converging on the cathedral faster than the Sisters at the firing apertures could shoot them down. The mob brought plasma guns and mining lasers up against the door, striving to burn a hole through its metal frame. Other bands of cultists employed similar tactics against the side doors and windows, burning through the outer shutters only to find the immense siege-plates lying behind. Gangs armed with picks and mauls climbed up onto the balconies, hammering away at the doors. It would need stronger measures to get through the heavy armaplas sheets. Trishala watched the motley throng with trepidation, recalling only too clearly the destruction wrought by the blasting charges they'd used to obliterate the perimeter at the base of the mountain. Even the Great Gate might not withstand such an attack. The rebels had shown evidence that they wanted the cathedral intact, but she couldn't depend on their plans not having changed.

From the firing apertures nearest the gate, Sisters with flamers sent sheets of fire pouring into the xenos mob, plasteel baffles preventing a backwash from spilling into the narthex. Frateris militia posted at other embrasures knocked cultists from the balconies with lasguns and shotguns. Grenades tumbled from the open mouths of gargoyles as acolytes pushed explosives out of their hollowed necks.

Like a rolling tide the cult was driven back only to come rushing in again. The ground was strewn with their dead and dying, yet still the fanatics came. Trishala wondered that they were so eager to accept such casualties. Throughout their rebellion, the xenos had exhibited a murderous cunning and subtlety. Was it zealotry that drove them to this extreme, stirred them to throw themselves again and again into the withering fire of the Battle Sisters? Or was there something more, something she'd failed to spot?

The temptation to send patrols through the cathedral nagged at Trishala's mind. She needed every fighter here, keeping the hybrids away from the Great Gate. The only Sisters not committed to that role were those posted to the sanctuary guarding the Warmason's Casket and theirs was a duty Trishala wouldn't compromise any more than she already had. She regretted hearkening to Kashibai's arguments and allowing Bashir's squad to go down into the catacombs with her. She needed them here.

The xenos were up to something, and it wasn't just to see if the Sisters would run out of ammunition. Trishala racked her brain trying to figure out what that purpose was, where the real attack would come from. Only when she had some clear idea, only then could she justify withdrawing any of her warriors from the outer defences. One of those blasting charges and the walls would be breached. She had to use every resource to prevent that.

It was that fact that troubled Trishala the most. Because she felt they were exactly where the cultists wanted them to be.

'God-Emperor help us,' Kashibai prayed as the roar of bolters swelled around her. The noble's tomb into which the Sisters had carried Palatine Yadav reverberated with the din of battle. When Kashibai reached Yadav, she'd found him injured from the fighting in the plaza. So too were some of the soldiers in his retinue. It had been her decision to take to the tombs leading off from the Rakesh Hall. If the rebels were following Yadav then the Sisters and soldiers could ambush them when they came into the hall and started down the false trail they'd laid.

Only the enemy pursuing Yadav wasn't a mob of cultists but a warband of Chaos Space Marines!

The musty gloom of the tomb was broken by the muzzle flashes from the Sisters' bolters and the bright glow of militia lasguns. Each burst of light threw eerie shadows over the murals painted across the stone walls and cast an uncanny luminance about the great crystal sepulchre at the centre of the room. The once flawless coffin, grown in a titanium mould by the highest arts of the tomb-cutters, was now pitted and gouged by the shots that had struck it. A jagged crack shivered across its side where Sister Bashir had been hurled against it after she'd been hit by a burst from the Iron Warriors. Her body lay crumpled on the floor, a malfunctioning servo in her left leg causing the limb to twitch with a ghastly semblance of life even though her chest had been ripped in half.

Kashibai rose from behind the sepulchre and blasted away with her boltgun. The shots raked the fearsome giants that were closing on the crypt. Her fire did nothing to stem their advance, only bringing a grinding roar from the autocannon one of the monsters carried. The stream of bullets sliced through the marble doorway, driving splinters into the face of the soldier who crouched there. The injured man toppled out from his cover, falling full into the lethal stream. His body flailed while the bullets tore him apart.

'Iron within! Iron without!' one of the Traitor Space Marines bellowed. The next instant there was a bloom of foul black smoke that spilled across the chamber. It was swiftly followed by another and still another. The Iron Warriors were laying down a veil of smoke to obscure their advance. Vainly the surviving soldiers and the Sisters loosed a fusillade into the swirling cloud. It was difficult enough to bring down the giants when they were visible. Unseen, the monsters were as good as invulnerable.

'God-Emperor protect us,' Palatine Yadav groaned from the far corner of the crypt. The priest's despairing utterance was like a blast of polar wind, chilling the Battle Sisters. If even the palatine had lost heart, what hope did any of them have?

Kashibai called them back to their senses. 'To reach us, they have to come to us,' she assured them. She knew there was no chance of outfighting the Chaos Space Marines. They had to out-think the monsters, lure them into overconfidence. Play upon their ancient hate and their superhuman arrogance.

Heartbeats stretched away into seconds, yet still the expected detonation failed to occur. The violence of the traitors' bolters persisted unabated, ploughing the head from the shoulders of one trooper and ripping a second apart at the spine. Screams rose from the other tombs as the soldiers posted there likewise fell victim to the oncoming Space Marines.

A blinding flare of light, a deafening roar of sound ripped through the crypt. The sensors in Kashibai's helmet dulled the impact of the assault, permitting her a hazy view of the crypt and an impression of sound beyond the ringing in her ears. She could see the figures of militia soldiers staggering about in confused agony, clutching at their heads and pawing at their eyes. The Iron Warriors cut down the disoriented men with a ruthless storm of gunfire. The blinding flash had come from a grenade thrown into the crypt by their enemy.

Marching in from the swirling smoke came the hulking Iron Warriors. Sister Sarala trained her bolter on the leading Space Marine, but before she could fire she was thrown back by a burst of fire that crunched through her breastplate and mutilated the body within. Sister Vimala fared slightly better, peeling off a shot that smashed the forearm of a looming Traitor Space Marine. He staggered back, dark blood jetting for a moment from his mangled limb before the chemical coagulants in his veins sealed the injury. Before she could manage another shot Vimala was torn in half by a blast from the autocannon carried by another Iron Warrior.

Kashibai and the last of Bashir's squad, Sister Ankita, rushed out from their cover, converging upon the horned Chaos Space Marine who commanded the others. Ankita's rush ended with a butchering sweep of the Iron Warrior's chainsword, the mangled ruin of her body strewn across the floor. At the same time, the giant met Kashibai's charge, seizing hold of her shoulder. As though her armoured weight was nothing to him, he wrenched her off the ground, holding her suspended in the air for an instant before flinging her against the wall. Stone splintered under the vicious impact, her helmet cracked and somewhere in her chest she could feel something splinter. Kashibai collapsed to the floor, sprawled upon the wreckage of her late comrades.

The rattle of bolters persisted a few moments longer as the Iron Warriors completed their massacre of the local militia in the other tombs. Kashibai struggled to rise but the Chaos Space Marine's attack had savaged her armour. No power flowed into the servo motors, leaving the heavy ceramite plates an inert bulk that weighed her down. Weakened by her injuries, Kashibai found herself unable to move. All she could do was watch helplessly as the traitors stalked through the carnage they'd unleashed.

Brother Mahar gestured with his weapon at the corner of the crypt. 'Warsmith Rhodaan, the priest.'

Rhodaan turned from the crystal sepulchre and stared into the corner of the tomb. Imperiously he marched across the litter of bodies and approached the cleric. He towered over Yadav, clutching him by the top of his skull and lifting him off the floor. The fingers of his gauntlet dug into the man's flesh, setting trickles of blood running down his face.

'The flesh can scream if it likes,' Rhodaan growled. 'The False Emperor can't help you now. He never could.'

Somehow Yadav summoned the courage to spit into

the beaked mask of the Chaos Space Marine's helmet. The defiance only amused the monster.

'The flesh thinks it can die quickly,' Rhodaan mocked. 'Perhaps, if it tells me what I want to know. I make no promises to flesh.' His fingers tightened and Yadav's face contorted in agony. 'It retreated into these catacombs with a purpose. There's another way into the cathedral, isn't there? If it wants the pain to stop, tell me the way.'

Again, Yadav fought through his anguish to glower at his captor.

'No need to question the flesh further, Dread Lord.' Cornak moved to join Rhodaan. 'He obligingly thought about what you wanted the moment you asked it.' The giant tapped a finger against the side of his helmet. 'Now that information is here. I know the way.'

Rhodaan turned his head and stared at the sorcerer. 'You are certain, Cornak?'

The sorcerer laughed cruelly. 'The mental anguish he feels now tells me his thoughts were true. Shame and guilt come quickly to those of limited perspective.' He brushed the butt of his staff against the Sororitas draped across the sepulchre, spilling the body to the ground. 'There is a way up into the cathedral. An entrance down in the roots of the building.'

'Then we are done here,' Rhodaan declared. His grip tightened about Yadav's head, crushing his skull into fragments. A fling of his hand cast the priest's quivering body into the ruined sarcophagus.

'This is as far as the priest was able to get,' Cornak stated. 'There is a safeguard at the entrance itself, however. Something he intended those already inside to disable for him.'

Rhodaan nodded. 'I would expect as much. It won't

keep us from getting inside. You've done well, hexmaster. I free you to raise your protective shields. Hide yourself from this xenos witch of your prophecy. Soon the Warmason's Casket will be mine and we can all be quit of this sorry little world.'

One by one, the Chaos Space Marines withdrew from the crypt. Kashibai listened to the sound of their boots crunching across the catacombs. Only when she couldn't hear it anymore did she try speaking into the vox. The Iron Warriors might still hear her or their sorcerer might discover her through his witchcraft, but by then she hoped to give warning to Trishala. She had to alert the Sisters that the Iron Warriors were coming.

All that rewarded her efforts was a crackle of white noise. Kashibai's impact against the wall had damaged the vox. She couldn't transmit to the cathedral.

The guides he chose from among the enlightened acolytes led Bakasur up through the heart of the cathedral. The retinue of hybrids and pure-strains that accompanied the magus made good time as they rushed through service corridors and maintenance halls. There were few who saw the cultists as they rose up through the cathedral. Those few were quickly silenced by genestealer claws and the psychic vibrations of Bakasur's mind.

At last, the magus was near his goal. The sanctuary to which Trishala had ordered all the relics of the Warmason gathered. It was true enough that she'd left guards to watch over the Celestial Chapel, but hardly enough to disrupt Bakasur's plans.

Dutiful, loyal in the extreme, utterly devoted to their master, Bakasur's hybrid bodyguards didn't hesitate when the magus ordered them to attack. The twisted aberrants stormed the Celestial Chapel, crashing through the towering doors, flinging their gilded panels inwards. As the panels came down, the cultists opened fire, defiling the pristine environs of the temple with blasts of plasma and the boom of shotguns. Alabaster pillars were blackened, elegantly carved pews were splintered. Rich carpets and lavish hangings were trampled and shredded by the rushing cultists.

The few acolytes present cried out in horror, shaken more by this desecration of the sanctuary than a true appreciation of their own peril. One acolyte evaporated in a burst of plasma, a second had his face extinguished by the blast of a shotgun. A score of black-armoured Sisters turned their zealous fury against Bakasur's guards, mowing them down with merciless disdain.

It was a necessary diversion. Much as those hordes throwing themselves upon the gate and thereby commanding the attention of the cathedral's guardians, so the sacrifice of his bodyguards distracted the defenders of the sanctuary. While the Sisters were cutting down the hybrids, the real thrust came.

Out of ventilation shafts and up from maintenance pits, the Inheritors came. The genestealers were upon the Sisters before they were even aware of this new horror. Scything claws raked across power armour, shearing through the flesh and bone beneath. Screams drowned out the bark of bolters as the marauding aliens mutilated their prey.

As complete as the slaughter of Bakasur's bodyguard had been, the massacre of the Sisters was equally thorough. It was over in a matter of minutes. The sanctuary was reduced to a shambles, its holiness now stained with the blood and offal of its guardians. Striding through the carnage, Bakasur entered the Celestial Chapel.

When Bakasur reached the middle of the sanctuary, the foremost genestealer hissed and lowered its gaze. The Inheritor led him through the havoc, prowling to the curtained alcoves beyond the altar. A shimmering haze surrounded each niche, a somehow menacing weave of distortion. The magus opened his awareness, drawing in the entirety of his surroundings and not merely what could be seen with his eyes.

Bakasur pointed to one of the pillars that rose beside the altar. The genestealer sprang at it, gouging the marble with a sweep of its claws. The dextrous, hand-like members reached into the exposed cavity, tearing at the machinery concealed within. As fragments of wire and pipe came spilling out of the pillar the haze surrounding the alcoves dissipated.

Sweeping his hand, the magus tore down the curtains. The exposed alcoves now displayed their hidden treasures. Bakasur had little interest in the jumble of religious relics the Sisters had brought from elsewhere and deposited in the sanctuary. Nor did he have any use for the artefacts of Vadok Singh that had always belonged here. There was one object and one object alone that he wanted.

Resting upon a pedestal of shiny obsidian, the Warmason's Casket was a metre long and half as wide. Precious metals and invaluable gems adorned its surface, ancient designs of tribal whorls writhed across its length. Depicted upon its lid was a representation of the Emperor crafted from some luminescent stone that had the shine of pearl and the vibrancy of moonlight.

This was the relic the Sisters had sealed away behind

force fields and firing lines. Bakasur thought again of the Great Father's design, his intention to harness the Iron Warriors and use them to ensure the cult's victory. They had yet to secure the cathedral, but with the Warmason's Casket in their possession they would break the soul of their enemies. This affront to the Imperial Creed would weaken them, leave them ripe for true wisdom and the glories of the Great Father. What had seemed dangerous to him once now filled him with awe. For once he forgot himself and when he motioned the genestealers to take up the Warmason's Casket it was a gesture of command rather than appeal.

CHAPTER XII

For nearly an hour the bombardment of Mount Rama had been faltering. What had been a vicious rain of annihilation had dwindled to a mere patter of occasional shells. Trishala had spoken with the Sovereign Spire and even reached the officer who'd replaced Colonel Hafiz as commander of the local militia. The defence forces were doing their best to maintain the barrage, but there had been complications. Ammunition supplies had been sabotaged, batteries had been overwhelmed and destroyed by cultist raiders. A few crews had even turned traitor, disabling their guns themselves.

Whatever the cause, Trishala railed against it under her breath. The barrage had become an asset in her defence of the cathedral, restraining to some extent the activities of the cultists. Now that the guns had gone largely silent, the cultists were bringing captured tanks and converted mining vehicles up to the square. The hybrids employed the machines as both firing platforms and mobile cover.

The acolytes and many of the frateris militia had their hands full keeping quiet the crowds of refugees packed inside the cathedral. Trishala had only a hundred and forty Sisters to fend off the attackers and guard the relics. Between them the Battle Sisters only had three multi-meltas to counter the enemy armour, a strain rendered even worse by the ferocious retaliation the cultists loosed against the heavy weapons any time they fired. After the first shot, they had to alternate fire to one of the other multi-meltas to avoid the immediate fury of the xenos horde.

Trishala still thought they could yet deny the rebels access to the cathedral. When a captured Leman Russ was disabled by the multi-meltas, the tank created a new obstruction on the steps. Or at least it should have if the cultists hadn't brought a massive recovery vehicle into play, some obscene metal behemoth designed to salvage damaged Goliaths. The gigantic wrecker soon had the tank dragged away, its crew cleverly using the Leman Russ to shield it from the Sisters. In a matter of minutes the way was again clear for the cultists to bring their machines towards the Great Gate.

Different scenarios played through Trishala's mind. What to do when the xenos battered their way in. What chambers to fall back to. Where to send the refugees so that they were out of the way. The narthex itself would have to be conceded to the enemy, but the Sisters could use the connecting corridors to fire into the first packs of cultists that desecrated the cathedral. They'd pay a high price for their achievement.

'Sister Superior!' The call came from Sister Archana. As she forced her way across the crowded narthex to the aperture Trishala had chosen for her own post, the question of why Archana had left her station in the gatehouse was forgotten. An ashen-faced deacon was rushing alongside her, his robes hiked up above his knees as he struggled to keep pace with the warrior. Decorum had no place in an emergency.

'The xenos,' Archana gasped as she rushed up to Trishala. It was odd that the Battle Sister didn't use the vox to relay her words, but as she continued it was clear her news was too dire to trust to any machine-spirit's keeping. 'They've violated the sanctuary.'

Sickness boiled up inside Trishala's belly. The genestealers! She knew for certain at least one of the creatures had been admitted by Debdan's traitors. There was no reason to believe there weren't more. It had to be them. Hiding from the patrols, skulking around in some corner until the defences around the sanctuary were at their weakest!

'I... I have seen it... Sister Superior,' the deacon stammered. 'Much death. There didn't seem to be anyone alive. So much blood...'

Trishala loomed over the petrified priest. 'What of the relics? What about the Warmason's Casket? What about the Shroud of Singh?'

The deacon's eyes fluttered, as though unable to comprehend the questions. Trishala swung away from him, looking instead at Archana. 'We must find out if they've destroyed the relics,' she told her. The honour of their order, the sombre vow that bound them all, was at risk. What did it matter if they held the cathedral if the sacred relics had been stolen? 'Get Sister Reshma.' Trishala paused a moment, wondering how many warriors she dared withdraw. If the defences here collapsed too quickly it would still come to nothing. The xenos had killed, had slaughtered, but would they recognise any value in the relics? It was just possible the monsters had left them alone.

In the end Trishala decided that ten Sisters were enough to investigate. She left instructions with Sister Nikhila, alerting her to listen for Trishala's signal. With that signal she would detach three more squads and send them to the Celestial Chapel.

Trishala led her retinue at a hurried pace, forcing their way through passageways and halls choked with the terrified survivors of Tharsis. Only when they were nearing the sanctuary did she allow their haste to slacken. Speed surrendered to caution as the Sisters fanned out, no warrior drawing nearer their goal unless she had the guns of her comrades keeping her covered. There was no need to remind them of the ghastly quickness and lethal claws of the genestealers. The only thought of comfort was that if the Sisters in the lead fell their deaths would be avenged by those who followed.

The Battle Sisters gained the sanctuary without incident. The xenos appeared to have left no guard behind. The bodies of several hybrids lay slumped near the entry, ripped apart by the bolters of the Sisters protecting the relics. The corpses of the defenders lay scattered about the rest of the sanctuary, huddled across pews, plastered against columns, and splattered along aisles. There was no mistaking what had killed them with such brutal abandon. Trishala had seen only too clearly how the talons of a genestealer tore through power armour and the carnage they visited against the flesh within.

Choking down her disgust at the slaughter of her warriors, Trishala focused upon the more pressing concern. The relics. Were they safe? Had the xenos been content with massacre or had they turned to desecration as well? Racing towards the altar, Trishala soon had her answer.

The column housing the field generators had been broken open and the mechanism itself savaged beyond recognition. The heavy curtains that concealed the alcoves where the relics reposed had been torn down. Most of the artefacts lay exposed upon their plinths and pedestals, seeming to Trishala's eyes almost naked without the distortion of their protective force fields. Even the stasis field that guarded the Shroud of Singh against the ravages of time had been disrupted. The ancient cloth of gold stood exposed upon its alabaster pedestal, the imprint of the Warmason's face still pressed upon the fabric.

The Shroud of Singh was untouched, even if it was undefended. The relief Trishala felt was soon erased when she looked to the pedestal of the cathedral's chief relic. There she found only emptiness. The Warmason's Casket was gone!

Shame. Guilt. Panic. All three briefly fought to overwhelm her. Trishala rebuked them all. On her lips were the tenets of the Imperial Creed, the litanies of the God-Emperor. In her mind she prayed to the Golden Throne for guidance, a way to redeem the trust she'd failed.

Casting her eyes to the floor, Trishala found her guide. Splotches of ichor, a slime that never issued from human veins. The splotches started near the altar and then withdrew towards the recessed ambulatory. One of the genestealers had been hurt and retreated. If the xenos had fled along with those that stole the Warmason's Casket, then the Sisters could pursue them. Catch them. Reclaim what the aliens had stolen.

'Sister Archana, wait here for Sister Nikhila,' Trishala ordered. 'She will be here soon with a detachment that will guard the remaining relics.' She looked over the rest of her retinue and pointed at the trail of ichor.

'The rest of us are going to find these thieves who've dared to defile the honour of the Order.'

Up through the buried cathedral crypts the Iron Warriors climbed. The giants set a pace no unaugmented human could have matched. In short order the Space Marines had penetrated Yadav's hidden door and followed the abandoned maze of corridors that ascended into the cathedral proper. Faintly they could hear the sound of gunfire in the distance.

'The xenos still fight to get inside,' Captain Uzraal suggested, contempt in his tone.

'You should be grateful they are so accommodating,' Rhodaan told him. 'With them to distract the defenders of this place it will make our task easier.' He swung around, fixing his gaze upon Cornak.

'What we seek is above us,' the sorcerer said, wagging his staff at the slanted ceiling. When he'd probed the mind of Palatine Yadav, Cornak had extracted not only the secret of entering the cathedral but also the location of the relic the Iron Warriors were seeking.

'Then let us be finished with it,' Rhodaan declared.

At his command the Iron Warriors pressed on, sweeping through galleries and vestibules cluttered with centuries of devotional paintings and religious sculptures. The worshipful depictions of the False Emperor and His vassals were repugnant to these veterans of the Long War, but there was no time to waste in obliterating the offending articles. The few acolytes bold enough to interfere were swatted away like insects. For the panicked masses of civilians who fled at their approach, the Iron Warriors didn't spare a second glance. So long as they weren't in the way the flesh held no interest for them. Let them spread the alarm. Nothing would stand between the Space Marines and their objective.

Reaching the Celestial Chapel, the Iron Warriors found far less resistance than they'd expected. The door leading into the chamber had been forced, torn from its fastening to lie sprawled across the floor. The sanctuary within was a charnel house. The iconography of the False Emperor's worshippers stared down from the walls upon the bloodied bodies of Sororitas, the pallid corpses of xenos hybrids and the mangled residue of robed acolytes. The light filtering down through the glassaic windows set an eerie panoply of colour across the carnage. At the far end of the hall, a white altar stood upon a raised dais, the remains of a cleric sprawled at its base.

The signs of violence provoked an increased urgency in the warsmith. Rhodaan roared at his followers, urging them inside. Brother Mahar, the first to rush through, was struck in the side by a burst of bolter fire. He crashed into the rows of pews, splintering them under his armoured weight.

Turu was close behind his fallen comrade, lunging through the doorway in a great leap that sent him hurtling deep into the room. He came up, loosing a burst from his own weapon at the foe who'd shot Mahar. The shells tore apart a line of pews and wore away at the face of a pillar. The violent assault drove the enemy from concealment. A lone Sister of Battle, her black armour coated in marble dust from the scarred pillar, tried to bring her gun swinging around to target Turu. In that brief instant she lost her view of the doorway. With her fire distracted, Rhodaan roared into the sanctuary. The warsmith's bolt pistol raked the woman, pitting her power armour and throwing her into one of the pillars. Her maimed body left a crimson smear against the marble as she dropped to the floor.

'Secure the room!' Uzraal barked at the Space Marines. 'If there're more of these viragos creeping about, make them regret it!'

Rhodaan stared across the destruction that had already been visited on the sanctuary. Before their arrival, this place had been the scene of fierce battle. The dead hybrids left little question who the Sisters had fought. The real question was who had prevailed and what their victory betokened for the Third Grand Company.

Cornak marched across the destruction, hastening towards the altar. As soon as Rhodaan noted the sorcerer's hurry he gave a warning sign to Uzraal and started after him. In all his dealings with Cornak, the warsmith always sensed a reserve, things the sorcerer didn't disclose. Seeing him make straight for the altar suggested to Rhodaan that the mystic had gleaned more information from Yadav than he'd let on, such as the precise situation of the Warmason's Casket and the other relics.

Rhodaan caught hold of Cornak's shoulder just before the sorcerer climbed the few steps of the dais. Cornak swung around, his staff half raised as though he'd considered braining his accoster until he discovered he faced the warsmith.

'The prize belongs to the Third Grand Company,' Rhodaan reminded Cornak. Behind him, Brother Gaos had aimed his autocannon towards the sorcerer. Uzraal had done likewise with his meltagun, slowly circling around to flank Cornak.

'The prize!' Cornak scoffed. He swung his staff around, thrusting its head towards a bare pedestal. He ignored the other alcoves and the other relics. Only the empty pedestal warranted his attention. 'Someone else has stolen it before we could!'

The sorcerer's agitation was so great as to allow his facade of servitude to slip, to sneer brazenly at the warsmith he'd sworn to obey. His discomfiture was such that he hadn't foreseen the cost of provoking Rhodaan. In a heartbeat, the horned Iron Warrior fell upon Cornak, bowling him back into the altar. Rhodaan's fist cracked against Cornak's helm, a kick of his boot sent the staff spinning from his grip.

'Another word, another breath that displeases me, hexmaster, and I will break you in half,' Rhodaan hissed. The pressure of his clutch pressed Cornak still farther across the altar. The sorcerer started to reach up at him, to thrust him back, but thought better of such resistance.

'After the long journey from Castellax,' Rhodaan said. 'After all the ordeals we've gone through and risks we've taken, now you tell me that what we've come for isn't even here?'

'But it was, Dread Lord,' Cornak insisted. He pointed again to the empty pedestal. 'It was right there. The xenos must have stolen it.'

Rhodaan leaned close, the fanged beak of his helm only millimetres from Cornak's optics. 'And why would the xenos want it? Of what use is it to them? Unless, of course, your psyker friend ripped those secrets right out of your mind.'

'I can find it again!' Cornak's entreaty rang out. 'If you give me the chance, I can track down these xenos, wherever they've gone.'

'How will you do that when you're afraid of their psyker?' Uzraal laughed.

'He will do it because he fears me more than a xenos witch,' Rhodaan told Uzraal. 'Isn't that right, Cornak?'

'Yes, Dread Lord,' Cornak replied. 'My spells will find where the Warmason's Casket has been taken.'

Rhodaan was silent a moment, weighing the sorcerer's words carefully. At last he released his hold upon Cornak and let him rise from the altar. 'You've promised me much, magician. Pray to your gods that you can deliver.'

Rhodaan turned from the sorcerer, growling new commands to the other Iron Warriors. 'Cornak will find a new trail for us to follow. It seems we must linger a bit longer on this miserable world.'

'Brother Mahar's wounds are minor,' Uzraal reported. Rhodaan looked past him, scrutinising the injured traitor. His armour was pitted and scoured by the shots the Sister had fired into him, but nothing that would slow him down. Nothing the artificers of Castellax couldn't repair once they were home.

Rhodaan looked again to Cornak. 'Now it is your turn. Lead me to the xenos and my relic.'

Scrambling down the side of the Warmason's Cathedral, Trishala felt her gorge rise. It wasn't a question of heights. Even as a girl on Primorus, she'd never felt anything but exhilaration staring down from the summit of the hive-city. No, what tore at her senses, what had her heart hammering inside her chest was the steep angle of their descent, seeming to make a mockery of gravity as well as perspective.

The path taken by the thieves was clear enough. First there was the alien ichor left behind by the injured xenos, but once they were outside the confines of the cathedral, navigating the layers of funerary barnacles clinging to the exterior wall, other traces left no doubt as to where the cultists had gone. Sides of crypts had been broken open, smashed apart to allow the thieves to pass through. Genestealer claws had gouged hideous furrows in the roofs of tombs onto which they'd dropped, marks that stood stark and barren against the weather-beaten stone.

It didn't take long for Trishala and Reshma to spot the purple-hued xenos scrambling along the tombs. Among them the Sisters could see a tall, lean figure in flowing robes, his arms locked about an object. Trishala's pulse quickened. Was it the Warmason's Casket the cultist was carrying away with him? Why else would the xenos be withdrawing from the cathedral instead of trying to force their way inside? Despite his burden, the hybrid moved with an even easier grace than his six-limbed companions.

Reshma paused in the doorway of a smashed crypt, sighting down the barrel of her bolter. She glanced at Trishala. 'Sister Superior?'

Trishala debated for only a moment. Reshma was a remarkably accurate shot. From this distance it would still need the Emperor's grace to hit the cultist with anything that resembled accuracy. Then there was the problem of the relic's fate. If it fell from this height it would be smashed against the slopes of Mount Rama. A sorry end for the precious artefact, but a better one than being a trophy for the cultists to gloat over. Grimly she nodded to Reshma.

Reshma leaned forwards, dipping her weapon and sighting just ahead of the robed hybrid, aiming not where he was but where he would be. The bolter roared and the shot sped downwards. A low gasp escaped Reshma. 'Missed,' she muttered before snapping off a second shot.

Trishala could see the hybrid plunging down across the tombs, unfazed by Reshma's attacks. The genestealers glanced backwards, glaring up towards the two Sisters. A few of them started to turn back, but a gesture from the robed cultist brought them short. Recalled by the hybrid, they followed him downwards.

'The range is too great for a boltgun,' Reshma apologised.

'We'll have to get closer,' Trishala decided. 'Make sure of our target. The xenos won't escape.' She roused Reshma to a renewed effort, leading her in the hazardous climb from their perch to the ring of tombs just beneath them.

As the two Battle Sisters started their descent, a lull in the artillery barrage enabled them to hear the snarl of gunfire from above. Trishala lifted her gaze, hoping to see Sister Nikhila bringing reinforcements to join the pursuit. Instead she saw why the genestealers had been called back. Their leader had other agents to guard his back. Emerging from the doorways of a dozen tombs were cultist fighters.

Trishala voxed an alert to the Sisters within the cathedral, telling them of the situation outside. The burst of fire the cultists sent down at Trishala's group was imprecise, but concentrated. Slug-throwers, lasguns, even a few bolters began smashing away at the exterior tomb where the Sisters were poised.

On her command the Battle Sisters sent a storm of bolter-fire up at the cultists. The explosive shells raked the hybrids and the tombs that sheltered them. The fury of the response caught them by surprise. A group of the cultists went hurtling earthwards as the tomb they were standing on disintegrated beneath the barrage. Another band was shredded under the righteous indignation of the Sisters.

The Sisters were to pay dearly for that brief moment of supremacy. The fire the cultists were directing down at them stopped abruptly. It took but a moment for the cause to manifest itself. Leaping up the tombs, using the fire from the cultists to cover its advance, one of the genestealers charged the Sisters. Alien claws sheared through ceramite and snapped bone in a frenzy of violence. One after another, the black-armoured Sisters fell, tumbling down the side of the cathedral or else sprawling amid the bones of the crypt. Soon Trishala and Reshma were the last ones standing.

Reshma's shots ripped at the xenos, crunching through its chitinous hide and exploding inside its flesh. She cried out as the genestealer sprang at her, its jaws snapping tight around her neck, its claws stabbing through her chestplate. Blood streaming from her wounds, she managed to raise her bolter and explode the head of the monster that dealt death to her.

Trishala started towards the stricken Reshma, but as she did a blur of motion caught her eye. A second genestealer came rushing into the tomb, crashing down through the roof rather than coming up from below. The xenos landed in a crouch, its eyes narrowing as it fixed its attention on Trishala. With a hiss, the alien rushed at her.

Bolter shells smashed into the genestealer as Trishala blazed away at the xenos. Despite the havoc her shots wrought on the creature's body, she couldn't blunt the impetus of its charge. The clawed alien slammed into her, propelling both itself and the armoured warrior through the rockcrete wall of the tomb.

Locked in the grip of a mangled genestealer, Trishala went hurtling down the side of the cathedral.

The death-shriek of an Inheritor rang through Bakasur's soul. The magus bit down on the anger and guilt that pounded in his heart. Emotion wouldn't serve any purpose. It wouldn't bring them any closer to the ascension or the design that the Great Father had planned.

Bakasur clung to the Warmason's Casket, keeping it safe as he descended the layers of exterior tombs and hastened through to the catacombs beneath the mountain. Only a few genestealers remained with Bakasur once they'd completed their descent. The others had been dispatched to aid the cult's forces already inside the cathedral. With the relic secured and some measure of victory guaranteed, it was time to focus on the greater objective. He wasn't certain where the Space Marines were, but if the Iron Warriors hindered the conquest of the cathedral, only the pure-strains had a chance to overcome them.

The remaining Inheritors clustered around the magus, hurrying him through the catacombs and into the tunnels below them. The Cult of the Cataclysm had been very careful about those tunnels; only Bakasur himself and the Inheritors were permitted to use them lest the humans suspect their existence. Now, however, the time for caution was past.

The hour of the Great Father would soon be at hand.

A dull red light greeted Trishala when she at last opened her eyes. Confusion roiled through her mind as she tried to unravel the sensations that racked her brain. There was that gruesome light, an emanation that seemed to pulsate from the very walls. The atmosphere was at once both hot and hideously moist, the air fairly dripping into her lungs when she drew a breath. There was a musty morbid smell, the odour of old bones and even older metal. For an instant she thought she must have crashed through the roof of one of the crypts clinging to the walls of the cathedral, but the sense of pressure against her ears made her reconsider. She was underground, and at some depth. Certainly further than she could have fallen and survived.

When she started to move, Trishala felt something damp and sticky dragging at her. Lowering her gaze she saw the pulped remains of a genestealer squashed beneath her. She was in no doubt that it was the same creature that had sent her hurtling down from the tomb. In their fall, the alien had been caught under her, its body dulling the impact enough to preserve Trishala's life. Lifting her gaze, she could see a jagged gash above her, a crater gouged into the ceiling by one of the artillery shells that had savaged the summit of Mount Rama.

The instant Trishala tried to rise she felt a weight pressing down against her chest. Twisting her head, she was treated to a grisly sight. Looming over her, one boot planted against her chest, was a huge, grotesquely disfigured hybrid. The cultist's head bore the worst aspects of both human and xenos, and from its shoulders sprouted four gangly arms with hands tipped by knife-like claws.

The hybrid hissed, glaring at her with hate and outrage. Opening its mouth, displaying its rows of needle-like fangs, the cultist leaned over Trishala. Looking like a scarlet worm, a tendril-like organ licked out from behind the teeth.

Horror filled Trishala, but decades of Adepta Sororitas training took that horror and turned it into violence. She wasn't the weak child of Primorus now, she was a Battle Sister. Boldly she kicked out with her legs, smashing the hybrid's pelvis with her armoured boots. The servo-enhanced might of her blow cracked the bone, viscous ichor splashing down on her as the surprised cultist recoiled in pain.

Trishala lunged at the enemy. She'd lost her bolt pistol in the fall, but she still had her power sword. Whether through ignorance or arrogance the cultist had neglected to take the weapon from her. She activated the sword and sent a destructive field of energy rippling across the blade.

Thrusting the sword upwards, Trishala felt a brief instant of resistance as it crunched through the hybrid's flesh and bone. A hot stream of ichor sizzled against the blade's power field as she drove the thrust home.

Trishala twisted the blade around in the wound, wrenching it across the hybrid in a vicious assault. All the fear, all the terrors that had lurked in her mind since her obliterated childhood were exorcised as she brought death to the monster. She saw again the xenos horde as they ran amok across Primorus, as their contagion consumed her parents and neighbours. This time, however, she wasn't helpless. This time she could fight back.

A look of almost human shock gleamed in the eyes of the hybrid as its corpse struck the ground. Muscular spasms rippled through its mangled body, causing its hands to claw at the floor, its talons to scratch at the wall.

The Sister Superior kicked the dead cultist away and rose to her feet. Certain that it would move no more, she looked away from the hybrid and at her surroundings. From the bones embedded in the walls she knew she was somewhere in the maze of catacombs that wound their way through the guts of Mount Rama.

How could she find the thieves who'd taken the Warmason's Casket? The recovery of the relic seemed impossible now. She voxed Sister Archana to report her condition and the situation. It was Sister Nikhila that responded.

'The cathedral is beset by enemies,' Nikhila voxed, the chatter of gunfire and the screams of the dying echoing behind her words. 'Cultists and genestealers, swarming in from above and below. Their efforts to take the Great Gate were only a feint, something to draw us away from the real attack.'

'What of the relics? Can you hold the Celestial Chapel?' Trishala asked.

'Chaos Space Marines,' Nikhila replied. 'They forced their way up to the sanctuary while we were fighting the cultists. Sister Archana is dead.'

The news made Trishala's blood go cold. It was enough to try to hold off the genestealers, but against the Chaos Space Marines as well she knew they would have no chance. 'Where are the Traitor Space Marines?'

'Gone, praise the God-Emperor,' Nikhila said. 'They fought their way up to the Celestial Chapel from the crypts, and then forced their way back down again. They must be insane.'

Trishala didn't think their actions could be explained so easily. Something had happened to divert the Chaos Space Marines. Their entering the cathedral from below lent a sinister significance to the inability to raise Kashibai or Palatine Yadav on the vox. The Traitor Space Marines could be responsible. If they were, then they could have discovered the entrance Yadav was trying to reach.

Why then had the Chaos Space Marines withdrawn? There was only one explanation that suggested itself. They'd come for the Warmason's Casket and, finding it stolen, they had no reason to stay.

'Nikhila, I am going to try to reach the Mourning Door,' Trishala said. She saw no way to pick up the trail of the missing relic, but if she could reach the cathedral, at least she could help her Sisters defend it.

Consulting her auspex, Trishala moved through the bleak catacombs, heading for the underground door. As she drew closer to her objective, she began to wonder how long ago the Chaos Space Marines had withdrawn from the cathedral and where they might be now.

As if in response to her unspoken questions, Trishala heard the tramp of armoured boots close by. When she neared the junction of two tunnels, she drew closer to the wall, holding her breath as she watched gigantic shapes stalking through the gloom.

She'd found the Iron Warriors. This close the Chaos Space Marines were even more monstrous, their armour adorned with grisly trophies and profane sigils. They exuded an aura of murder and massacre, the ignominy of treacheries ancient and obscene.

Trishala watched them pass, seven giants arrayed in ancient power armour. She heard the deep snarl of their horned leader as he gave the others their orders. Hearing his words brought clarity to the lurking Battle Sister.

From his words, Trishala knew the leader of the Iron Warriors was looking for the Warmason's Casket. They were on the track of the xenos thieves, intending to seize the relic from them.

A new intention filled Trishala's heart with grim determination. If she was careful she might follow the Iron Warriors, let them lead her to the stolen relic. When they confronted the xenos, when traitor and alien fought, she might find opportunity in the confusion of battle. She might steal back the Warmason's Casket or at the very least destroy it so that no enemy could defile its purity more than they already had.

Steeling herself for the ordeal ahead, Trishala stalked down the passageway, following the armoured step of the Iron Warriors as they marched deeper into the catacombs.

Rhodaan kept close to Cornak as the sorcerer guided the Iron Warriors ever deeper into the catacombs. If the hexmaster faltered in his purpose now, Rhodaan would emphasize the cost of failure. Seizing the Warmason's Casket would render a great honour to Perturabo. This close to achieving that ambition, Rhodaan wasn't about to be thwarted. Not if all the xenos witches on Lubentina were howling for Cornak's blood.

'We're getting close,' Cornak advised, strain in his tone.

Almost the moment the sorcerer spoke, the catacombs erupted with gunfire. Hybrid cultists came charging out from side passages, blasting away with shotguns and lasrifles, bolters and stubbers. The whirring snarl of Gaos' autocannon reduced one pack to a tangle of gore, but other cultists came surging through the carnage. Las-bolts and shotgun pellets glanced off their power armour as the Iron Warriors met the rebel charge.

A snarl from Periphetes' bolter brought a pair of cowled hybrids plunging to the floor, their bodies quivering in a final paroxysm. Captain Uzraal's meltagun evaporated a burly hybrid lugging a heavy bolter. Turu and Mahar were beset by a pack of zealots swinging energised picks and hammers, and fended off the mob with bone-breaking swings of their fists and mangling swipes with the stocks of their bolters.

A snarling monstrosity with three arms hurled itself at Rhodaan. The hybrid's claw slashed at the warsmith's face, but the intervening parry of his chainsword blocked the strike. The blade's whirring teeth dug into the chitinous limb, partly severing it and leaving it dangling from the cultist's shoulder. While the hybrid sent shots from its laspistol glancing off Rhodaan's armour, the Space Marine's bolt pistol punched holes through its body.

'Iron within! Iron without!' the warriors of the Third Grand Company bellowed as they butchered their way through the cultists. Even Rhodaan lost count of how many fell before their assault as the Iron Warriors smashed their way through the rebels. Ahead he could see that the tunnel branched off. To the right there was a continuation of the morbid, bone-encrusted passages of the catacombs. To the left, angling downwards, the path took on a raw, rugged appearance, walls of compressed spoil fused and hardened by the pressure of millennia.

'This is what the cultists tried to keep us from finding,' Uzraal observed as he aimed his weapon at the mouth of the sunken tunnel.

'They failed,' Rhodaan said. He turned towards Cornak, pointing to the tunnel. 'They must have taken the relic this way.'

Cornak nodded his head. 'The magus is near,' he declared. 'He thinks to block our advance with his powers.' He reversed his staff, bringing it slamming down against the floor. Immediately a blast of force swept forwards, roaring down into the tunnel. Rhodaan could almost see the moment when the sorcerer's magic slammed into an opposing force. There was a flash of energy, a tremble that rolled through the earth. Dirt and bones clattered from the ceiling.

'Keep the xenos witch's magic in check a little longer, hexmaster,' Rhodaan ordered Cornak. He hefted his chainsword. 'His spells will end when his head leaves his shoulders.' The warsmith led the way as the Iron Warriors descended into the lower tunnels.

CHAPTER XIII

Bakasur clutched at his head as the psychic vibrations issuing from his brain met the arcane surge expelled by Cornak's magic. He could feel the black tendrils of sorcery seeping through the power he'd evoked, splitting and fracturing it, partitioning its strength until there were only feeble motes of energy left. The mental blast that would have brought the roof of the tunnel crashing down instead only provoked the slightest shifting of the ancient spoil heap. Instead of tonnes of earth crashing down there were only a few streams of dirt and dust.

The magus opened his mind, reaching into the consciousness of the cultists around him. A dozen hybrids staggered against the earthen walls of the cavern as Bakasur drew from their brains the energy he needed. He focused the siphoned power into his effort to collapse the tunnel, but even this wasn't enough to overwhelm Cornak's sorcery. The Space Marine was on his guard now, wary of allowing Bakasur to draw him into the magus' mental defences. Cornak concentrated only on combating the manifestation of his power, not on the alien mind that produced it. The sorcerer wouldn't let himself be exposed to the consciousness of the cult, to have his mentality dispersed among thousands of minds. He was content to keep the tunnel open.

It was no stretch of imagination for Bakasur to understand why. The sorcerer was counting on the other Iron Warriors to deal with the magus.

Dread of such an encounter briefly made Bakasur consider drawing upon the minds of the Inheritors with him to add to his power as he'd done with the hybrids. The thought of defiling the essence of a pure-strain with such a trespass made him repent the very thought. There was a better way. A way that would draw the Space Marines into a trap of their own making.

Still keeping a part of his mind fixated on bringing down the tunnel so as to distract the sorcerer and keep Cornak occupied, Bakasur gave speedy commands to the hybrids and genestealers with him. The half-human cultists spread out across the cavern, taking up positions from which they'd be able to ambush the Iron Warriors. The Inheritors scurried away down the side passages, ranging through the burrows they'd excavated long ago. The genestealers would be ready when Bakasur needed them.

Rhodaan's chainsword came snarling down into the neck of the cultist sprawled at his feet. The hybrid screamed, struggled to bring his alien claws slashing into the Space Marine's power armour. By that time the teeth of Rhodaan's blade had already ripped through the chitinous hide and were shredding the fibrous tendons within. The cultist's head sagged obscenely against his shoulder, dangling by a clutch of unsevered muscles and veins. The warsmith kicked the twitching carcass aside and waved his followers forwards.

The narrow tunnel opened into a large cavern lit by a hellish luminance pulsating from the walls. The crimson glow sent weird shadows playing across the rough columns of rockcrete that supported the ceiling overhead. Pockets of darkness stretched away on all sides, shadowing niches and cavities, obscuring passageways and tunnels. About the cavern was strewn a jumble of cannibalised machinery, the detritus of scores of mining implements stolen and scavenged by the cult.

It was from these jumbles of wreckage that more attackers emerged to confront the Iron Warriors. The sentinel killed by Rhodaan at the entrance was but a precursor to the ambush that had been prepared for them. Up from behind the piles of scrap, out from the shadowy holes that lined the walls, a mob of pale-skinned hybrids confronted the intruders. Lasguns, autoguns, shotguns, all blazed away at the armoured giants. A pair of cultists kicked over the corroded frame of an ore-cart to expose the vicious muzzle of a heavy stubber. A huge rebel with three arms leapt atop the chassis of a mine-cart to rake the Space Marines with a bolter captured from the Sororitas.

The furious fire crackled against the thick armour of the Iron Warriors. Before the hybrids manning the heavy stubber could open up, Uzraal sent a blast from his meltagun into their faces, reducing cultists and cover alike to a puddle of molten waste. Mahar blasted away at the rebel with the bolter, sending him tumbling down to the floor in a gory heap.

Rhodaan loosed a burst from his pistol, ripping through a hybrid that rushed at him from one of the alcoves, a shock maul clenched in her hands. The maimed cultist flew back, crashing against the jumbled machinery behind her. The warsmith's gaze was drawn to the gaunt figure that stood exposed when the scrap collapsed under the corpse. He was a tall and emaciated example of the xenos-infected cultists, adorned in a robe of dark purple. Rhodaan could sense the strength rippling around the hybrid, but his attention was quickly diverted to the golden box he held tucked beneath one arm.

'You should have left that where it was,' Rhodaan told the hybrid. He lumbered towards the robed cultist, his chainsword cleaving through the bodies of those rebels who rushed out to block his path. The thin treacle of hybrid blood dripped from the whirring teeth of his blade as Rhodaan advanced. The almost placid way in which the cultist watched him draw near gave the warsmith pause. He had no time for whatever trickery gave the fanatic such confidence. Raising his pistol, he was ready to wither the thief in a burst of shells.

Pain! Raw and unrelenting, as searing as a hot blade pressed against his skull, brought Rhodaan to a halt. The bolt pistol dropped, his arm falling to his side as every nerve in the limb screamed at him in agony. The same torment rippled down his sword arm and it was only with a fierce determination that he forced his fingers to retain their grip on the chainsword.

Rhodaan could see the awful grin that showed on the

inhuman visage of his foe. No mere cultist, this was the magus himself, the xenos witch Cornak had feared for so long. Bakasur was using his psyker powers to afflict the warsmith, to violate his very mind and reduce him to helplessness.

Grim pride swelled within Rhodaan. He was a veteran of the Long War, a champion of the IV Legion. By his own hand he'd risen to become warsmith of the Third Grand Company and Lord of Castellax. It was more than determination that enabled an Iron Warrior to survive and achieve so much. Tenacity, endurance, and, above all, defiance were the things that kept him going, the bitter compulsion to prove his martial quality against any foe. He would not submit to a xenos witch on some ignominious shrine world!

Rhodaan had the pleasure of watching the smile evaporate from Bakasur's face as he forced first one foot forwards and then the other. By will alone the warsmith was smashing his way through the psychic torment. Even as the pain swelled, as the magus poured more suffering into his nerves, Rhodaan kept advancing.

He moved forwards and raised his chainsword. 'Give me the casket, xenos.'

Bakasur shifted his grip on the Warmason's Casket, fingers curling around the lid as he held it at his side. The sensation of pain racking Rhodaan dwindled while at the same time a ripple of distortion flowed down the magus' hand and across the box. 'But a thought from me and your treasure will be destroyed,' the hybrid warned. 'Relent if you would save it, Space Marine.'

A growl of amusement rasped from the mask of Rhodaan's helm. If the magus thought he could threaten Iron Warriors then he understood little of the Third Grand

Company and even less of their purpose on Lubentina. 'It needs better than you to threaten me,' he swore as he marched onwards.

At that instant the ceiling overhead split open. Rhodaan looked up to see a shape of claws and chitin dropping down on him. Across the vox he could hear the rest of his Iron Warriors crying out in surprise.

Once again, the cult had prepared a layered ambush. While the Iron Warriors cut down the hybrids, Bakasur's real protectors had moved into position.

The genestealers were on the attack.

Down from the ceiling above, up from the floor below, the Inheritors lunged into action. Bakasur had played for time to allow the genestealers to spring their ambush with the smallest amount of risk to themselves. Into their minds he'd sent the image of each Iron Warrior in the cavern. Timed properly the pure-strains would have been on their enemies from the moment they ripped their way into the chamber from the overlapping tunnels.

The menace posed by Rhodaan and his refusal to be cowed by either mental tortures or threats against the relic had stirred Bakasur's mind with weak mammalian fear. The genestealers responded to that fear, launching their attack an instant before all was ready. One of the Iron Warriors went down, his legs torn from under him by the genestealer that erupted from the floor at his feet. The other Space Marines, however, were given enough warning to fall back from the immediate danger. Their bolters barked as they fired bursts at their attackers, compelling the genestealers to evade the murderous retaliation. One Inheritor collapsed as the deadly flare from an autocannon ripped through its carapace and sent it pitching across a pile of scrap.

Immediately before him, Warsmith Rhodaan was caught in the talons of the genestealer that had dropped onto him. The rending claws raked across his power armour, scouring the heavy ceramite. But they did so with less power and force than they should have, scratching the plates rather than gashing them, unable to tear through to the flesh within. The answer to the faltering assault was the chainsword that impaled the Inheritor's chest. In that split second when the genestealer came hurtling down at him, Rhodaan had raised his sword, piercing the creature's body.

Savagely, Rhodaan wrenched the dying genestealer from his sword. Though the sounds of battle rang out across the cavern, he didn't turn aside to see how his comrades were faring. His attention was focused, as it had been before, on Bakasur and the relic he held.

'The casket is mine, xenos,' Rhodaan stated, a slime of genestealer ichor dripping down his armour.

Bakasur withdrew from his advance. Even if the Inheritors prevailed against the other Iron Warriors, it wouldn't help the magus. He would be dead, a death that would accomplish nothing to further the schemes of the Great Father. A death that wouldn't bestow on him the glory of ascension.

As his mind strove for some escape, the sweep of his thoughts brushed across all those nearby. Bakasur found something there that he could use, a thought so keen and vigilant that it blazed like a beacon even through the barriers that guarded the brain that gave it form. Swiftly Bakasur dropped his own psychic defences, stilled his thoughts, folded his mentality down to the faintest ember of awareness.

Rhodaan continued to advance. 'The casket is mine, xenos,' he repeated as he raised his chainsword.

He started to swing his blade down at Bakasur when a cry across the vox stopped him.

'No!' Cornak howled from across the cavern. The sorcerer stormed out from the tunnel. 'It belongs to the Circle!'

A blast of psychic force slammed into the warsmith, bowling him over. Rhodaan slammed to the floor, his chainsword digging at the ground. A second blast threw him against the wall. The pain Bakasur had so recently sent to afflict him was nothing beside the agony that now racked his body. Every muscle, every tendon felt as if it were on fire.

Cornak stalked across the cavern, moving with a speed incredible for one burdened down by power armour. When a genestealer sprang at him, a blast of magic from his staff sent it spinning away into the junk piled about the chamber. When Uzraal tried to intercept him, he was thrown back by an invisible malignance that found him slamming against one of the columns.

The sorcerer stopped to glare down at Rhodaan. 'You've been most obliging,' Cornak mocked. 'Your little warband has been my sword and shield, my horse and chariot. Now, at the end of things, you kill my enemy and cheat the prophecy.' He gestured with his staff to where Bakasur stood. 'But the prize is not for you, and so you've outlived your usefulness to me.'

Rhodaan stared up at Cornak, confused by the sorcerer's words. 'You're mad, traitor,' he snarled. 'Mad and blind. I never touched the xenos witch.'

Cornak spun around, Rhodaan's words alerting him to the psychic deception Bakasur had played upon him. Feeding the sorcerer's treachery, the magus had made him believe the task he required of Rhodaan had been accomplished. To cheat fate and escape the doom he'd foreseen.

The sorcerer hurriedly raised his staff, muttering incantations as he banished the illusion provoked by the magus. Rhodaan could see the ripple of distortion leap from Bakasur's hand into the ancient staff. The shaft vibrated wildly, the head affixed to it beginning to smoulder and crack. Cornak's arcane retaliation sent splinters from the staff slashing Bakasur's pallid skin.

Perhaps the sorcerer should have prevailed despite all his fears and omens. Rhodaan didn't give him the chance. Lunging up from the floor, he brought his chainsword slashing down across Cornak's hand, lopping it off at the wrist. The staff, the focus of his powers, slid to the floor. For an instant, the sorcerer's magic faltered.

It was all the time Bakasur needed. He was gesturing at the sorcerer with a clawed finger, directing a holocaust of mental malignance into Cornak's undefended mind. The enmity of every cultist on Lubentina fed the magus' assault. The afflicted sorcerer ripped the helm from his head as he roared in pain. Wisps of vapour steamed away from his boiling brain, colour dissipated from his eyes as they became lifeless, milky things. With an expression of utter disbelief frozen upon his once gloating visage, Cornak crashed to the ground.

The doom the sorcerer had thought to cheat had claimed him just the same.

Rhodaan had no time to capitalise on Cornak's destruction. Even as he turned towards Bakasur a genestealer came scrambling out from the mounds of junk. The four-armed xenos lunged at the warsmith, hurling itself at him in a cataract of rending claws and gnashing fangs.

Trishala stole down the tunnel following the rearmost of the Iron Warriors. She was as afraid of losing contact with the terrifying Chaos Space Marines as she was of drawing their attention. To confront them would be throwing her life away, but if she lost them she would lose what she knew had become her only chance to recover the Warmason's Casket.

The roar of combat grew louder as she approached a wide cavern littered with debris from mining machinery. Trishala saw the Iron Warriors striving to defend themselves from a pack of genestealers that lunged at them from behind the piles of scrap and the rockcrete columns that supported the roof. One of the Space Marines had been brought down already, lying mangled at the edge of a pit in the floor. As she watched, a genestealer scrambled up the side of a column and launched itself at another of the Iron Warriors. The alien's claws ripped down the side of his armour, opening the ceramite along his left arm and raking the flesh within. The stricken Space Marine pressed the muzzle of his bolter against the creature's head and exploded its skull before it could visit further mutilation against him.

Trishala's attention shifted from the fighting between Chaos Space Marine and xenos and instead focused on the duel between sorcerer and magus. Sight of the purple-clad hybrid made her pulse quicken. Tucked beneath his arm was the Warmason's Casket!

The finale of the duel saw the Chaos Space Marine

sorcerer felled by a combination of the magus' powers and the chainsword wielded by one of his fellow Iron Warriors. Trishala didn't know what provoked the infighting, but it gave her an opportunity. The sword-wielding Chaos Space Marine was soon beset by the genestealers, compelled to defend himself against the lethal xenos claws.

Only one prospect offered any chance to redeem the Order's honour. The Warmason's Casket. If Trishala could recover that artefact then at least the disgrace wouldn't be complete. She looked from the embattled Chaos Space Marines to where the hybrid magus had been. Bakasur hadn't lingered after slaying the sorcerer. Setting the genestealers against the Iron Warriors he was now retreating down an earthen tunnel. Under one of his arms the jewelled panels of the relic glittered in the crimson light.

Scrambling across the room, Trishala set off in pursuit of the magus. She ignored the threat of the Iron Warriors and their alien adversaries as she dived into the rough tunnel. All that mattered to her now was catching Bakasur and reclaiming the relic he'd stolen.

Sounds of combat receded into the distance. The dull, hellish glow became more pronounced, the air hotter and heavier than it had been in the catacombs. The sensor fitted to Trishala's arm alerted her to rising radiation levels in her surroundings, enough to prove lethal to an unshielded human if they lingered in such an atmosphere too long. She wondered if these delvings of the cult had reached down to the power plant that supported the Warmason's Cathedral. She took some comfort in knowing that her power armour would act as a buffer between herself and the radiation, and even greater solace in the fact that once she caught up to the magus she'd have no reason to hang around these toxic caverns.

Ahead, the tunnel opened wider, expanding into a large hall dominated by the gigantic housings of atomic converters, colossal cylinders of titanium and plasteel that rose from the floor to expand into networks of cable and pipe that vanished into the ceiling. Here the reddish glow was more pronounced, vibrating from the walls and pulsating upwards from the floor. Patches of deep shadow filled the corners and the far side of the room. Trishala could see something more than just the barren rock when she peered at the opposite end of the chamber. There was a dull, corroded quality to the surface, suggestive of immense plates of metal buried and forgotten long ago.

Bakasur had stopped running. The magus was actually kneeling before that darkness, extending the Warmason's Casket towards the blackest patch of shadow. The worshipful attitude of his posture inflamed Trishala's senses. The hybrid was rendering up an offering.

Before Trishala could set upon a course of action, Bakasur swung around. The magus's eyes fixated upon her, an eerie light shining behind them. 'I didn't know it would be you, defiler,' he said. The light behind his eyes expanded, enveloping Trishala's vision completely.

Through the blinding glare, Trishala struggled to bring her surroundings into focus. When she did it was with an abruptness that was nearly as overwhelming as the light had been – and far more disorienting.

She was no longer in the power plant under the Warmason's Cathedral. Trishala instead found herself in a chamber with ferrocrete walls, pressed on every side by a mass of terrified humanity. The stink of fear was too great to be washed away by the overworked recyclers that struggled to pump air into the security shelter. The moans of fear, the consoling murmurs, the desperate prayers merged into a susurrus of dread. The vision of hundreds packed into the shelter, filling it from wall to wall.

Trishala saw her parents, felt her mother's hand squeezing her own, heard her father enjoining her to pray to the God-Emperor and hold to her faith in Him. Then there came the screams, the rending sound of alien claws. She saw the traitors among the refugees, watched them holding the rest back while they opened the door.

In a blur of purple and crimson, the genestealers came rushing in. Their jaws agape, the hideous tongue darting out to strike those they came near. It wasn't death they brought, but something much worse.

Trishala's father fell silent, grabbed by the cultists and drawn towards the xenos. Her mother's hand lost its hold. She was pulled towards one of the monsters and Trishala cried out when she saw the thorn-like tongue jab her mother's neck. Then she was herself being pushed towards the xenos...

Only it hadn't happened that way! The aliens had ignored her, focusing their attentions on the adults in the shelter. She'd escaped their clutches. She'd survived. Praying incessantly to the God-Emperor for deliverance, she'd been spared the taint of the xenos.

Trishala prayed again, reciting the mantras that had been instilled in her by the Ecclesiarchy. She fought against the force that compelled her towards the genestealers, struggled against the disorienting sensations that filled her mind. This wasn't reality, nor were they memories. This was delusion, a manifestation conjured by the magus. Against the psychic illusion, Trishala pitted her own resolve, her faith in the Emperor. By degrees she was brought closer and still closer to the genestealers. She could see one of them turn towards her, its mouth open, the spike-like tongue licking out.

With a scream, Trishala broke the illusion. Before her she saw not the face of the genestealer, but that of Bakasur. His face was an abominable fusion of human and alien, an atrocity of flesh that could not fail to evoke memories of Primorus in Trishala's mind. The magus drew back in surprise when he saw that Trishala had broken free of his psychic hold.

'You've seen us before. Our brethren on Primorus have been suppressed,' Bakasur declared. 'It is to be regretted that they shall never know the wonder of ascension.' He craned his head to one side, as though listening to some faint voice. 'The Great Father mourns their sacrifice. Such a waste.'

Trishala shook off the lethargy that lingered in her limbs from the psychic attack. As she moved towards Bakasur, the magus warned her back with a threatening display against the Warmason's Casket. One motion, and he'd destroy the relic.

'Lubentina will be different,' Bakasur said. 'Here we will be triumphant. Here we will rise to our destiny.' His pallid hand reached out to her. 'You were denied the gift of ascension before. This time will be different. Even a defiler such as yourself may serve the Great Father.'

A feeling of obscenity coursed through Trishala as the magus pointed. With all her being she wanted to rebuke his profane declarations, but her tongue was frozen. The urge to split Bakasur's skull thundered through her heart, but her arm remained at her side. She felt as helpless as the child cowering with her family in the security shelter, watching as the xenos came to destroy her world.

The roar of a bolter boomed through the cavern. Trishala was struck in the side, sent crashing to the floor by the impact of explosive shells. She could see Bakasur leap back, still holding the Warmason's Casket before him. Striding into the power plant were the Chaos Space Marines.

'Tell me xenos, is your arrogance such that you think *we* will serve your little father?' The voice was that of Rhodaan, the horned lord of the Iron Warriors.

Trishala heard the growl of the warsmith's chainsword as he agitated its machine-spirit and set the whirring teeth into motion.

'Kill the half-breed filth,' Rhodaan bellowed to his followers.

At Rhodaan's command, the Iron Warriors surged forwards, rushing at the magus. They'd had a taste of the hybrid's abilities already, and seen for themselves that he could ward away their gunfire. When the Space Marines came close enough to get to grips with Bakasur, it might be a different story.

'Warsmith! At our flank!' The warning shout came from Uzraal and a moment later the Iron Warriors captain was discharging his meltagun into a clutch of charging genestealers. The foremost of the aliens was reduced to a smoking husk, the ones immediately behind it flailing on the ground with portions of their carapace melted away. Periphetes and Gaos opened up on the alien throng, holding them back, but Turu fell under a carpet of slashing claws. This time there was no timidity in the xenos attack.

A buzzing inside his head made Rhodaan turn from the

aliens rushing out from the shadows and charge at the magus instead. Bakasur had witnessed Cornak's sorcery and seen how effective the magic was at crippling Space Marines. Now, with his psychic abilities, he was trying to manifest a similar effect. Rhodaan intended to finish him before he could make good the effort.

Bakasur realised his peril as Rhodaan came at him. Desperately he lifted the Warmason's Casket, holding it before him like a shield. Without hesitation the Space Marine brought his chainsword screaming down. Its edge chewed into the magus' arm, hewing through it to savage the body of the robed hybrid. The buzzing in Rhodaan's head evaporated as the maimed cultist slumped to the ground, the relic pressed close to his bloodied breast. This time Bakasur wasn't feigning death with a psychic illusion.

Before Rhodaan could reach down and seize the relic, his mind was beset by a different kind of assault. It was like a mental avalanche, a psychic scream of monstrous fury. The offence of the entire cult, their concentrated hate and anger at the fall of their prophet, all condensed and focused by a mentality even more powerful than that of Bakasur. A merely human mind would have been liquefied under that psychic storm. A mind attuned to psychic vibrations would have been stunned into idiocy. Rhodaan was neither of these things. He was staggered by the assault, felt blood gushing from his nose and ears, heard his hearts struggling to recover their equilibrium after the attack rushed through them. But the warsmith didn't fall; he was able to face the gloom where he sensed the perpetrator of the attack lurking.

'Iron within! Iron without!' Rhodaan shouted the war cry of his Legion as he dashed towards his hidden assailant. A genestealer lunged at him, the warsmith's chainsword slashing out to rend its limbs and open its skull. The litter of the dismembered creature strewed his path as he drove into the darkness.

The optics of his helm compensated for the radioactive glow cast by Rhodaan's surroundings. Shadows couldn't hide the bulky frames of mighty turbines or the armoured shells of atomic nodules. The power source of the Warmason's Cathedral had become the heart of the xenos cult.

The nodules were aglow with the decaying half-life of their fuel cells, creating the reddish glow that pulsed through the walls and ground. Several of them had spilled from the broken turbines, embedding themselves in the rock. Tangles of twisted metal created a spider web of plasteel overhead, support beams stretching down to create a deranged forest of columns. When a crouching genestealer launched itself downwards from one of the overhangs, Rhodaan's chainsword caught it in mid-leap, hewing away the limbs of its left side and leaving the rest to flop about on the ground.

'You would have been wise to let us leave,' Rhodaan shouted into the darkness. 'You should have contented yourself with the flesh of this world. Now I'll have to kill all of you.'

The threat was meant to goad the lurking Great Father into the open, but when the creature came at him, Rhodaan was unprepared for its wrathful cunning. After the attack of the genestealer, his attention had drifted upwards, searching among the twisted metal for some trace of his foe. The atomic nodules had been dismissed from his thoughts as a refuge too deadly for any enemy to choose.

Up from one of the glowing pits, the Great Father climbed. It possessed the same shape as its four-armed spawn, but its carapace was discoloured with age, darkened until it was almost black. Old scars criss-crossed its chitin, standing out in stark comparison to the darkened hue. Its claws were immense talons, each the length of Rhodaan's forearm. Its head was a bloated swelling of cranium and jaw, the fangs as long as knives. The eyes that stared from the creature's face were hoary with age and filled with an inhuman malevolence. Gigantic in its proportions, the patriarch easily twice the size of even the pure-strains that had accompanied it across the stars, the huge genestealer lashed at Rhodaan once more with its tremendous mentality.

Rhodaan felt the awful spectacle the patriarch presented. He'd faced the fearsome broods of the tyranids before and the sensation he now felt recalled to him the experience of meeting one of the xenos tyrants in battle.

The warsmith stumbled, knocked back against one of the columns by the patriarch's mental assault. He swung around, sighting the huge genestealer as the alien leapt at him from the edge of the nodule. The monster's enormous claws slashed out, only Rhodaan's genetically enhanced reflexes and mechanically augmented speed enabling him to duck their murderous sweep. The talons raked across the column, shearing through the plasteel.

Rhodaan struck at the Beast, bringing his chainsword slashing for the creature's belly. Exhibiting a speed and agility that contrasted with its enormous size, the patriarch darted away, swiping at the Space Marine as it retreated. Rhodaan was knocked back by the glancing blow, a deep gouge running the length of his helm's fanged beak.

Lunging at him once more, the Great Father allowed Rhodaan no respite. A psychic screech assailed his brain, threatening to overcome his mind while the patriarch's claws slashed at his body. By the narrowest margin, the warsmith darted out of the monster's path. This time the rending claws only caught one of his pauldrons, disfiguring the insignia of his legion. The chainsword did better, rending across one of the patriarch's arms and leaving it hanging limp and bleeding.

The patriarch glared at Rhodaan, the amber-coloured eyes sunk deep in its chitinous skull possessed of a primordial degree of malevolence. The monster reared back, giving ground before Rhodaan. The Space Marine pursued the Great Father warily, watching for whatever trickery it intended. He wasn't lulled by the fiend's display of caution. The patriarch wouldn't concede this fight until one of them was dead.

The nearly blinding flare of Uzraal's meltagun rushed through the patriarch's lair, for a brief instant banishing the shadows and overwhelming the crimson glow. From above there sounded the anguished shrieks of pure-strain genestealers. A litter of partially melted aliens crashed to the floor amidst the slag of their perches. The Great Father's ploy was clear – to lure Rhodaan into an ambush.

'More of them up in those girders,' Captain Uzraal cautioned Rhodaan. 'They seem leery of dropping down in range now.'

'Keep an eye on them,' Rhodaan told Uzraal. He kept his eyes on the patriarch, trying to guess what it would try next now that the ambush had failed. The Beast's gaze kept shifting from the warsmith to Uzraal and back again. 'If their leader goes for you, melt his face off. We'll worry about the ones above after.' Rhodaan noted the quick shift of the patriarch's gaze, the way the genestealer's eyes glared at him. As he had with Cornak, he buried his intentions deep within his mind, layering his thoughts to deceive a psychic spy.

'If he gets me, withdraw to the spaceport,' Rhodaan ordered Uzraal. At once he saw that his suspicion was right. The Great Father shifted its massive bulk ever so slightly, positioning itself for another rush at the warsmith.

Uzraal was an old comrade of Rhodaan's, serving as one of his Raptors before he became warsmith. He didn't need Rhodaan's intention explained. He knew what was expected of him, and it wasn't a retreat to the spaceport. Swinging the meltagun around, he poised the weapon at the patriarch. The huge genestealer's attention was diverted once more, the alien monster jumping away from the path of Uzraal's aim, putting several columns between itself and the captain.

As the Great Father was moving, so too was Rhodaan. Driving through the cluster of twisted metal, he flanked the hulking monster. Explosive shells sped from his bolt pistol, pelting the Beast's side, drawing streams of treacly ichor from its carapace. Then the warsmith was bringing his chainsword swinging around, its teeth chewing into one of the columns just as the patriarch spun around to combat its original antagonist.

The severed length of column came stabbing down, impaling the charging patriarch like a spear. The Great Father reared back, flailing at the corroded metal that pierced its side. The scything talons of its clawed hands raked across the thick metal, splitting it and leaving much of its length to crash to the floor. By then, however,

Rhodaan was capitalising on the patriarch's distress. The chainsword came chopping down, gnawing into one of the monster's legs, chewing through chitin and muscle, shredding flesh and bone. The hulking xenos brought both talons whipping around, but all they found was the broken stump of the column Rhodaan had brought down. While its claws raked the ancient metal, the warsmith's gun pumped rounds into the patriarch's body.

A keening shriek rang out from the Great Father, urging the pure-strains down from the web of steel. Uzraal was ready for their descent, waiting until the swift-moving xenos were in his sights and then loosing a blast from his meltagun. The second shot wrought even more destruction upon the nest of twisted plasteel. The structure collapsed in upon itself, smashing and crushing the genestealers that had avoided the direct effect of Uzraal's shot.

'Warsmith, the whole place is coming down!' Uzraal barked, already drawing back towards the crimson-lighted chamber.

Rhodaan heard the warning, but even as he turned the maimed patriarch was coming at him once more. The monster's talon sheared the right horn from the Space Marine's helmet before his chainsword was raking across the Beast's wrist, sending the alien claw spinning away in the dark. The patriarch's head darted forwards, its fangs scraping across Rhodaan's breastplate, scarring the ceramite and defacing the combat honours affixed to it. A burst from the bolt pistol answered the xenos violence, punching a line of craters down its shoulder and side.

The Great Father roared, a cry of agony as well as fury. Gone was the crafty Beast that had lurked like a spider in its web while minions fought its battles. Gone were the psychic tricks and the appeals to its multitudinous spawn. All that was left was the spite and bitterness of the vanquished, the dying belligerence of hate. The patriarch slammed into Rhodaan, bowling him onwards. The genestealer ignored the biting teeth of the chainsword and the havoc visited on it by the bolt pistol. The debris crashing down from the disintegrating nest didn't give it pause as it plunged across the collapsing lair with its enemy.

The sensors in Rhodaan's armour flashed in warning, alerting him to the swelling radiation. The Great Father was driving him towards one of the nodules, seeking to bear him down into an atomic tomb. He glared at the monster, then brought his armoured helm crashing into the patriarch's face, raking his remaining horn cross-wise until he pierced one of those amber eyes. In his battles against the tyranids, Rhodaan had found few points as sensitive as the eyes.

The patriarch was staggered for an instant as its eye burst beneath Rhodaan's savagery. A heartbeat of weakness, but it was enough for the warsmith. Raking his chainsword along the Beast's shoulder, he ripped away both arms on that side. Freed from the monster's clutch, he emptied his pistol into the Great Father's back, piercing the dark chitin to penetrate the soft tissues within.

Even in its anguish, the Great Father turned to confront its foe. Strength, however, was swiftly failing that huge xenos body. Rhodaan brought his boot slamming into the patriarch, tumbling it sidewise. The Beast crashed down at the edge of the glowing pit. Before it could struggle up again, Rhodaan had slapped a fresh clip into his pistol. A burst of explosive shells provided the momentum to pitch the alien headlong into a radioactive grave.

'When we win the Long War,' Rhodaan snarled down at the patriarch, 'we will see that all your xenos breed burns.'

Rhodaan marched out from the patriarch's lair only a moment before the compromised nest of twisted plasteel came crashing downwards. The warsmith didn't glance back at the destruction. If any of the Great Father's brood had survived the collapse they'd be in no condition to cause trouble. By the time they could dig themselves out, the Iron Warriors would be long gone.

Captain Uzraal joined Gaos and Periphetes around the mangled body of Bakasur. None of the Iron Warriors had been impertinent enough to retrieve the relic from the hybrid's corpse. That was an honour they knew belonged to the warsmith alone.

Rhodaan stalked past his followers, letting his gaze linger on each in their turn. Then he was looming over Bakasur's bloodied body. He brushed away the lifeless hands and took up the Warmason's Casket. He held it reverently before him, carefully displaying it to the surviving Iron Warriors. 'This is what we came here for.'

Contemptuously Rhodaan snapped the broken box in half and tossed the jewelled pieces aside. Uzraal sputtered in disbelief. Periphetes tried to reach out to stop the action with his mangled arm. Gaos simply cried out in protest.

The warsmith ignored them all. It wasn't their place to understand, only to obey. He cared nothing for the vessel or the veneration the people of Lubentina had shown it. The treasure that had lured him from Castellax was what the casket contained.

'The Dekatherion,' Rhodaan announced as he held up a rod of onyx laced with silver. A bulb of some shimmering crystal tipped one of its ends while the other was ringed with a series of switches and knobs.

The Iron Warriors were awed simply gazing on the device, but for Rhodaan the effect was even more pronounced. He held in his hand a relic, but not the sort the flesh of Lubentina would venerate if they knew its origin. The Dekatherion wasn't the creation of Vadok Singh even if it had come to reside in a relic devoted to the Warmason. It was the invention of Perturabo, primarch of the Iron Warriors.

Rhodaan's grip tightened around the relic. He glanced across at his followers. 'We have what we came for. Let us be quit of this place.'

Solemnly, the Iron Warriors turned from the havoc of the catacombs and the xenos tunnels. With their leaders slain, the cultists would be a disorganised rabble of small consequence to the Space Marines. Such forces as the Imperial authorities had remaining to them would know better than to challenge their departure.

Rhodaan had learned many times over the Long War that most of the flesh who bowed to the False Emperor weren't nearly so ready to die for Him as they claimed.

Painfully, Trishala rallied her flagging strength. The shots the Iron Warriors had fired at her had shattered her shoulder and arm. The pain her injuries caused her was nothing beside the agony she suffered as she watched Rhodaan smash open the Warmason's Casket. The heretic's claim about what the relic had contained only magnified the hurt. Her mind fought to reject the very possibility that such a sacred relic could have housed anything belonging to the Chaos Space Marines.

As Trishala rose to her feet she stumbled to where Rhodaan had so contemptuously tossed the fragments of the casket. While part of her railed against the desecration and her inability to prevent it, she was pragmatic enough to understand that there was nothing she could have done. One Sister against five Space Marines. All she would have done was die to no purpose and the Iron Warriors would still have despoiled the Warmason's Casket.

Tenderly she knelt and retrieved the gilded fragments. Trishala would carry them back to the cathedral and put them with the other relics. That much at least she *could* do. She cast an uneasy look at the wreckage under which the Iron Warriors had entombed the Great Father and its ilk. The catacombs would be filled with the cultists corrupted by the patriarch and the genestealers that had been absent when it met destruction. Unable to raise the cathedral on the vox, she couldn't even be certain the Order of the Sombre Vow still held control of it.

Duty. Obligation. Faith. These were the things that demanded her fealty now. Trishala would return what remained of the Warmason's Casket, set it beside the Shroud of Singh and the other relics. Whatever else happened, this purpose at least was within her ability to fulfil.

EPILOGUE

Havoc was consuming the streets of Tharsis. In every quarter and district, hordes of hybrid cultists surged up onto the surface from the Cloisterfells and the old mine tunnels. Regions the local militia thought safely under their control again became cauldrons of violence. Mobs of cultists tried to penetrate the perimeter around the Sovereign Spire and, for the first time since the rebellion broke out, there were attacks against the spaceport.

The soldiers tasked with keeping order at the spaceport were compelled to forsake all other duties as they hurried to defend the perimeter. In their absence the masses of pilgrims seeking to escape the embattled planet on the transports fell into complete anarchy. All pretence of discipline crumbled as they surged towards each ship, trying to force their way onto the vessels, trampling the new arrivals that had just been brought to Lubentina.

The Cult of the Cataclysm had become a crazed, wild

beast after the deaths of its leaders. The grand strategies of the Great Father and Bakasur no longer flowed through its gestalt mentality. Restraint was gone and in its place there was wrath. Reserves long kept in the darkness now swelled the ranks of the fighters. Hidden traitors now revealed themselves in acts of sabotage and murder. In hundreds of places across the city, the rebels sought revenge against their oppressors, against the humans they held responsible for killing their god and his prophet.

The troops holding the spaceport knew there'd be no reinforcement of their position. With three-quarters of the city under attack and the Warmason's Cathedral itself in the hands of the xenos, there was no longer any ground route to the spaceport still in Imperial control. Communications reached them that such units as could were falling back to the Sovereign Spire or else withdrawing from the city entirely. It was hoped that a counter-assault could be organised once the militia was regrouped. If such an effort was successful, then perhaps it would provide some relief to the soldiers on the perimeter.

For hours the soldiers held the line, fending off repeated cultist attacks. Only the disorganised and quasi-independent fashion in which the attacks were staged allowed the militia to repel them. Had the cultists surged against the whole of the line in a united effort, the position would have been overwhelmed quickly.

As a still greater tide of rebels swarmed towards their line, the soldiers braced themselves for the finish. Before the storm of cultists could strike them, it suddenly faltered. From the streets beyond the hybrid horde, a withering gunfire sounded. At first the wave of cultists turned back, swinging around to pour into the darkened street, then the rush faltered, crashing against an obstacle both irresistible and unstoppable.

The soldiers on the line cheered. Against all hope, it seemed relief had been able to reach them. Unable to raise the fighters shooting their way through the rebels on their vox units, the troops could only wonder about their identity. Had a regiment of their comrades fought their way across the city? Was it the frateris militia or had some of the Battle Sisters escaped the fall of the cathedral?

The reality silenced the cheers and sent a knot of dread rising in every man's throat. The fighters who'd butchered a path through the cultists were armoured giants only too familiar to the men at the spaceport. The Iron Warriors had returned.

The soldiers hurriedly opened a gap in their cordon, clearing a way for the Chaos Space Marines as they marched through the perimeter. There were a handful of them now, but the soldiers had just seen that handful gun down scores of cultists. They weren't going to provoke the Iron Warriors into doing the same to them.

As the Iron Warriors advanced, the rioting pilgrims forgot their desperate effort to leave Lubentina. They fled before the Space Marines, the panic hammering in their hearts spreading into even those who couldn't see the giants as they marched across the landing pads.

The transport closest to the Chaos Space Marine gunship had become the scene of a tense standoff. Minister Kargil, with a retinue of guards and an entourage of servants laden down with his valuables, had been trying to bully his way onto the flyer. Kargil's elocution had done less to cow the masses of pilgrims than the threat of the shotguns borne by his guards. Even that threat paled, however, beside the terror provoked by the Iron Warriors as they drew near. The crowd of pilgrims that had been blocking Kargil's path to the transport now became a frantic mob as they stampeded away from the ship and away from the Chaos Space Marines. Kargil and his minions were trampled under the avalanche of frightened pilgrims, all of the minister's valuables crushed underfoot along with the man who'd thought to escape with them.

The Iron Warriors paid no notice to the panic around them. It was of no consequence. They had what they'd come to Lubentina to recover. When they were back aboard their gunship and rising into the darkening sky, the Space Marines lost all interest in the planet below. Over the course of the Long War they'd fought on thousands like it.

Before the war was over, they would fight on thousands more.

In the darkness of the crypt, Sister Kashibai called weakly into her armour's vox. She didn't know if anyone could hear her, or even if there was anyone left to hear. Had it been minutes or hours since the Chaos Space Marines had fought them? It was all a blur to her, a confusion of exhausted sleep and semi-lucid instants of pained wakefulness. The Space Marine's attack had ruptured something inside her. She could feel her vitality ebbing away with each blood-specked cough that left her throat.

Kashibai wasn't certain that the vox was still functional. Perhaps its machine-spirit had dissipated, leaving the mechanism inert. Perhaps it lacked the strength to cast her voice more than a few metres and made it impossible to reach the cathedral above and her Sisters. She wasn't worried about herself, about being lost in the catacombs. It was concern for them and the masses of refugees taking sanctuary in the cathedral that forced her to persist. Trishala had to be warned. She had to know that the Iron Warriors were going to penetrate the cathedral from below rather than above. The Order of the Sombre Vow had to know that the Chaos Space Marines were coming.

The urgency of getting word to her Sisters provoked another fit of coughing. In the whirr of pain, Kashibai struggled to hold on to her awareness. She couldn't reach her chronometer, had no way of gauging how much time had passed. It might already be too late. It would certainly be too late if she fell unconscious. Maybe her earlier lapses had been longer than she imagined. Perhaps she'd been alone in the tomb not for hours but for days? The possibility sent a flare of terror rushing through her.

Through the pain, Kashibai began to sound the warning once more. Again, there was no response. Were they all dead then? Had the Iron Warriors run amok through the Warmason's Cathedral or had the Cult of the Cataclysm finally breached the Great Gate and unleashed a horde of ravening xenos upon the God-Emperor's children? She denied the sense of despair that welled up inside her. She had a duty, an obligation, to perform. Dire conjecture and desperate fear had no room in her mind. Resolutely, she called the alarm once more. Even with her voice dry and cracking, she continued to call out to her Sisters.

At length, Kashibai's perseverance bore results. Not the kind she anticipated, for when an answer came to her, it sounded from the door of the crypt rather than across the vox. Amazed, the wounded Sister looked towards the doorway, watching as the speaker limped into the crypt.

Trishala's armour was stained with blood and alien ichor, battered and gouged in several places. Her face was cut and a savage bruise discoloured her left cheek. Her left arm was cradled close against her chest.

'There's no need to call out, Sister Kashibai. What has been done has been done.' Trishala paced around the shattered crystal sarcophagus, inspecting the dead soldiers and Battle Sisters. She paused when she spotted Palatine Yadav's body. 'You found Yadav.' She turned towards Kashibai. 'You did what you could to bring him back to the cathedral.'

Kashibai struggled to turn herself so that she could face Trishala. 'The Chaos Space Marines found us. We were too few to resist them.' She displayed her blood-specked teeth in a grimace of anguish. 'I could only watch as their sorcerer ripped Yadav's secrets from him. They took what they wanted, then they killed him.'

Trishala walked to Kashibai. She had seen death often enough to recognise that Kashibai was fading fast. There wasn't much time left to her. Soon she would be drawn into the Emperor's light. It could serve no purpose to tell her everything that had happened. To let her know the Iron Warriors had destroyed the Warmason's Casket, or that the genestealers had stolen it from the Celestial Chapel. It could do her no good to know that Trishala had been unable to raise anyone in the cathedral on her vox and that it had likely fallen to the cultists.

'All the God-Emperor expects of His children is that they do their utmost,' Trishala told her. 'That we think not of ourselves, but of our greater duty to Him and to the Imperium that is His legacy to us. That we fight to the last breath defending what He built for us.'

Kashibai's head sagged against her chest. For an instant, her eyes closed, then snapped open in a paroxysm of fright. 'The cathedral!' she cried. 'They must be warned! The Chaos Space Marines are coming!' She gazed up at Trishala, a confused expression pulling at her pale visage. 'We tried to stop them, Sister Superior. We did try...'

Kashibai's words dripped away in a fit of coughing. Blood trickled from her mouth. When she shifted her body, Trishala could see a slick of crimson staining the floor beneath her.

'You did more than I could have ever asked,' Trishala said. She knelt beside Kashibai, clasping her hand in her own. She held tight as another fit of coughing racked Kashibai's body. She held tight as the dying Sister again warned her that the Iron Warriors were heading for the Mourner's Door. She held tight as she felt the strength ebb from Kashibai's fingers.

'Do you recall the Sombre Vow sworn by all in our order?' Trishala asked. The question spurred a greater awareness in Kashibai's eyes. For an instant she was free from the pain and confusion.

'By the blood of my heart, do I swear to defend the Imperial Creed,' Kashibai recited.

'By the honour of my soul, do I swear to guard the sacred and protect the holy,' Trishala joined in Kashibai's recitation. Through the intricacies of the vow that bound them as Battle Sisters, their two voices were united.

'And ever shall I give glory unto Him who rests within the Golden Throne,' Trishala completed the ritual. Kashibai's voice had fallen away before reaching the end.

It was some time before Trishala released the limp, lifeless hand that she held.

Rising from her fallen comrade, Trishala looked at the ceiling overhead. Somewhere above them was the Warmason's Cathedral and the xenos cult. She didn't know if any of her order remained, if they were still fighting to protect the relics entrusted to them. But she did know she was going to find out. To join them in death or glory.

The sound of artillery intruded even into the halls of the Sovereign Spire. The militia was doing its utmost to clear the overrun scholarium. Any restraint, any notion of salvaging something from the vast seminary had been abandoned. Destruction of the cultists was the only objective, regardless of what was destroyed with them. Eradicating rebel strongpoints that could threaten the Sovereign Spire and the other concentrations of Imperial strength yet remaining in Tharsis had become the utmost priority.

There were few enough of those, Cardinal-Governor Murdan reflected as he listened to the shells smashing down. The Warmason's Cathedral had become a stronghold of cultists, an impregnable fortress behind its thick walls and solid plasteel siege shutters. The spaceport had been overrun shortly after the fell Iron Warriors departed Lubentina. The soldiers there simply weren't able to maintain the perimeter and suppress the panicking pilgrims.

A few parts of the city had become citadels of local militia forces. The most prominent was the convent that had headquartered the Order of the Sombre Vow. Almost a thousand soldiers and frateris militia had assembled there, fending off the cult's repeated attacks. The citadel would have benefited from a few squads of Battle Sisters, but it seemed all of them had perished in the fighting on

Mount Rama. Only Sister Superior Trishala had made her way back to the convent.

Murdan took the rescue of the Shroud as a sign from the God-Emperor that, as dire as things might seem, all was not lost. Whatever happened, the Cult of the Warmason would endure. Lubentina would live on... and not as some xenos-infested rock.

The entrance of a hall-serf into the council room roused Murdan from his reflections. With the rest of the council either dead or fled, the governor had become accustomed to the isolation. He felt a twinge of annoyance at the servant's trespass into this solitude. Then he spied the message resting on the silver tray the man carried. Murdan stared at the copper scroll the hall-serf had brought him. The message etched into the thin metal sheaf had issued from the Crystal Turret. Rakesh the astropath had been contacted by Imperial forces. Librarian Abigor of the Flesh Tearers Chapter of the Adeptus Astartes was responding to the plea Rakesh had issued. Their fifth company was en route to Lubentina. Granting no caprice of the immaterium, the Space Marines would make planetfall in several weeks.

Murdan reread the message, feeling every letter branding itself upon his soul. Dreams of having his name ensconced with such paragons of courage and devotion as his predecessors Gaurang and Rohak crumbled before his very eyes. All he had worked towards, all he had sacrificed, it would count for nothing now. He was finished. He would be stripped of his title, cast out from the Ecclesiarchy. He could almost hear the priests passing sentence on him, declaring him apostate and expelling him from the Emperor's grace. As the prestige of Lubentina had grown, he'd cultivated many enemies, men who would be only too eager to exorcise their jealousy by pursuing his downfall.

Space Marines! They'd deemed the crisis on Lubentina so dire that a company of the Emperor's mightiest warriors was being dispatched to assess the situation! Murdan felt an icy dread gnawing at his spine. Three months to wait for their arrival, to discover what his own fate would be. Vindicated for his efforts or condemned for his losses.

At least Trishala had saved something from the cathedral. The Shroud of Singh might not be as prestigious as the Warmason's Casket, but it was a sacred relic in its own right. Something to offer up to the Ecclesiarchy.

Another comforting thought came to Murdan as he read over the communication once more. These would be real Space Marines, not the Chaos heretics that had added to Lubentina's agonies. When they arrived, he could expect the Flesh Tearers to be noble and disciplined champions of the Imperium.

The bright glow of Lubentina's sun filled Rhodaan's vision as he gazed out from the gunship's viewports. He motioned with his hand, waving at Uzraal to launch the torpedo.

'It is done, warsmith,' Uzraal reported a moment later. The torpedo moved with too great a speed to be more than a brief flash as it streaked away from the gunship. Rhodaan looked down at the targeting cogitator, watching its display as the missile sped towards the sun.

'From Iron, cometh Strength,' Rhodaan intoned, clapping his hand against his chest in salute.

'From Strength, cometh Will,' Uzraal continued, following the warsmith's example.

Brother Gaos bowed his head and added his part to the Litany of Iron. 'From Will, cometh Faith.'

'From Faith, cometh Honour,' Periphetes added, awkwardly repeating the salute rendered by the others with his left hand.

Rhodaan stared out through the armourglass window. 'From Honour, cometh Iron,' he swore as a bright flash flickered at the edge of the sun's corona. Honour had been rendered to Perturabo.

It was a strange sensation for Rhodaan, knowing what he'd done. There was a part of him that was tempted to follow the same path that had lured Cornak to his doom. Claim the Dekatherion for himself, find some way to unlock its abilities and harness them for his own benefit. Considering the ignominious fate that had struck down the sorcerer, there was little to recommend such a path. He was an Iron Warrior and there was one thing that set him apart from the renegades and daemon-worshipping madmen of the other Legions. He still remembered what loyalty was, still obeyed the onus of duty. Whatever power he hoped to accrue for himself, he wouldn't claim it at the expense of the Legion or by betraying his primarch.

Perturabo was a master craftsman and had made many devices over the millennia. The Dekatherion had been crafted during the Great Crusade, a time when many wonders had been shaped by the primarch's hands. All had been wanting, falling short of the perfection Perturabo intended. In time he'd repented their fabrication and sought to destroy them. The simple fact of their existence was a point of vexation, a slight upon his sensibilities.

The blip that represented the torpedo vanished into the sun. Under Rhodaan's supervision, the warhead had been hollowed out, allowing the despised relic to be sealed away inside. He'd drawn inspiration from his combat against the genestealer patriarch and the Beast's demise in the atomic nodule. Once the Dekatherion was propelled into the burning maw of the sun it would be obliterated utterly.

'It is done,' Rhodaan repeated Uzraal's words as the blip winked out, the torpedo and its contents consumed by the sun. He turned and growled a command to the pilot. 'Now we return to Castellax.'

As his ship turned away from Lubentina's sun, Rhodaan was thinking past the honour paid Perturabo. It would take more to rebuild the prestige of the Third Grand Company. Campaigns and atrocities that would far eclipse their activities on the shattered shrine world.

As guardian of the Shroud of Singh, a place was made for Trishala on the Ecclesiarchy mission ship when it departed Lubentina. The priests had heard the stories circulating about her one-woman assault of the Warmason's Cathedral after the rest of her order had been killed and the xenos held control of the building. She'd fought her way up to the Celestial Chapel and there, amid the ruin of the violated sanctuary, she'd recovered the Shroud of Singh. Through her bravery and perseverance, the holy relic had been saved. It would remain a subject of wonder and adoration to the Cult of the Warmason.

It was an epic tale that had built up around her, but as Trishala sat alone in her cabin recovering from her wounds, she could only wonder how such a story had come to be. Certainly she'd struck out for the cathedral after leaving Kashibai in the catacombs. It had been her intention to join her Sisters in a last stand against the cultists. She could remember passing through the Mourning Door and advancing through the crypts.

What followed was simply a blur, a jumble of images and sensations. She knew there had been pain and horror and death, but the details refused to make themselves clear to her. She knew it was miraculous that she'd survived. Doubly so when she managed to claim some slight measure of victory from the carnage. She'd rescued the Shroud of Singh and brought the holy relic back into the keeping of the God-Emperor's children.

Trishala could feel the pulse of the ship's engines as it started away from Lubentina. She didn't have a viewport to watch as the planet receded into the distance, but she could sense the increasing gulf just the same. The connection she shared with the God-Emperor had been bound into her duty as defender of Vadok Singh's relics. As she drew away from the place where she'd failed in that duty, she could feel a hideous sense of isolation and loneliness wailing through her brain. She'd lost that sense of community, of belonging. Even with the rest of her Battle Sisters fallen in combat, while she was on Lubentina she hadn't felt alone. They were with her, as close to her as her own thoughts.

Trishala glanced about her humble surroundings. Her power armour lay heaped against one wall, immense within the confines of the cabin. There was a bed, only somewhat more substantial than a cot, and a small bit of furnishing that was at once both desk and stool. The previous occupant of the cabin must have been a scribe of some fashion, for the surface of the desk was covered in sheets of parchment and an array of quills and other materials. Trishala paced towards the desk, glancing across the columns of figures scrawled across the pages, the records of cargoes and payments, expenses and tithes.

The feeling of isolation swelled inside her mind. Trishala rested against the desk, dropping down on the metal stool. She bowed her head in prayer, seeking the comfort of communing with the God-Emperor. Since escaping with the Shroud, she had prayed incessantly, repenting her failures and asking for the strength that seemed unequal to the trials ahead.

It was more than simply the Shroud of Singh she was taking from Lubentina. Wherever the relic went, wherever the Ecclesiarchy decided to send her, she would bear with her a new discipline. A new understanding of the Imperial Creed and the God-Emperor and the glories that He had intended for His children.

In the midst of war, she'd unexpectedly found enlightenment. Trishala had been blessed to carry that gift within her.

That one day she might bring others the glory of ascension.

ABOUT THE AUTHOR

C L Werner's Black Library credits include the Space Marine Battles novel *The Siege of Castellax*, the Age of Sigmar novel *Overlords of the Iron Dragon*, and the novella 'Scion of the Storm' in *Hammers of Sigmar*, the End Times novel *Deathblade*, *Mathias Thulmann: Witch Hunter*, *Runefang*, the Brunner the Bounty Hunter trilogy, the Thanquol and Boneripper series and Time of Legends: The Black Plague series. Currently living in the American south-west, he continues to write stories of mayhem and madness set in the worlds of Warhammer 40,000 and the Age of Sigmar.

WARHAMMER 40,000

THE EYE OF MEDUSA

DAVID GUYMER

READ IT FIRST
EXCLUSIVE PRODUCTS | EARLY RELEASES | FREE DELIVERY
blacklibrary.com